"I—I think it's best if we say goodbye, Grant."

The words took him like a punch to the gut. He stiffened, stared at her rigid back. "You mean, for us to go our separate ways?"

She flinched, nodded.

"Then turn around and look at me and tell me that's what you want."

She shook her head. Her hand, pale against her dark gown, fisted. "I can't."

His heart jolted. He sucked in air. "Why not? It should be easy enough if it's what you want."

"But it's not!" She whipped around, her eyes anguished, wet tracks of tears glistening on her cheeks. "It's what has to be. And I'm not—not strong enough to do what I must, when you—when I'm— I have to go." She spun back around toward the dock.

He caught her hand, took her into his arms. She pushed against him, then grabbed fistfuls of his shirt, buried her face against his chest and burst into tears.

Award-winning author **Dorothy Clark** lives in rural New York. Dorothy enjoys traveling with her husband throughout the United States doing research and gaining inspiration for future books. Dorothy believes in God, love, family and happy endings, which explains why she feels so at home writing stories for Love Inspired Books. Dorothy enjoys hearing from her readers and may be contacted at dorothyjclark@hotmail.com.

Books by Dorothy Clark

Love Inspired Historical

Family of the Heart
The Law and Miss Mary
Prairie Courtship
Gold Rush Baby
Frontier Father
An Unlikely Love

Pinewood Weddings Series

Wooing the Schoolmarm
Courting Miss Callie
Falling for the Teacher
A Season of the Heart

Visit the Author Profile page at Harlequin.com for more titles

DOROTHY CLARK

An Unlikely Love

HARLEQUIN® LOVE INSPIRED® HISTORICAL

Recycling programs for this product may not exist in your area.

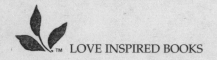 LOVE INSPIRED BOOKS

ISBN-13: 978-0-373-28307-1

An Unlikely Love

Copyright © 2015 by Dorothy Clark

www.Harlequin.com

Printed in U.S.A.

Let us not therefore judge one another any more: but judge this rather, that no man put a stumbling block or an occasion to fall in his brother's way.
—*Romans* 14:13

This book is dedicated with affection
and deep appreciation to all of the talented
Love Inspired Historical authors who graciously,
unfailingly rush to cheer for, help, commiserate with
or pray for each other as the occasion demands.
You ladies are the best!

And Sam.
This is the tenth book since we joined forces
as critique partners and you've stuck with me
through them all. Ten books, Sam!
How do I thank you for that?

"Commit thy works unto the Lord,
and thy thoughts shall be established."

Your Word is truth. Thank You, Jesus.

To God be the glory

Chapter One

August 1874
Chautauqua Lake, New York

The steamer lurched, vibrated. The whistle blew. They were under way. It wouldn't be long now. Marissa caught her balance and pressed her hand hard over her stomach. Laughter and excited chatter rose around her. It seemed as if everyone on the boat was talking about the Chautauqua Assembly program. Snippets of conversations about the Bible studies, teacher training classes, musical entertainments, recreational activities and lectures the assembly offered swelled to an uncomfortable din.

The lectures. She squeezed the small velvet purse dangling from her wrist, felt the stiffness of the two letters inside and took another breath against the roiling in her stomach. The hum of voices drowned out the patter of the rain against the window at her back. She swept her gaze over the people crowded onto benches or standing shoulder to shoulder in the large cabin and gauged her chances of making it to the door.

"Excuse me." She turned sideways, edged through the crowd and slipped outside. The hubbub of the other passengers aboard the *Colonel Phillips* faded to a low murmur. A cool mist from the falling rain swept under the floor of the upper deck and peppered her face. She took a deep breath of the fresh air and looked around. Lantern light from the windows spread a golden gleam across the wet deck, glistened on the railing. She pulled the hood of her waterproof coat forward, took a cautious step toward the front of the ship, another, then stopped.

"Are you all right, miss?"

A man strode toward her out of the darkness. Obviously, he had no problem walking aboard a moving vessel. She nodded, wiped the moisture from her face. "I'm fine. It's only that I'm unaccustomed to walking on a floor that quivers beneath my feet. It's a little unnerving."

The light from behind her washed over the man's strong, well-defined features, flashed on his white teeth when he smiled. *My, but he's handsome.* Warmth climbed into her cheeks. She turned her face away from a lantern hanging from the upper deck that would, no doubt, reveal her blush.

"It's the thrust of the steamer's engine you feel. The occasional lurch is caused by the paddle wheels when there is a steering correction." The man stopped a few steps away from her. "The deck is a bit slick. May I assist you to your destination?"

He was younger than she'd thought. Perhaps in his midtwenties. A few years older than herself. She glanced across the distance to the railing and weighed her unease against propriety.

"Allow me to introduce myself." The man removed his hat and dipped his head in a small polite bow that revealed a mass of short brown hair with deep waves crested by sun streaks. "Grant Winston, at your service." He replaced his hat and flashed his smile again. "At least I am if you will permit me to be, Miss…"

"Bradley." She drew her gaze from his disarming grin, nibbled at the corner of her lip. "I am going to the railing at the front of the ship. If you wouldn't mind walking beside me…"

"It would be my pleasure."

"Then, thank you, Mr. Winston. I accept your kindness." She offered a silent prayer that she wouldn't slip on the wet deck and stepped forward. Grant Winston moved beside her, matching his steps to her uncertain ones. She let out a sigh and took a tight hold when they reached the railing.

"Feel safer now?"

"I will as long as I don't look down."

He chuckled. A deep, pleasant sort of rolling sound that had a smile tugging at her lips.

"I take it you're not a veteran steamer passenger?"

"I'm strictly a landlubber." She laughed to cover the nervous tremor in her voice and peeked over the railing. Dark water flowed beneath the ship, brushed along the side in a sinister-sounding whisper. Her stomach flopped. "I didn't know how intimidating water could

be. I should have made Lincoln teach me to swim."
The name slipped from her lips without thought. Pain
rose, squeezed the air from her lungs. She blinked,
thankful for the rain that would hide any betraying
shimmer of tears.

"Lincoln?"

The band of pain squeezed tighter. "My brother."
Bitterness tainted her voice. She drew a shallow, ragged
breath, lifted her gaze and watched the lights on the
shore morph to yellow blurs as the ship steamed toward
the middle of the long lake. *Don't let him ask about Lin-*
coln, Lord. Please, don't let him ask. The ship lurched.
Her kid gloves slipped against the wet rail. She gasped
and tightened her grip.

"It might help if you look at the land ahead, instead
of behind. See how it curves around? That's why the
captain changed course. The ship will steady now."

His deep voice was calm, reassuring. The tension
left her shoulders. *Thank You, Lord.* She gingerly
shifted her position and searched for the spot he described.

He gestured ahead toward the right. "When we pass
that outcropping, you'll see lights among the trees on
the hills at the Chautauqua campgrounds at Fair Point,
though it's still quite some distance away."

The wind gusted. He swiped the water from the
collar of his mackintosh and tugged it up around his
neck. "I understand there are already a great number
of people in attendance, though the assembly does not
officially begin until tomorrow. And, of course, there
are still people coming by steamers both from here in

Mayville and from Jamestown at the other end of the lake. Two or three hundred on every ship. A friend here in Mayville told me the captains are leaving port at full capacity."

If he was trying to distract her, it worked admirably. "So many?"

"Yes. It's quite amazing really." He turned toward her, leaned his hip against the railing. "The Chautauqua Assembly program seems to have caught the interest of people from all over. I've spoken with a family from Canada. And people from Ohio and Virginia. And, of course, New York and Pennsylvania."

Oh, my! What had she gotten herself into? She swallowed hard and stared toward the outcropping he'd pointed out. The more people who attended her lectures, the better, of course. But she was no orator, only—

"Am I right?"

She started out of her thoughts, glanced up at him. "I beg your pardon?"

"I asked if you are attending the assembly."

Her stomach clenched. "Yes, I am." *Because of you, Lincoln. And Father.*

"I thought as much."

She took a steadying breath, thrust her dark thoughts away. "And why is that?"

"Because I believe everyone aboard this ship, save the captain and crew, is headed for the Chautauqua campgrounds. And—" his gaze dropped to her hands gripping the railing "—I figure it had to be something like this advertised assembly to entice you to step foot on the *Colonel Phillips*."

"You are correct, Mr. Winston." *Though not because I'm afraid of the water.* The conversation had gone far enough. She wanted no questions about her reason for attendance—not with tears threatening. Nor did she want him to find her lacking in proper manners and judge her to be a woman of low behavior. She gave him a polite smile. "Thank you for your kind reassurance and assistance, sir. I'm most appreciative."

He took a step back and made her a polite bow. "My pleasure, Miss Bradley."

The steamer gave another lurch, headed into the wind and started around the outcropping. The rain slanted in between the decks. She clung to the railing and stared out over the water until Grant Winston's footsteps faded away and there was only the patter of the rain against the hood and shoulder cape of her waterproof coat, and the whisper of the water against the ship. A well-brought-up young woman did not look after a young man—not even a kind, helpful one.

She let out a long breath and turned her thoughts to the two letters in her purse. Who had prompted those in charge of the Chautauqua Assembly to send her an invitation to lecture on temperance? Could it be the Mrs. Tobin Swan who had written asking her to lead a group of women in protest against the local vineyards and wineries? Her lips lifted in a grim smile. Wine had destroyed her family. It would be a pleasure to stop its production at its very source.

"Grant me success, Lord, I pray." Her determination firmed. The solitude of the rainy deck was the perfect place to rehearse her lectures. The more she practiced them, the less chance that she would make an error or miss including an important point when she was speaking.

Grant leaned on the rail and watched the foaming water churned up by the side wheel. It was hard to imagine having a fear of the water. Going for a swim was his favorite way to end a summer workday. But then, he'd learned to swim when he was four years old. Of necessity. Of course, he'd been plenty afraid that day.

He stared down at the lake water and thought back to the moment when he'd stepped on the wet mud at the edge of their pond and slid into the cold water. Fortunately, he'd instinctively pushed hard when his feet hit the stony bottom. A grin slanted his lips. That push combined with the frantic flailing of his arms and legs had brought him back up to the top of the water where he could gasp in air. He'd stretched his arm out in an effort to reach the bank, kicked his feet and stretched out his other arm trying to get closer, and suddenly he was swimming on top of the water instead of sinking to the bottom. Of course, the pond was shallow at that end. Not more than five feet deep even during a spring runoff. Things would have ended differently had he fallen in the deep end.

His grin faded. He'd not thought about that before. He'd best fence that pond if he ever married and had children of his own. He straightened and moved down the railing, leaned against a post and watched the lights of Mayville disappear as the steamer rounded the outcropping. His mother and father were eager for him to marry and produce an heir. Being an only child had its responsibilities—a fact that they pointed out to him more and more frequently of late. It wasn't that he had any objections to being married. He wanted a wife and family the same as any man. He just hadn't met a woman he'd found interesting enough to hold his attention. Although Miss Bradley was definitely intriguing. And she *was* a "miss." She hadn't corrected him when he addressed her as such. And she hadn't simpered about it, either. He hated that coy behavior.

Muted laughter and voices drifted his way from the crowded passenger lounge at his back. He wiped the rain from his face, stepped over into the silence by the side railing and slid his gaze toward the front of the steamer. She was still there. A dark silhouette against the flickering, rain-streaked light of one of the ship's lanterns.

Miss Bradley was different all right. He wasn't accustomed to a young woman dismissing him from her presence. And he'd never known any woman who shunned society for solitude. Or one who didn't hurry inside as quickly as possible when it rained. So why was she standing out in the chilly, rainy night alone? And what had caused the sadness he'd seen in her eyes? Her lovely blue eyes.

The steamer cleared the outcropping. Pinpricks of light flickered against the darkness ahead. He pushed back the edges of his mackintosh, shoved his hands in his trousers pockets and leaned back against a post studying the shifting pattern of lights. He'd intended to find out the schedule and attend only the science classes at the Chautauqua Assembly in the hope of finding a way to increase yield at the vineyard. But that was before his chance encounter with the intriguing Miss Bradley. Now he would come to Fair Point as often as he could get away from the vineyard. Foolishness perhaps; the assembly would last for only two weeks. But that would give him time enough to find out the answers to those questions.

A ship's whistle floated through the dark, rainy night. Bells pealed. Tiny lights danced on the water, approached the docking area miles ahead at Fair Point. A frown tugged his brow down. Another steamer was bringing a couple hundred or more attendees to the Chautauqua campgrounds from the other end of the lake. The swarm of people would make finding Miss Bradley difficult. But he liked a challenge…

Marissa stared at the lights gleaming along the shore and peeking through the trees on the hill. The assembly was much larger than she'd imagined. "Oh, my! There are so many lights they look like a swarm of fireflies."

"And I should think most of those who will be attending the assembly have not yet arrived." The young woman crowding against the railing on her left smiled and tilted the umbrella she held against the changing direction of the wind. "I know some are staying at the hotels in Mayville. They don't care to live at the camp. And I'm certain there are many others who will live in their accustomed comfort and only attend daily—when they so choose. My aunt is numbered among them. As for me, the next two weeks should be very exciting. I've never spent time in the woods. And with all the meetings and entertainments—"

The steamer's whistle drowned out the young woman's voice. Bells ashore pealed out an answer to the ship's signal. The steamer lurched, slowed. Water slapped against the side then rolled off to wash up onshore. They came to a full stop.

"We've arrived! I must find my cousin." The young woman spun about and joined the other passengers.

The deck seethed with people clutching their bags and umbrellas and jockeying for position in the line to disembark. She pulled her small dangling purse into her hand and pressed back against the side railing to wait for the crush of people to thin.

Shouts came from all directions. Crew members jumped to the dock, caught ropes that were thrown to them from aboard the ship and wrapped them around thick posts. The disembarking plank hit the dock with a thud.

"All ashore for Fair Point and for the Chautauqua Assembly!"

The hum of conversation aboard ship died. People pressed forward, umbrellas bumping. Farther down the deck, crew members hefted trunks onto their shoulders and carried them ashore. Hers was riding on the beefy shoulder of a man twice as broad as the plank they trod. She held her breath when the plank sagged beneath the man's weight and hoped her trunk didn't leak.

"Come along, miss."

A deckhand motioned her forward. She tugged her hood farther down over her forehead and stepped into the line at the top of the wide gangway. Lantern light from posts at the end of the dock shone on the water between the steamer and the shore. It looked deep. Rain pocked the dark surface, danced on the plank and the dock. Was the plank slippery? An image of her sliding off the side into that dark water flashed into her head. She frowned and moved forward with the line, grateful she'd worn her boots instead of packing them. The couple in front of her stepped onto the gangway. She was next. She clenched her fingers about her purse and wished for a railing to hold on to.

"We meet again, Miss Bradley."

Grant Winston smiled and moved away from the steamer's railing, stepped into line beside her. Had he been waiting there for her? Such forwardness was unacceptable. But she was too grateful for his strong, solid presence to demur. She nodded and moved onto the wide gangway, her steps steadier and less timid because he walked beside her.

"Those with admittance passes go to the line on my right please. Those without passes go to the line on my left."

She lifted her gaze beyond the man standing in the center of the dock a short distance ahead directing passengers. A small shingled building stood at the far end of the weathered boards, the lanterns hanging from hooks on the small structure illuminating the two lines flowing toward open gates at each side. The dark tree-covered hill sprinkled with lights rose a short way beyond. Her stomach flopped. How was she to find her way? Unless…She drew her gaze back, hoping. "I'm to be on the right, Mr. Winston."

"And I on the left. I've decided to purchase a pass for the full two weeks." He smiled and bowed her across in front of him, stepped into the other line.

Her hope flickered then steadied. Perhaps Mr. Winston would find her again when they had both cleared the gates. She swallowed her trepidation, extracted her speaking invitation with its attached pass of admittance from her purse and followed those ahead of her to the gatehouse.

"Next, please."

A quick glance to her left showed Grant Winston's line was moving much slower. The prospect of receiving any help from him vanished. She stepped up to the side window and handed her invitation to the man inside the small house.

"Ah, you are one of our speakers. It's good to have you with us, Miss Bradley." The bearded man smiled and motioned behind him. "Mr. Johnson will show you to the accommodations for teachers and speakers. Tell him about your baggage."

"Thank you." She breathed a sigh of relief as he waved her through the gate, then paused as a man garbed in a black waterproof with a piece of blanket draped over his shoulder stepped forward.

"Mr. Johnson at your service, Miss Bradley. Have you any baggage?"

She nodded, scanned the piles of trunks. "That al-

ligator, camelback Saratoga sitting on top of the near
pile is mine."

"Very good, miss. If you will follow me please."
The man hefted her trunk to his blanket-draped shoulder and started across the narrow strip of flat land to a
beaten path that disappeared into the trees on the hill.
She stopped and glanced over her shoulder. Mr. Winston was standing by the gatehouse looking her way.
Her cheeks warmed as their gazes met. She averted
hers lest he think her bold and stepped onto the path.

"Watch your step, Miss Bradley. The rain makes
the fallen leaves slippery."

It was an understatement. *Everything* was slippery.
And dark. Torches sitting in boxes of what looked like
sand atop posts spaced along the way sputtered out
light useful only for guidance. She stopped trying to
hold her skirt hems up to keep them from becoming
soiled and simply tried to maintain her balance and not
become separated from her guide among the throng of
people on the path.

"Thank you for your help, Mr. Johnson." The flap
door of the tent fell into place behind the departing
guide. Rain pelted the sloped canvas roof, dripped off
the overhanging eaves outside. Marissa shivered and
cast a wary glance up at the sagging pockets where
the edges of the four roof sections met the tent walls.

"Don't touch those! It makes them leak."

She shifted her gaze to the slender, dark-haired
woman with whom she would live for the next two
weeks. Light from a lantern sitting on a small writ-

ing desk revealed a glint of amusement in the young woman's gray eyes.

"I don't mean to sound bossy, but I learned that lesson the hard way. That's why I'm working here in the center of the floor." The young woman laughed and gestured toward a large wet spot on the rough board floor beside the far tent wall. A drop of water hit the wood, splattered.

Marissa glanced up at the sagging canvas above the wet spot. Another drop formed, fell. *Oh, dear...*

"I thought it would be smart to push up on that sagging part of the roof and shove the pooled water over the side. I was wrong. When I let go, it started dripping where my hands had touched the canvas." The woman pulled a face and waved her hand toward the juncture of roof and wall. "As you can see, it's still dripping. But only there—nowhere else, though it looks as if it will. Anyway, I'll move the desk back as soon as the rain stops and the canvas dries."

"Thank you for the warning." She looked at the woman and laughed. "I thought, perhaps, I would have to sleep in my waterproof."

"Let's hope it doesn't come to *that*."

"Indeed." She swept her gaze over the furnishings in the surprisingly spacious tent. There were two cots, two chairs, a desk and, thankfully, a washstand equipped with a pitcher and washbowl. A bucket of water holding a tin dipper sat on the floor beside it.

"There's a pump and a stone fire pit with a huge iron pot two tents down that way." The woman swept her hand to the right. "We're to get our water there.

Someone from the camp tends the fire that keeps the water in the pot warm. It's a luxury I didn't expect."

"I'm not familiar with tent living, so any further bits of wisdom you care to share will be appreciated." She shoved the hood of her waterproof back off her head and shot a wary look at the unmade cot. The guide had placed her trunk beside it. Both sat beneath one of those sagging pockets of rain. "It will also be to your advantage as we are to be housemates—or perhaps I should say tent mates." She looked back at the young woman and smiled. "Thank you for sharing your quarters with me. I'm Marissa Bradley."

The woman's eyes narrowed. "Temperance?"

"Yes." She braced herself, resisted the temptation to ask how the woman knew. Temperance was not a favored subject with many women. They preferred to hide from the truth. She had done so for five years. And her mother.

"You're very young and pretty to be a crusader. I admire your courage. And I'll be writing about you and your lectures. Make them good, for if they're not, I'll not hesitate to say so." The young woman came forward, peered straight into her eyes. "I'm Clarice Gordon. I write articles for the *Sunday School Journal*. And for other papers on occasion, so you must take my warning seriously."

"I shall, Miss Gordon."

"And, as we'll be sharing living quarters for two weeks, I suggest we dispense with formality and call each other by our given names. Would you agree, Marissa?"

How forward! Still, it made sense. "I would indeed, Clarice."

"Good. Then the air is clear between us. Now—" Clarice Gordon gestured toward a tall, clean section of tree root standing upright beside the flap. A blue waterproof dangled from one of the high roots. "Behold our coatrack. Why don't you hang up your waterproof and I'll help you make up your bed? You did bring bed linens with you?"

"Oh, yes, indeed. They were on the list." She shrugged out of her coat and hung it up to drip-dry, shivered in the damp air and hurried to her trunk to get her quilted cotton jacket. "What do we do for meals, Clarice?"

"We go to the hotel."

She jerked erect, her bed linens in her hands. "A hotel!"

Clarice laughed and shook her head. "It's only called that. It's a rather poor excuse for a building, but it is made of wood."

"I see." She shook out a sheet and spread it over the mattress tick, placed her hand on the surface and felt for the stuffing material. *Cornhusks.* "And the food?"

"I haven't had the pleasure of dining at the hotel. I only caught a glimpse of it when my guide showed me where it was located. It's downhill a short way from here."

"*Everything* is downhill from here." She shot Clarice a wry look, spread the top sheet and reached for a blanket.

"That's true." Her tent mate grasped the edge of the blanket, looked up and grinned. "But there is one advantage. Your prayers will have a head start over those offered from below."

As if that mattered. She smoothed the blanket over her side of the cot then pulled out the pillow she'd jammed into the trunk lid and fluffed the feathers. It was too late for prayers—Lincoln was dead.

"What do you mean you're going to this Chautauqua Sunday School Assembly thing? Isn't going to church on Sunday good enough for you?"

Grant placed his wet shoes on the hearth, looked at his father's set face and braced himself for a long discussion. "The assembly is not only about church. I went to Fair Point tonight and bought a pass for the entire two weeks."

"Besides, more church teaching is always a good thing, Andrew." His mother looked at his father and smiled. "And I'm sure there are a lot of lovely young Christian woman attending the Chautauqua classes."

Oh-ho. He tugged off his damp socks and glanced over at the settee. His mother always had such a lovely, serene look about her, but there was a she-bear inside her that reared up and charged to his defense whenever his father was displeased about something he said or did. He was her only child and could do no wrong in her sight—with the exception of his not getting married.

He dropped his socks beside his shoes and rushed to defuse her implications. "That's true, Mother. But it's the science classes being offered at Chautauqua that interest me. I'm hoping by attending I will learn something that will help me better care for the vines and increase their yield and thus our profits." A pair of beautiful but sad blue eyes flashed before him. *And to satisfy my curiosity about Miss Bradley.*

"We're doing all right."

His father's gruff words pulled his thoughts away from the intriguing young woman and focused them on their situation. He shot a glance toward the settee and tempered his response. His mother did not know about the demand note his father had taken against the coming harvest to meet expenses after the killing cold last winter had destroyed so many of the old vines.

"We can always do better." *As the concords prove.* He stopped himself from uttering the words aloud and stepped close to the fire to dry his pants legs. "Scientists discover all sorts of new ways to make crops healthier and increase yield."

His mother rested her needlepoint on her lap and smiled up at him. "I'm sure that's true, son."

His father snorted, shook his head. "You're sure whatever comes out of the boy's mouth is true, Ruth. If these scientists are so smart, let them figure out a way to control the weather. Now, *that* would help."

"Perhaps one day they will."

His mother's support of him was automatic. He aimed a smile her way.

His father leaned sideways in his wheelchair, picked up a piece of wood and placed it on his lap, then turned and wheeled himself along the hearth and added the wood to the fire. "This damp gets into a man's bones and makes them ache. And it's not good for the grapes, either." A piercing look accompanied the words. "You need to see to the vineyard, Grant, not go gallivanting off to some science classes that are nothing but a waste of time."

He let the criticism go. It was his father's frustration with his own inability to go out into the fields talking. A change of subject was in order before his father became overheated and jeopardized his health. "The stems of the concords are turning woody, but the seeds are still a little green. The full-bodied flavor and sweetness hasn't quite developed yet, either. I figure to let them hang another three or four days. It'll be time to start harvesting the south slope then."

"Sounds about right." His father nodded, rubbed his knees with his palms then looked up at him. "I'll send word out to the wineries. The vintners will want to come take a look at the grapes so they can make their bids. We need to give the winner enough warning so he can get his schedule together and hire pickers to harvest the grapes."

He nodded and glanced toward the window, thought about a solitary figure standing on the steamer's deck in the rain. *Perhaps, if he found Miss Bradley as intriguing as she seemed, he would invite her to join him for a picnic and watch the pickers.* "I'll bring in a few clusters before I go to Fair Point tomorrow and we'll make our final decision. And you've no need to worry. The science classes are scheduled late in the day. I'll be here to oversee the harvest. And there's something else…" He reached into his pocket, withdrew the list of lectures being offered and held it out to his father.

"This is another reason for my going to the assembly. They are holding a series of lectures on temperance. I plan to attend them."

"Temperance!" His father snorted, shoved the list away. "A waste of time. Men drink. Always have, always will. You need to spend your time here, tending the vines."

"There's nothing to do for the next few days except watch for the grapes to ripen to maturity. I'll check them every morning." He turned to dry the front of his pants, frowned down at the fire. "There are a lot of taverns and inns in the surrounding towns and villages, and I've no doubt a good many of the owners will attend those lectures. Mix them in with those people in favor of temperance, and it wouldn't surprise me if there are fireworks that will rival those I've heard they're planning to shoot off on one of the boats in the middle of the lake." He wiggled his toes against the warm stone beneath them and glanced down at his father. "What's that old saying… 'A wise man knows his enemy'? I don't intend to miss those lectures."

Chapter Two

Grant whistled his way along the path at the top of the low, rolling incline of the vineyard's south slope. The sun warmed his shoulders, glinted on the knife in his hand and gleamed on the grapes in his basket. It was perfect weather for finishing the ripening of the grapes. And for the opening of the Chautauqua Assembly.

He glanced up, checked the sun's position in the blue sky and smiled. He had plenty of time to meet with his father, clean up and eat, then ride into town and catch the steamer. The science class was scheduled last in the afternoon. A vision of lovely blue eyes above a pert nose wiped off his smile and furrowed his brow. Where would he find Miss Bradley? It was too much to hope that she was interested in science.

He quickened his steps then turned onto a path between two of the rows of vines that flowed down the gently sloping incline in long, regimented courses. Healthy, hardy vines clung with tenacious tendrils to the strung wire trellises at his sides. He looked left and right, scanning the new vines he was starting between each of the ones he'd planted over the past five years. The new ones would be ready to be replanted in the spring. And there were enough of them that they would finish the rows in the new field he'd started. And that would double the size the vineyard had been when he took over its care after his father's crippling accident.

Satisfaction surged. He cast a proprietary gaze over the clusters of purple fruit peeking through the lush growth of leaves and puckered his lips to blow out another tuneless melody. Of the different vines he'd introduced into the vineyard to prove to his father that scientific methods of experimentation could be applied to growing crops, these concords had proved the best. They had survived last year's harsh winter that had killed the canes of most of the other new varieties and also a large portion of the vineyard's old, original vines. None of their neighbors' vines had fared as well. And the concords yielded a crop that ripened earlier than the others he'd tried. They'd have no worries about an early killing frost this year.

A grin slanted his lips. His father was getting excited about the concords. Being the first to market put him in position to negotiate a good price from the competing vintners. Perhaps they could make profit enough to pay off the demand note *and* have money left to carry them through next year. And with his percentage of the profit that was his year's wages, his plans for buying a business of his own would take a leap forward.

He reached under the canopy of leaves on his right,

cut off a heavy cluster and placed it in the basket with the others. One more bunch from farther down the row and he'd have the sampling they needed to make up a harvesting plan to present to the winning bidder. He hurried down the path, his mind already jumping ahead to the late afternoon science class. Perhaps today he'd learn other ways to improve the vineyard. And he would for certain meet the intriguing Miss Bradley again.

Marissa frowned, shot an uneasy look in the direction of the rumble of male voices and tugged her dressing gown closer around her shoulders. It was a little unnerving to prepare for the day when you could hear strange men talking and walking about.

She finished fastening her skirt, moved back to her bed for her bodice, slipped in one arm, shrugged off the dressing gown and slipped her arm in the other sleeve in the same movement. A few quick twists of her fingers buttoned the bodice down the front. She craned her head to look over her shoulder, reached her hands around to the back of her skirt and shook out the gathered folds of fabric that fell from the center of the waistband into a short train at the hem.

"These bustles are so impracticable! How am I supposed to keep my hem from dragging in the mud left by last night's rain as I go from tent to tent? It's impossible!" She muttered the complaint into the empty air, snatched up her dressing gown and folded it. "At least the dirt won't be so noticeable on the dark colors of my mourning clothes."

She looked down at her dark gray day dress and blinked away a rush of tears. *I miss you, Lincoln.* She pulled her thoughts away from her deceased brother, picked up her brush, swept her hair to the crown of her head and gathered it into her hand. A glance into her small mirror showed her hair had formed its usual soft waves with curls dangling around her forehead and temples. It made her look less serious. She sighed, secured the hair in her hand with a gray silk ribbon, let the thick mass fall free then caught it up again into a loose bunch at her crown. Two quick wraps of the ribbon about the hair held it in place while she tied the bow. When she lowered her hands the freed curls frothed over the back of her head. They always did, no matter how she tried to secure them. She'd given up the battle and ceded them victory years ago.

The hem of her gown swished softly across the rough boards as she set to work using the housekeeping activity to hold at bay the sadness that still overwhelmed her at times. She folded her nightclothes, placed them under her pillow and straightened the covers on the cot, forcing her thoughts to the day ahead. What would this morning's meeting for the teachers and speakers hold in store for her? Perhaps she would learn why the leaders had invited her here to Chautauqua. She had written them that she was not a professional speaker but had only addressed a few small women's meetings at various towns around her home. Still they sent her a second invitation. And she couldn't refuse. Not when it meant a chance to spare others the pain of—

She broke off the thought, opened her trunk and withdrew the enameled pendant watch she'd borrowed from her mother. An expensive Cartier watch. The symbol of her father's remorse for abusing her mother while in a drunken state. She had only to look at the watch to remember her father's uncontrolled anger, the sounds of her mother's pleading voice, the cries she tried to muffle. Her face tightened. She pinned the watch on her bodice, pricked her trembling fingers on the clasp. How many times had she and Lincoln heard or seen...? And then Lincoln—

Tears welled into her eyes. "Dear Lord, I pray You will give me the words to speak to convey the dangers inherent in the use of strong drink. And that You will use those words to bring comfort or conviction to the hearts of those who hear that they may be spared the suffering my family has known. Amen."

A sense of purpose swept away her concern over speaking before such large numbers. It was the message that was important, not how eloquently it was presented. She settled her small unadorned black hat forward of her clustered curls, picked up her purse, pushed aside the tent flap and stepped out into the sunshine.

The rustle of people taking seats filled the tent. A hushed murmur floated on the air. Marissa clutched her purse and walked midway down the aisle between rows of benches to an empty spot at the end of a pew on her left. "Excuse me. Are you waiting for someone to join you, or is this seat available?"

An older woman looked up and smiled. "I'm not expecting anyone. You're welcome to the seat. I'm Mrs. Austin…from Cleveland, Ohio."

She smiled her thanks, eased the folds of her bustle beneath her and slipped onto the bench. "I'm Miss Bradley. I'm from Fredonia—a small town not far from here. Are you—"

"Good morning, ladies and gentlemen."

She shrugged an apology for her unfinished question and turned her attention to the platform at the front of the tent.

"For those of you whom I've not yet met, I am Dr. John Austin."

Austin! She slid her gaze toward the woman seated beside her, received a smile and a whispered "My brother-in-law," nodded and again faced the speaker.

"I want to welcome you to Fair Point, and thank you for coming. You teachers, speakers and entertainers are the heart of this Chautauqua Assembly. It could not take place without you. And now for an explanation of our purpose and some rules about your classes or lectures." Dr. Austin clasped his hands behind his back and leaned forward, his bearded face sober. "It is our belief that every facet of a person—spirit, soul and body—should be ministered to in order to promote an abundant life. Therefore, this assembly will devote itself to Bible study, teacher training classes, musical entertainment, lectures on important issues of the day and how they relate to the church, recreational activity, praise meetings and devotional exercises."

Important issues of the day. That would include her subject of temperance.

Dr. Austin cleared his throat, stepped to the edge of the platform. "It is also our belief that education should be available to every man, woman and child for the enrichment of their lives and the betterment of mankind. Therefore, reading and the discussion of books shall be an ongoing class. Also, the advances in the sciences will be demonstrated and taught."

She took a breath and glanced around. All of the people looked so competent and accomplished. And she felt so inept and uncertain. As if she were still walking on the *Colonel Phillips*'s quivering deck.

Grant Winston. A vision of him walking toward her out of the darkness slipped into her mind. It was strange how safe she had felt with him beside her. And how reluctant she was to see him go when they'd been separated onto their different paths after disembarking. Would she ever see him again? She frowned and fingered the cord on her purse. That was highly unlikely. There were so many people attending the assembly it would be impossible to— *The assembly.* She jerked her thoughts back to the speaker.

"—in addition to the Bible readings." Dr. Austin glanced down at the paper he held. "Today's topic for the late afternoon featured lecture will be moral ideas. Tomorrow, it will be on drawing caricatures. And the day following will feature the first of the lectures on temperance."

There was an audible intake of breath among those listening, a general stirring as people glanced at one another. She caught her breath at the reaction, looked down at her lap. *Two more days to prepare.*

"And, of course, every day there will be nature walks in the woods and promenades along the shore, boats for rowing and all manner of entertainments—music, steamer rides, fireworks..."

Steamer rides? Not for her. Unless... She closed her eyes, pictured Grant Winston standing beside her at the rail of a steamer with sunshine warm on their faces and a soft breeze riffling their hair. A smile touched her lips. He had sun streaks in his hair, the way her father did before he moved them into town. Was Grant a farmer? Or perhaps a logger? Or—

She started at movement beside her and opened her eyes. People were standing. She hastened to her feet, stepped out into the aisle and joined the flow of people exiting the tent. She had missed the rules for speakers Dr. Austin had spoken of! How could she—

"Marissa!"

She stopped and turned at the soft call. Her tent mate was hurrying up the aisle toward her. She released a soft sigh and waited for Clarice to catch up to her. Clarice would have notes.

"Well, that was interesting! What a crowd!" Clarice paused, motioned her into the line of people in the aisle and headed for the tent opening. "Are you ready to eat something, Marissa? I wasn't able to get a seat at a table earlier and I'm starving!"

Marissa smiled and dipped her head to a man who stepped aside to let them precede him through the tent's entrance. "I am a bit hungry." No doubt because she had two more days before she spoke. She paused, looked around. People were entering the woods in all different directions. "Which way do we go for the 'hotel'?"

"Up." Clarice laughed and stepped into the trees.

Grant strode along the dock, showed his admittance pass to the gatekeeper and hurried across the flat shore area, his empty stomach rumbling. Discussing the grape samples with his father had taken longer than he expected. Not that it surprised him. His father was set against his coming to this assembly. How could the man still be so against science when he had proven to him with the concords that experimentation worked?

He frowned down at the line map on the back of his pass, tucked it in his pocket and started up a wooded path at a fast pace taking his frustration out on the hillside. He was a grown man with his own ideas, but the doctor had warned against any heated confrontations because of his father's ill health. One fit of anger could overstress his weak heart. It made his obstinance doubly hard to deal with. If it hadn't been for his father's crippling accident, *he* would be a scientist by now, not a vineyard manager trying to cope with old-fashioned ideas.

He halted. People were clustered at a crossing of paths ahead. He glanced at the sign nailed to a long building made of rough boards. The Hotel. This was the dining hall? Hopefully, the food was better than the building.

He glanced inside and looked for a young woman

with blond curls dangling at her forehead and temples. It wasn't much to go on, but he'd find Miss Bradley. He had time. The science class wasn't scheduled until later. And she had to eat. He stepped back outside, took up a place by the door and scanned the people entering the clearing. His pulse jumped at the sight of blond curls and a pair of lovely but sad blue eyes. She was with another lady. Well, he'd met the challenge of finding her. That was enough…for now. He smiled and stepped forward, dipped his head. "I see you survived the steamer ride, Miss Bradley."

She glanced up at him, surprise in her blue eyes. "I did. Thank you again for your assistance on that slippery deck, Mr. Winston." She smiled, glanced at her companion. "May I present Miss Gordon?"

There was a shyness in Marissa's smile that tugged at him. He bowed an acknowledgment and shifted his gaze to Miss Gordon. A pair of gray eyes with a speculative gleam in their depths studied him.

"It's unpleasant dining alone. Perhaps your friend would like to take his meal with us, Marissa." Miss Gordon ignored Miss Bradley's soft gasp and continued to gaze at him. "Unless you were waiting for someone, Mr. Winston?" There was a challenge in her tone.

Marissa. He tucked the name into his memory and slid his gaze to its owner. Her cheeks were pink. She was obviously embarrassed by her friend's boldness. He hurried to smooth over the social misstep. "I would be honored to escort you both to dinner, if you have no objection, Miss Bradley."

She dropped her gaze and shook her head. "I should

be pleased at the sight of another familiar face at the table, Mr. Winston. The crowds of strangers are a bit overwhelming."

"Then I am happy to serve." He stepped to the door, motioned them into line before him.

Sunshine streamed through the cracks between the boards of the walls to stripe the dried mud on the floor. The crude benches alongside long tables covered with oilcloth were filling with people. He ushered them to one with three empty places, helped them onto the bench, then took his place and looked around.

"I'm glad it's not raining today."

"Me, too."

He glanced at the women across the table.

The younger of the group smiled and pointed toward the ceiling. "Last night we had to eat while holding umbrellas."

"Which was no easy feat!"

He looked from the laughing women to the roof. There were streaks of blue sky showing between many of the boards. It didn't take much imagination to picture rain pouring through those wide cracks to drown the plates of food on the tables below. "I see what you mean. Thank you for the warning, ladies."

Marissa slanted a look up at the ceiling and laughed. "It looks as if they would be wise to plan soup for the daily meal when there is inclement weather."

She had a quick wit. He chuckled, admiring the sparkle of bright flecks in her blue eyes.

A man walking in the aisle behind them stopped, cleared his throat. "What's that you say, young lady?"

The women across the table lifted their heads, and their eyes widened.

Marissa gasped. "Dr. Austin!" Pink flowed into her cheeks. "Please forgive me, sir. I meant no—"

"Do not apologize, young lady. I am in your debt." The leader of the Chautauqua Assembly smiled. "Good strong soup that will not be harmed by the addition of a bit of rainwater is an excellent idea. I shall pass it on to the cooks." He gave a polite bow and walked off.

The women stared after him.

Miss Gordon burst into laughter. "You should see your face, Marissa!"

In his opinion she looked beautiful—if a bit chagrined.

Marissa lifted her hands to cover her cheeks, glanced down at the table. "What are you doing, Clarice?"

He shifted his gaze to the box Miss Gordon had opened. It held all manner of writing supplies.

"I'm making a note to include this story in my article. It's the sort of personal touch that will make my report on this assembly lively and entertaining as well as factual. I shall title it 'The Chautauqua Experience.'" Miss Gordon pulled out pencil and paper, dashed down words. "This is exactly what I was looking for. Something that will make my article stand out from all the other dull, factual reports and gain the editor's and publisher's attention."

His eyebrows rose. "Publisher?"

Marissa Bradley glanced at him, something akin to apprehension in her eyes. "Clarice is a reporter for the *Sunday School Journal*." She turned back to Miss Gordon. "You'll not mention me by name?"

"Not if you don't wish me to. Let me think…" Miss Gordon stopped writing, looked up and grinned. "Ah! I've thought of the perfect name! I'll call you 'Miss Practical.' Do you agree, Mr. Winston?"

"With your choice of the name 'Miss Practical' for the article? Yes, indeed. But as the perfect name for Miss Bradley…" He drew his gaze slowly over her face, his pulse leaping as pink again stole across her delicate cheekbones. "It is too early in my acquaintance with Miss Bradley for me to have an opinion as to that."

A pudgy hand holding a plate of food inserted itself between them. He nodded his thanks as a woman placed tin plates holding boiled potatoes, green beans and two-tined steel forks in front of them, then looked back at Marissa Bradley trying to judge her reaction to his intimation that he would like their budding acquaintance to continue. She had her gaze fixed on her plate. No encouragement there.

He frowned down at his food, stabbed a bite of potato. There was something about Marissa Bradley that drew him in a way no other woman had done. Perhaps it was the mystery of the sadness in her eyes. Whatever it was, he intended to see her again—though instinct warned him she was a very proper young lady and would refuse a direct invitation. *Propriety!*

He jabbed a forkful of green beans, lifted them to his mouth as he pondered the problem. How could he overcome the social conventions of propriety? Another "chance" meeting? He worried the idea around a bit, smiled and impaled another potato. With all of its activities, the assembly should offer ample opportunity. He would find a way.

Marissa rose from the bench and slipped out of the tent to avoid the crush of people when the lecture was over. What a wonderful speaker! The woman had been so concise in making her points about each moral idea she presented. Envy struck, brought forth a long sigh. If only she could be that succinct when she was speaking. Unfortunately, memories always came swarming into her head and her heart got involved. Her subject was not an academic one. It was personal. She lived it.

Grief rose in a sickening wave. Tears stung her eyes. She lifted her hems and ran down the short, narrow path to the larger main one. It was crowded with people. The hum of their voices, chatting and laughing, caused her tears to overflow. She looked around, but there was no place to go where she could be alone. Dusk was falling, and it was too dark to go into the woods, even if she dared.

She drew a long steadying breath, wiped the tears from her cheeks and joined the flow of people going downhill.

"…saw them putting up the canopy on the shore."

"…the concert…"

"…perfect end to the day."

Bits of conversations about the evening entertainment flowed around her. She eavesdropped shamelessly, using the distraction of learning more about the concert to get her emotions under control. Sorting the pieces of information from the general hum of conversation was challenging, like putting a jigsaw puzzle together, and it kept her from remembering. The tightness in her chest eased.

Light flared against the dark trees beside the path ahead. She looked up at the man who had lit the torch in its box of sand, watched as he closed his lantern and climbed down the ladder of short cross boards nailed to the post. A young dark-haired woman stood in the flickering light writing something on a piece of paper that rested on top of a slender wooden box.

"Clarice!"

Her tent mate turned and looked up the path.

She waved her hand and hurried forward. "I see you are taking notes for your 'Chautauqua Experience' article." She peered down at the paper. "What did you call the man—Mr. Lamplighter?"

"No. I named him Mr. Torch Man. It's more accurate and colorful." Clarice slipped the paper into the box, latched it and held it against her chest. "Are you going to the concert? If so, we can walk together."

It would be better than sitting alone in the tent remembering. She took a breath and squared her shoulders. "Yes, I am." She started back down the path, glanced over at Clarice. "Would you like me to carry that box for a bit? You must get tired of carrying it around."

"No, thank you—though you are kind to offer." Clarice looked down and patted the box. "I always keep these writing supplies with me. I never know when something will happen that will fit into an article, or even become one."

"Such as when I embarrassed myself in front of Dr. Austin?" *And Grant Winston.* Her stomach sank at the thought, though he'd been most kind and treated her faux pas with humor.

"Exactly! That incident inspired me to go an entirely different direction with my article for the *Sunday School Journal.* And it will make it ever so much better. Thank you."

Marissa dipped her head. "You're very welcome— as long as I remain anonymous."

"You shall." Clarice stepped out from the cover of the trees along the path. "Oh, my! Only look at that crowd! How am I ever to make my way to a place by the musicians?"

"How are you ever going to *find* the musicians?" She stepped close to the trees, out of the way of the people coming off the path, and stared in amazement at the land on their right. People surrounded the striped canopy that had been erected at the edge of the lake, and from the canopy to the trees at the base of the hill there was no land visible, only people. Most of them were seated on the ground. Those coming were milling about, looking for a place to sit. The blend of their voices as they chatted with one another put her in mind of a swarm of bees.

"Well, I'd best hurry. Dusk is falling and the concert will be starting soon." Clarice looked at her. "Are you coming?"

"Not I!" She smiled and gave a fake shudder. "You

shall have to brave that crowd by yourself. I will listen to the music from over there—" she gestured to the empty shore on the other side of the path "—in solitude."

"Coward." Clarice clutched her box tight to her chest. "I'll see you at the tent if I survive!"

Grant glanced over his shoulder again. People were still streaming by on the path outside. Something was drawing them. Perhaps this was the opportunity for the "chance" meeting with Marissa he'd been thinking about. He slipped off the bench and stepped out from under the canopy making as little disturbance as possible. He'd already lost track of the experiment, but it didn't pertain to farming anyway. There was nothing in today's session that would help him with the vineyard, and it was getting dark. He frowned at the dusky light and pulled his watch from his pocket. The steamer would be leaving soon. The "chance" meeting with Marissa would have to wait until tomorrow. With all the people crowding the path, he'd be fortunate to reach the shore in time to catch the steamer for home. Unless there was another way.

A narrow trail on his left parted the woods. Light filtering through the branches of the trees lit its downward slope. He glanced back at the crowd on the main path, entered the woods and followed the winding way. The sound of voices faded, gave way to birds twittering their night songs. He stepped cautiously through a cluster of pines where it was too dark to see clearly and entered a clearing. Tents formed rows laid out like streets to his left and right. Children laughed and played games, chased one another in and out of the trees. Adults talked over cooking fires. The smell of coffee tantalized his nose. He took a deep sniff, looked around. The path had disappeared.

A woman wearing a long apron straightened from a cooking fire, rubbed her back and looked his way. "You took the wrong path if you're going to the concert. Or else you don't care if you get there late." She motioned to her left. "The main path is a short piece that way."

He smiled his gratitude. "Thank you. I thought this trail might be a faster way to the shore. Obviously, I was wrong." He gave her another smile. "Did you say there was a concert tonight?"

The woman nodded and brushed a strand of hair off her forehead with the back of her hand. "Down on the shore. Isn't that where you was headed? It seems like everybody is going—except those of us with young'uns to watch over. You'd best hurry if you hope to attend. It started at dusk."

"Thank you. You've been very helpful. Perhaps I will attend." He smiled and dipped his head. "Have a good evening."

"And you. Mind your step, there's pines along that path and their roots will trip the unwary."

The woman's words followed him into the darkness beneath the pines. He picked his way to the wider path and started down, joined with others coming out of narrow side paths and clearings to merge with the crowd ahead of him. He wasn't the only one late for the concert. There had to be a hundred or more people within his limited scope of vision.

He scanned the crowd for Marissa's blond curls as he walked, though he knew it for a fruitless effort. The dusky light made all of the ladies' hair seem dark. He snorted at his own foolishness and glanced up at the darkening sky. It wouldn't be long now until the *Colonel Phillips* made its last run of the day. He'd sit on the dock and listen to the music until they ran out the gangplank and he could go aboard.

Music sounded in the distance. He followed those ahead of him out of the trees onto the shore, stopped and stared. The failing light made it difficult to see, but he was almost certain… He smiled and started forward.

Marissa lifted her hems and moved closer to the lake. A warm, gentle breeze carrying soft music from the concert down the lakefront caressed her face and fluttered the curls at her forehead and temples. She stopped and brushed back the curls, gazed at the *Colonel Phillips* floating on the silvered water at the end of the dock, its lanterns golden orbs against the evening sky.

May I assist you to your destination? Sun-streaked hair above a handsome face with a disarming smile rushed back from the oblivion to which she'd assigned them. Seeing Grant Winston at the dining hall this afternoon had brought back the memories of him on the boat. She sighed and shook her head. It was foolishness to entertain romantic thoughts about a man she would likely never see again. But he was so nice. And it was such a perfect night for dreaming…

"Miss Bradley?"

She froze. It couldn't be. She turned, stared at the object of her dreaming. "Mr. Winston!" Heat rushed across her cheeks.

"At your service." He smiled and dipped his head.

She nodded a greeting, pressed her hand over her pounding heart and struggled to order her scattered thoughts.

A frown pulled his straight dark eyebrows together. "I'm sorry if I startled you, Miss Bradley. But you were so lost in thought you didn't notice me."

Thoughts about *him*! The heat in her cheeks increased. She fussed with a fold in her skirt for an excuse to put her head down. "I was admiring the sight of the *Colonel Phillips* against the night sky." *Don't mention the steamer!* "And the lake, of course. Even the silvered water is lovely—from a safe distance." She pressed her lips together to stop her babbling. There was no point in letting the man see that the unfortunate timing of his appearance had her completely undone. It served her right for dreaming about him.

A smile curved his lips. "There is no quivering deck under your feet here."

It wasn't her feet that were quivering. It was her stomach. She lifted her head, gave him a polite, if somewhat forced, smile and groped for a change of subject. "How did you find me?" *Oh, dear. She'd made it sound as if he were on a quest of some sort!* "I mean, what do you want?" *And that was worse!* She stared at him, aghast at her lack of manners.

His gaze traveled slowly over her face, came to rest on her eyes.

The apology she was about to offer died on her lips.

"You have a penchant for standing alone away from the crowd, Miss Bradley. And you are the only person on this part of the shore. I took a chance that it was you."

His gaze held hers. He had warm brown eyes. So... warm... The quivering spread to her knees. She broke the eye contact, clenched her hands to keep from pressing them against her stomach and wished he'd stop talking long enough that she could gather her wits together.

"Would you care to stroll with me along the shoreline until it is time for my steamer to leave, Miss Bradley?"

Did he think her bold like Clarice? She pushed at her curls, pretended to adjust her hat to stall for time. His request was innocent enough to be acceptable. What could she say? *I'm sorry, Mr. Winston, but you make me nervous?* It wasn't his fault that she'd been dreaming. She looked down at his offered arm, nodded and slipped her hand in the crook of his elbow. It felt natural and secure, as if it belonged there. She thrust the thought from her, lifted her hems with her free hand and strolled beside him.

"Did you come to the shore for the concert, Miss Bradley? Or only to admire the view of the lake by night?"

"I came for the concert—along with everyone else here at Chautauqua, it seems. I've never seen so many people in one place. Which is why I am on this side of the dock." She gave a small laugh, focused her thoughts on answering his question to keep from thinking about his closeness. "The loveliness of the lake view was a pleasant surprise." She looked at the water slipping along the shore at his side. "Although I cannot say I find it so at the moment. Now that I'm close, the water simply looks dark and dangerous."

"It's not that way once you know how to swim. It's really quite refreshing to dive into the water on a hot summer's day."

His smile was too charming. "Ah…" She gave him a sidelong look and shook her head. "I shall no longer be ashamed of my cowardice concerning water, Mr. Winston. I see now why you were so comfortable on the steamer. You live on the lake. Though I still cannot see how that can make diving into its water enjoyable." She gave a mock shudder.

He chuckled and turned so that they headed back toward the dock. "I have misled you, Miss Bradley. I live in Mayville and our home is not on Chautauqua Lake, though our land borders it. I learned to swim in a small pond on our property when I was four years old."

"So young?" She halted and looked up at him. "Weren't your mother and father concerned for your safety?"

That deep chuckle rolled from his chest. "They no doubt would have been, had they known about it." A grin slanted across his mouth. "I fell in the pond."

She gasped, pressed her hand to the base of her throat. "Who saved you?"

"No one. My wild flailing and kicking eventually got me to the bank. After that I dove in the pond on purpose." He laughed, tucked her hand back through his arm and started walking again. "I can tell by your horrified expression you've not had any similar experience."

"I should hope not, Mr. Winston!"

"There are no lakes or ponds for swimming where you live?"

Not after we moved from the farm. The thought sobered her. She closed her mind to the memories. "No. I live in Fredonia."

"Ah. Then it is more likely that you are surrounded by vineyards than lakes or ponds."

"Our home is in the town." The answer was curt, bordering on the impolite, but she wanted no questions about her home. And no conversation about vineyards!

He stopped, looked down at her. "I hope you won't think me overly forward, Miss Bradley, but I sense that these two weeks at the Chautauqua Assembly are different. People have come from all over the country, and we must make friends quickly. Thus, strict rules of etiquette have to be relaxed. Would you do me the honor of addressing me by my given name—in private, only if you choose?"

"Why, I—"

"I would not ask such freedom of you, but for the special circumstance of Chautauqua. My name is Grant."

There was sincerity in his voice and in his eyes. Dare she defy propriety? She caught her breath and nodded. "Very well. Because of Chautauqua…Grant." Her cheeks warmed. She looked away.

"Thank you, Miss—"

"Marissa." *Forgive me, Mother.* She made herself look up at him, to read what was in his eyes at her boldness.

"Marissa…"

The *Colonel Phillips* blasted its horn.

She jumped.

He looked at the steamer at the end of the dock, frowned and looked back at her. "The gangplank's being set in place. I have to go." He released her arm, stepped toward the dock, then returned to her. "I will be back for the science class tomorrow evening. May I see you when it's over, Marissa? If you will tell me where you're living—"

The steamer's horn gave its last warning.

"There's no time for directions." He trotted backward toward the dock. "Will you meet me at the hotel? At dusk tomorrow?"

She swallowed the last of her inhibition and nodded. "Yes. I'll be there."

"Until then!" He smiled, turned and ran up the dock and onto the steamer.

She stood rooted to the spot, shocked by what she'd done. But when he'd looked at her…

"There you are, Marissa."

She started, glanced over her shoulder.

Clarice walked up beside her and looked toward the steamer. "Was that Mr. Winston?

"Mr. Boat Man." She laughed and hastened to change the subject, lest Clarice start taking notes for her story. She'd embarrassed herself enough. Her plunge from the rules of society would remain her guilty secret. "Are you through working for the day?"

"I am. Until I get back to the tent and put my notes in order." Clarice waved her hand back toward the hill. "Shall we leave the throng?"

"Yes, of course." She glanced back at the lake. The *Colonel Phillips* was rounding the point. Grant was gone. Until tomorrow night. Her pulse skipped. Her guilt swelled. She composed herself, lifted her hems and followed Clarice up the hill.

Chapter Three

He'd done it. He'd found Marissa Bradley. Well, truth be told, it wasn't his efforts that had brought them together tonight. Grant threw his tie over the back of the Windsor chair, sat and yanked off his shoes. His mother would say the Lord had taken a hand. He frowned, shook his head. He was a man of faith, but he was also a man of science, and that was difficult to swallow. Still…

He *had* given up. The lateness of the hour and the multiple hundreds of people sitting on the grass or milling around listening to the concert had him admitting defeat. But seeing her standing on a deserted portion of the shore was serendipitous, to say the least. His mother would, of a certainty, say it was God.

He crossed to his bed and flopped down onto his back. Marissa was beautiful. His pulse quickened. He laced his hands behind his head and stared up at the plastered ceiling, remembered the way she'd looked with the soft evening light falling on her upturned face, glowing in her blue eyes. Truly beautiful. The delicate cast of her features, the cleanly arched eyebrows over her long-lashed blue eyes, her finely molded nose and cheekbones, soft, full mouth and small, rounded chin were perfection.

He jerked to his feet and walked over to his window, opened it to the warm August night and looked toward the lake. He'd met beautiful young women before. Paid court to a few until he'd lost interest. That was what he had intended to do with Marissa Bradley—see her a few times, satisfy his curiosity about the sadness in her eyes and then say goodbye. But tonight, when he'd looked into her eyes in that first, unguarded moment, something had happened—something beyond the jolt of his heart. There'd been a *knowing* in him that was irrefutable. A sort of…*connection* he didn't understand and couldn't explain. Whatever it was, it was foolish in the light of reason and knowledge. It was also undeniable. It was still there.

He frowned, looked down at the grapevines silvered by the moonlight, turned and headed for his dressing room. He was a young, healthy man. Miss Bradley was a beautiful young woman. His was a simple physical reaction, easily explained by science. He had no reason, time or inclination to examine his response to her more fully than that. He had a busy day tomorrow with the coming harvest to prepare for. The matter of Miss Marissa Bradley would straighten itself out. The odd feeling was, no doubt, because of the circumstances of their meeting—a chance encounter in highly unlikely circumstances was intriguing. That's all it was. The attraction of mystery. He was a man who liked to find answers. The feeling would go away after his planned meeting with Marissa tomorrow night.

"Marissa…" He turned on the tap, shrugged out of his shirt and splashed water on his face. The name suited her. It was soft and beautiful and…haunting. He toweled off, tugged on his nightshirt, turned down the wick in the oil lamp and headed for bed, Marissa Bradley's name and beautiful face lingering in his mind.

Marissa tugged the quilt up closer around her chin and stared at the sloping canvas roof over her cot.

I took a chance that it was you.

A tingle ran up her spine. Grant had come to walk with her. The other meetings might have been accidental, but tonight, he'd chosen to come and spend time with her. And he wanted to see her tomorrow night. Her pulse quickened, shot energy through her. She turned onto her side, winced at the crackle of the corn husks in the mattress and glanced over at Clarice. Her tent mate was sound asleep in spite of the snores and snorts issuing from the tents around them. Nothing seemed to disturb her.

She edged closer to the side of her cot and slipped her legs out from under the covers, froze at the sound of footsteps outside their tent. She drew her legs back under the covers and waited. Moonlight threw a misshapen shadow on the canvas. She watched it float across the wall and disappear, then quickly climbed out of bed and pulled on her dressing gown and slippers. A quick flick of her wrist freed the mass of long curls she'd secured with a ribbon at the nape of her neck from beneath the collar so she could close and button the quilted gown.

Six steps took her from one side of the tent to the other. She turned, careful not to bump against the small writing desk, and walked back again. It was not very satisfactory pacing, but she couldn't stay in bed. She had to *move*. At least with the moonlight shining on the canvas she could see well enough.

Would you do me the honor of addressing me by my given name?

She frowned, fiddled with the top button on her dressing gown. Had she done the right thing when she agreed to Grant's request? And to meet him at the hotel at dusk tomorrow? Oh, what had she been *thinking*! She did not want to demean herself in Grant Winston's eyes. She wanted him to respect her. To hold her in high regard. To—her breath caught—to be attracted to her as she was to him.

She stopped, clasped her face in her hands and blew out a breath. Had she lost all common sense? She knew nothing about Grant Winston except that he was handsome and charming, polite and thoughtful and kind… And that he lived in Mayville and knew how to swim.

What if he indulged in wine or other strong drink?

The thought wouldn't be denied. It hung there in her mind. She closed her eyes, wrapped her arms about herself and endured the pain of the memories that swarmed in silence. There was no room in the tent for tears.

The sadness and grief drove her back to her cot. She

curled up under the covers and stared at the canvas wall. How could she have allowed herself to become so besotted by the beauty of the warm August night and her foolish, romantic dream—so enraptured by Grant's sudden appearance and charm that she forgot the promise she'd made herself—that she'd never fall in love, never marry? She knew what could happen. Her father was charming, too. Until he drank wine. And Lincoln—

She curled tighter, pressed her hand over her mouth to hold back the sobs pushing up her throat. She would meet Grant Winston at the hotel tomorrow night as she promised. And she would tell him that her lectures were to begin the following day and she would not have time to see him again. It was better...*safer* for her that way. And nothing, not even Grant Winston, must be allowed to interfere with her work, to dilute her concentration on her message.

"Good afternoon, Miss...Bradley, is it?"

Marissa looked up from the paper she held and gave the older woman coming into the small, shaded clearing a polite smile. How did the woman know her name? Her memory clicked. Ah, the teachers meeting. "Yes, Bradley is correct. How may I help you, Mrs. Austin?"

"If you wouldn't mind sharing your bench for a brief spell, my dear? The woman smiled and leaned on an ebony walking stick. "I'm afraid this hill is a little too much for me to manage in one try. I find I must pause and let my breath catch up to me every so often."

"It is a bit steep in places. I'm sure that's the reason

for these strategically placed benches." She moved toward the end of the wood bench and pulled her skirt close. "Please sit down and rest yourself."

Mrs. Austin sat, leaned back and sighed. "My weary body and sore feet thank you." She gestured toward the paper with the knob of her walking stick. "I'm sorry to disturb your reading, Miss Bradley. Do go on with it. I shall remain silent."

"No please, that's not necessary, Mrs. Austin. I will be glad of your company." She folded the paper, looked up and smiled. "I have been studying these lecture notes all day. A break from them will be very welcome, I assure you."

The woman nodded, leaned her walking stick against her knees and reached up to adjust the pin in her flower-bedecked hat. "There is keen interest in your lecture tomorrow afternoon, Miss Bradley. Temperance is an issue that touches us all. And people have strong opinions about it—both for and against."

And have no trouble expressing them. "That's certainly true." She straightened, stared at the woman. "If I may ask, how did you know I am lecturing on temperance, Mrs. Austin? The lecturers' names are not printed on the schedules."

"I recognized your name when you introduced yourself to me yesterday. My daughter attended a lecture you gave in Dunkirk. She wrote me all about you. She's here with me." Mrs. Austin's blue-gray eyes focused a kindly gaze on her. "As we learned during the teachers' meeting, debate is to be encouraged after a lecture is concluded. Are you prepared for that, my dear?

Your speaking engagements thus far have been to small welcoming women's church groups. That will not be the case here. These lectures are open to all, men *and* women. And temperance is such a volatile subject."

"Yes…" *What if the debate got out of hand? What if she couldn't handle it?* She drew a breath, opened the drawstring on her purse and slipped her notes inside.

Mrs. Austin reached over and rested her gloved hand on hers. "It was not my intent to discomfort you when I proposed your name to John as a worthy speaker on temperance, my dear. But now, since I've met you, well…you look so young, close to my daughter's age. Please forgive this meddlesome old woman for putting you in a position that may be…upsetting."

So it was Mrs. Austin who had recommended her. "There's no need, Mrs. Austin." She tamped down her nerves and pulled up a smile. "I thank you for telling Dr. Austin about me—for gaining me the opportunity to spread the temperance message to so many people. And I appreciate your thoughtfulness in warning me of possible unpleasantness during a debate. But I have faced irate saloon owners and their equally angry patrons and survived. I am sure I will survive the lectures and debates here at Chautauqua, as well." *And the protest she was to lead?*

"Here you are, Mother. I despaired of finding you. It's time you returned to our tent for supper."

Marissa turned her head, looked at a young woman who stood at the edge of the clearing, her back to the people walking on the path behind her. She took in the young woman's cowed posture, the shawl draped around her thin shoulders though the day was warm, the downward cast of her eyes. She looked closer, gripped her hands together.

Mrs. Austin stirred beside her. "I'm coming, Rose. I've been resting here with Miss Bradley. You remember her from—"

"Yes, of course I do, Mother."

The young woman gave her a polite nod and a shy smile but made no effort to come closer. It wouldn't have mattered. She could see the fading bruise beneath Rose's blue-gray eyes so like Mrs. Austin's—except for the shadow of fear in them. Her heart squeezed. She smiled and nodded a return greeting, remained seated despite her desire to go and put her arms about the young woman. It was obvious Rose was uncomfortable and only wanted to leave. How well she understood Rose's need to hide. She reached up and touched her mother's pendant watch, closed her fingers around it.

"I will be praying for you, Miss Bradley." Mrs. Austin gripped her walking stick, rose and looked down at her. The older woman's face was taut, her eyes overbright. "May the Lord bless you for what you are doing on behalf of women everywhere, Miss Bradley. And may He give you courage and strength as you carry on."

Her throat swelled. Her chest tightened. "Thank you, Mrs. Austin." She smiled and rose to her feet. "I hope we meet again before the Chautauqua classes are over and we all go our separate ways."

"Oh, you may rely on that, Miss Bradley." The older woman's eyes flashed, her mouth firmed. "Rose and I

will both be attending your lectures. *And* taking part
in the after debates. A woman can stay silent only so
long! Good evening."

"Good evening, Mrs. Austin." She resumed her seat
on the bench and waited while Mrs. Austin and her
daughter joined the flow of people going up the hill.

*Debate is to be encouraged after a lecture is con-
cluded...temperance is such a volatile subject...*

Her stomach knotted. She took a breath and straightened, ran her fingers over the smooth enamel of her
mother's watch. Her mother had eyes like Rose's—
except they were green. Once they had sparkled with
laughter; now they were shadowed with grief and fear.

*Don't go to Chautauqua, Marissa. Please don't go.
Stop this insane traveling around to strange towns to
speak about temperance. You cannot bring Lincoln
back, and you may be hurt!*

The memory of her mother's plea brought the answer she hadn't given bursting forth in a furious whisper. "What does it matter if I am made uncomfortable,
or even injured, Mother? It is far less than you and
other women like you suffer! And if it helps to stop
young men like Lincoln from wasting or losing their
lives—" Her voice broke on a sob. She spun about so
those walking on the path couldn't see, covered her
face with her hands and waited for the pain to ease.

Muted chatter and laughter came from the people on
the path. Birds twittered. A chipmunk rustled through
the dry fallen leaves looking for provender. She drank
in the peace, absorbed the strength of it into her heart.

The tears on her cheeks dried. She clasped her hands in her lap and closed her eyes.

"Lord, please help me when I speak tomorrow evening and the days following. Please don't let me disappoint Mrs. Austin and Rose and all of the other women who are ashamed or afraid and need someone to speak for them. Please let these lectures bring them comfort and strength in the knowledge that they are not alone. And please let them steer young men like Lincoln away from paths of destruction. Amen."

Fresh dedication to the temperance cause erased her fears and strengthened her determination. She opened her eyes and glanced up at the sky. The light was beginning to fade. But there was still time to go to the tent and freshen up before going to the hotel to meet Grant Winston.

She rose and shook out the skirt of her plum gown, closing her mind to the question of why freshening her appearance should matter when she was only going to tell Grant goodbye.

Grant's strides ate up the distance to the hotel. The science class had been interesting, but disappointing as far as information about improving crops was concerned. So far he had learned nothing with which to counter his father's continued assertions that he was wasting his time coming to the Chautauqua classes.

A crowd blocked the intersection of paths ahead. People milled about waiting to get into The Hotel. Others came out and walked across the clearing to the path.

He swept his gaze over the moving lines, frowned

and looked to the side of the building. Marissa was talking with an older woman. She glanced around and their gazes met. His heart slammed against his rib cage. He yanked his hat from his head and started toward her, an eagerness to be with her driving his steps.

She said something to the woman, lifted her hems and came toward him, a picture of shyness and dignity that stole into his thudding heart.

"Good evening. I hope I haven't kept you waiting, Marissa." Pink flowed into her cheeks when he spoke her name. His fingers crunched the brim of his homburg. He put it back on his head out of danger.

"Not at all. I only arrived a few minutes ago." She looked down, brushed at the front of her long skirt.

He pulled his gaze from the mass of blond curls that fell to her shoulders from under the small excuse for a hat she wore, and looked toward the building. "I didn't have time last night to make proper plans. Would you like to get something to eat?" She looked up, and his mouth went so dry he'd have choked on a bite of food.

"Thank you, but I was uncertain about our…plans, also, so I dined earlier with my tent mate." She took a breath. "Mr. Winston, I—"

"Grant." The pink spread across her cheeks again. He made a manly effort to ignore her blush. It was either that or give up breathing. "We seem to be blocking the exit route standing here." He smiled and offered her his arm.

She looked up at him, started to say something, then glanced at the people coming out of the hotel and slipped her hand through the crook of his elbow.

He had the distinct impression she'd been about to refuse his company. He started across the clearing toward the downhill path before she could change her mind. "I'm afraid our choice of entertainment is sparse. We can go to the drawing class being offered by Mr. Paul Frank. Or perhaps go for a walk." He looked down at her and grinned. "I'm doubtful you would like to go rowing on the lake."

"You are correct, sir." She tugged him to a halt, a small frown creasing her brow. "Grant, I need to—" Her frown deepened. He watched fascinated as she nibbled at her lower lip with her teeth. "Did you say the artist conducting the drawing class is Mr. Paul Frank, the famous caricaturist?"

"That is my understanding." *He'd never known God made eyelashes so long...*

She sighed, seemed to come to a decision. "Then I should very much like to attend his class. Do you know where it is being held?"

"I do. But that knowledge is not necessary. All we need do is to follow the largest crowd. And that would be this way." He guided her off the downhill path and they followed a long line of people to an enormous canopy ringed with posts capped by blazing torches.

A large blackboard, a small table covered with crocks and boxes and a wooden chair were on a platform in front of long rows of benches. Posts with lanterns atop them lit the platform and shone on a small, portly gentleman standing in front of the blackboard and speaking.

"—call out as soon as you recognize *what* or *who* I am drawing."

Grant looked over the filled benches and frowned. "I'm afraid we're too late to find a seat under the canopy. But I see something that might serve. Be careful of the uneven ground." He took her elbow and led her to a small rise off to the side of the structure.

"It's a chicken!" A man in the audience shouted out the guess.

They paused, looked toward the platform.

"A chicken?" The artist stepped back from his work, raised his hands into the air and gave an exaggerated shrug. "Is my drawing that bad?" Laughter erupted.

Grant glanced at the disconnected lines on the blackboard, shrugged and started forward again. "It looks like a chicken to me."

She shook her head. "If it's a chicken, what is that wavy line at the bottom?"

He stopped himself from taking a deep sniff of the lavender scent that rose from her hair, glanced at the blackboard again and grinned. "A broken branch?"

"A *branch*? Is that the best you can do, O ye of little imagination?"

He pulled his eyebrows down in a mock scowl. "You cast aspersions on my artistic sensibilities?"

"Not at all. There's no need. Your lack thereof is evident." She grinned and nodded toward the blackboard. "Mr. Frank is drawing a woman's hat. That wavy line is the brim."

He stopped, gave a soft cackle and flapped his elbows. "Chicken!"

Her laughter was like music. She patted her head. "Hat!"

"We shall see."

"Indeed, we shall." She looked back toward the canopy. "This is much better than if we had stayed in the back. I can see over the heads of everyone."

"Good." He removed his coat, spread it over the leaf-strewn ground at their feet and made her an exaggerated bow. "Your seat awaits—if you don't mind sitting on the ground, that is." He held his hand out to her. She looked at it, caught at her lower lip with her teeth. The impression came again that she was about to refuse. He braced himself.

"As long as the ground doesn't quiver." She gave a little laugh and placed her hand on his.

It was trembling. The slight tremors traveled all the way to his toes. *Blushes. Trembling. Miss Marissa Bradley was not as calm and detached as she acted. So why was she feigning disinterest?* He curled his fingers around her soft, delicate hand, helped her seat herself on his coat, then lowered himself to the ground as close to her as he dared.

"It's my hat!"

A woman on a front bench shrieked out the words.

"You're right, madam. And this…is you." The artist connected two lines, and the face of a woman appeared beneath a hat trimmed with feathers. The audience burst into applause.

Marissa shot him a smug look from the corners of her eyes and grinned.

His pulse leaped. He returned her grin and shrugged. "I'll get this next one." He pulled his face into a mock frown, stared at the new lines on the blackboard and stroked his chin. "I've got it!" He leaned forward and placed his lips close to her ear. "It's a chicken."

She burst into laughter.

He sat and drank in the sight of her. He could look at her all night.

"It's amazing how Mr. Frank does that." She tilted her head, studied the blackboard, then looked at him and shook her head. "I believe, *this time*, your 'chicken' is a man."

He narrowed his eyes at the blackboard. "And I believe you may be right." He pulled his eyebrows into another mock scowl. "It's beginning to look like President George Washington—with a *chicken* feather in his *hat*."

She glanced over at him, her eyes twinkling. "A plume straight from his plantation no—"

Two quick blasts from a steamer's whistle rent the air. A few people rose from their seats and made their way into the aisles between the rows of benches.

"Alas, we shall never know. That's the warning from the *Colonel Phillips*." He looked up at the sky and frowned. "The lanterns make the canopy area so bright I lost track of the time."

He rose and helped her to her feet. His pulse raced at the feel of her hands in his. He locked his gaze on hers and cleared his throat. "I'm sorry to make you miss the rest of the entertainment, Marissa, but I've only time enough to walk you to your tent before I leave."

"That's not necessary." She lowered her gaze and gave a little tug. He relaxed his grip, and she slipped her hands from his, stepped back and shook out her long skirts. "You'd best hurry."

It sounded like a dismissal. He nodded, leaned down and picked up his coat. He'd never had to beg to court a woman and he wouldn't start now. But right was right. "A gentleman doesn't leave a lady to find her own way home, Marissa. So, unless you have made plans for another escort, I'll see you to your tent on my way down the hill."

"Plans for another *escort*? You think—" She stiffened and tugged at the waist of her gown. "Good evening, and *goodbye*, Mr. Winston."

He stared at her rigid posture, hastened to apologize. "I didn't mean to offend, Marissa. I only thought—"

She lifted her hand. "It's not your fault, Mr. Winston. I gave you the wrong impression when I broke the rules of propriety. But…so you will *know*." Her chin lifted. "I do not live *down* the hill. If I did, I would have been pleased to have you see me home."

The past tense was not lost on him. Nor was the fact that she would have accepted his escort. "Marissa—"

"I live *up* the hill—at the very top. And I *do* have another escort, of a sort. My tent mate. You remember Miss Gordon. She is there—"

He winced as she waved a hand toward the bench in front of the platform.

"—taking notes for her article in the *Sunday School Journal*. I will walk home with her when the class is over and her work is done. Now, I suggest you hurry, lest you miss your steamer. Thank you for a pleasant evening."

He grinned. He couldn't help it. She was the cutest thing he'd ever seen standing there with her chin jutted, her eyes flashing blue sparks and her cheeks so flushed they matched the color of that gown she was wearing.

"You find me amusing, Mr. Winston?"

Whoo! An ice-cold voice and a red-hot anger. Quite a combination. He shook his head, held her gaze with his. "No. I find you intriguing, Miss Bradley. And I, also, find you a lovely, very proper young lady I look forward to seeing again. You mistook—"

"I mistook nothing, Mr. Winston. Your meaning was quite clear!" Her chin raised another notch. "As for you seeing me again—I'm afraid that will not be possible. I shall be too busy. I begin lecturing tomorrow and—"

"You're a speaker?" That information drove his explanation from his thoughts. "Then I shall attend your lecture. What subject—" A long single blast of the steamer's whistle sounded a final warning of imminent departure. His time was gone. "No matter. I shall find you. Until tomorrow afternoon, Marissa!" He spun on his heel and sprinted for the path that led to the lake.

Chapter Four

"Winston!"

Grant looked over his shoulder to find the person who had called out to him. A man waved his hand above the heads of those crowded on the trail. He stepped aside and nodded as John Hirsch, owner of the Stone Tavern in Mayville, strode up to him.

"You going to this temperance thing, Winston?"

"I plan on attending, yes." Hopefully, he'd find Marissa there. He had to try to repair his faux pas of last night and he'd already missed his chance of attending her afternoon lecture, thanks to his father. He fell into step and headed up the hill beside the tavern keeper. "I've read the temperance people are growing in numbers, and I'm curious to hear one of them speak."

"So am I. I've heard they close down taverns and men's clubs, wherever liquor is sold. I'm here to find out if that's true—and if this speaker has any plans to cause trouble around here." John Hirsch's face darkened. "There'll be plenty of trouble if she riles up local women to try and shut down my place. And the other bar owners in the area feel the same. There's a group of us going to be here. You're welcome to join us."

"Sorry, I'm meeting someone." *I hope.* He shot the tavern owner a questioning look. "How do you know the speaker is a woman?"

"Stands to reason, don't it? Men are the ones that do the drinking. No women come to my place."

"That's true." He acknowledged the hand John Hirsch raised in farewell, looked at the people overflowing the canopy into the clearing and frowned. Hopefully, he could work his way to a spot where he'd be able to hear the speaker while he searched the attendees for Marissa. Would the subject even interest her? He veered to the right, spotted a space beside an outside support post and edged into it. People crowded in behind him, muttering about being late, about not being able to get closer to the speaker.

He scanned the profiles of those seated under the canopy looking toward the platform at the front. There was no beautiful face with a pert nose and a small determined chin in sight. A grin tugged his lips into a slanted line. She'd jutted that chin at him like a weapon last night. Marissa Bradley had spunk to spare. He liked that. He'd never cared for coy, simpering women.

The desire to see her strengthened. He glanced over the crowd again. If she wasn't here, he didn't know where to look for her, beyond the vague "top of the hill" direction she'd thrown at him in her anger. Ah! She could be sitting up by the platform with Miss Gordon. He frowned and glanced over his shoulder. If he could get through those who were vying for position behind him, he could make his way to where he could see the faces of the people seated on the front benches. He inched around the post, glanced toward the front and froze, stared at the slender, black-garbed woman on the stage. *Marissa?* Shock held him rooted in place. He fastened his gaze on her face, strained to hear what she was saying over the rustle and bustle of the other latecomers seeking a place to stand.

"I am not telling you anything you do not already know. We are gathered here from many different cities and towns in many different states. Think of your hometown. How many churches are there? How many taverns where strong drink is sold? In most towns, for every minister there are three or four or more barkeepers, and while churches meet, at most, a few days a week, the taverns and bars and men's clubs sell their products of destruction all the days of the week."

There was a murmur of agreement from many around him. But it had always been so. He scanned the nearby faces. If Marissa's aim as a temperance speaker was to plant seeds of discontent among those listening, she was doing a good job.

"And what happens inside those shops? The proprietor tucks the coins offered into his till and gives the patrons drinks that numb their brains and dull their senses. When the patrons go home to those who love them above all others, their drunken state causes them to inflict pain with their words and their hands. The same is true of those who drink only in their homes. And though I am aware that not all who drink to excess turn mean or abusive, they still inflict pain and shame upon their family by their very state."

There was a collective gasp followed by furtive looks and bowed heads. A woman in front of him blinked tears from her eyes. Another rubbed at her upper arm and winced. He glanced from face to face of the people in front of him, noted frowns and set jaws on the men, overbright, downcast eyes on some women, lips pressed into firm lines and heads held high in others. He leaned forward and slid his gaze over the attendees on the seats that had been blocked from his view by the post, focused on a woman who sat clutching a handkerchief, her head slowly nodding as if it had a will of its own. Sarah Swan? Why was the grocer's wife here? Toby Swan was a friendly, jovial man—

"—brother died an untimely death because of the ravages of strong drink."

The pain in Marissa's voice jerked him from his thoughts. He slid around the post for a clearer view of her, remembered her speaking of her brother that first night on the steamer.

"Lincoln is the reason I stand before you today. I want you to know you are not alone in your hurt and your shame. And to *implore* you to take steps to help your loved ones before..." Marissa's head bowed then lifted. "...before it is too late."

So *that* was why she was lecturing on temperance. Grief was in her voice, the line of her slightly bowed head, her rigid posture. He clenched his hands, wished he could comfort her. He locked his gaze on her, willed her to look his way, to notice him, to at least know that he was here and that he cared that she was hurting.

"Ladies and gentlemen, the consumption of strong drink in all its forms is more prevalent today than it has ever been in our nation. It is destroying families and ruining young people's lives. And it has to stop! I know many of you feel helpless and alone, but you're not. And if you will only find the courage to speak the truth at church meetings and women's clubs, at sewing and quilting bees when you return to your towns, you will find others will gather strength from your honesty and stand with you. There is comfort and strength in knowing you are not alone. And there is power for change in numbers. The temperance movement is growing. I urge you to add your voice to our protest against the damage done to families by strong drink and those who provide it."

Whoa! Grant swept his gaze to the other side of the canopy, found John Hirsch and his cohorts standing in a group on the edge of the crowd. They did not look pleased.

"That concludes my message. Are there any questions or—"

Voices erupted into a cacophony of called questions and challenges. He darted a look back at Marissa. Her hands rose for silence.

"I will be pleased to answer your questions, ladies and gentlemen. But I cannot hear when you all call them out at once. Please keep order while presenting your questions. I will answer all that time allows tonight. And if it becomes too late, I will answer any remaining questions after my next lecture." She nodded toward someone on her right. "Have you a question, madam? Please stand and speak out so all can hear."

A woman stood, her back straight as a ramrod. "Do you include wine when you speak of 'strong drink'?"

Wine? He shook his head. That was ridiculous. They drank wine in church during Commu—

"I do indeed, madam. Wine can alter a man's judgment and personality the same as all strong drink."

A man shot to his feet, his chin thrust out in a belligerent jut. "Who are you to vilify wine, when Jesus Himself made wine at the wedding feast at Cana?"

A murmur spread through the crowd. Grant stared at the man's angry face and his gut tightened. This could get nasty. He glanced at Marissa standing alone at the edge of the platform, slipped back behind the post and edged through the cluster of people behind him. He had to get to her in case things got unruly. He hurried along the space between the people and the edge of the woods toward the platform, paused as Marissa's voice rose clear and firm above the muttering.

"It's true that Jesus made wine at Cana. But, as that wine was *freshly* made, I do not believe that it 'biteth like a serpent, and stingeth like an adder' as does wine 'at the last' as we are told in Proverbs, chapter twenty-three. That chapter carries a strong warning against drinking that type of wine. It says we are not to look upon it, and warns us of the consequences."

He searched his memory but couldn't recall ever hearing of such a warning.

"'Who hath woe? who hath sorrow? who hath contention? who hath babbling? who hath wounds without cause? who hath redness of eyes? They that tarry long at the wine; they that go to seek mixed wine.' Ladies and gentlemen, I *know* these things are true! And not only for those who drink the wine, but for those who live with them also. *That* is why I include wine when I speak against strong drink! Next question please."

One of the men with John Hirsch pushed forward. "I've heard you people close down taverns and bars. You close churches that hold Communion services, too?"

Another of the group thumped the man's shoulder, looking pleased at the trap his cohort had sprung. "That's right! Fair's fair." The group snickered.

Grant started forward again. Marissa was no match for—

"We do not. The warning says, 'They that tarry *long* at the wine…' That does not happen at a church Communion service, sir."

There was a burst of applause. A woman surged to her feet. "I want to start a temperance group when I go home." There was a chorus of agreement. The woman looked around, stood straighter. "Will you tell me—"

A blast of a steamer's horn drowned out the rest of the woman's words. He looked toward the lake, glanced back at Marissa. She was holding her own, and he had no choice. At least John Hirsch and his friends had to leave, too. He blew out a breath and headed for the path to the lake.

The jet buttons that fastened the bodice of the dress she'd removed shimmered through her watery gaze.

Marissa blinked away the rush of tears. She hated the black dress. It made Lincoln's death real. Not that it wasn't every minute of every day. But the dress brought back the raw pain of his passing. And talking about it this evening...

She drew a breath and gave a quick tug on the black ribbon that restrained her curls. They fell onto her shoulders and tumbled down her back. She stared down at the ribbon in her hand, played it through her fingers. Grant had been there. She'd thought after their tiff last night that she'd seen the last of him in spite of his declaration. But he'd come. She'd seen him standing beside a support post at the back, and the tightness in her chest had eased, her pain had dulled. How could the mere sight of a man she'd known for such a short time make her feel better?

She tossed the ribbon on top of her black hat lying on the dress draped over her open trunk and slipped beneath the covers. Clarice would be back from the necessary any moment, and she was in no mood to talk. Sadness for all those women who had come to her lecture seeking answers and asking for help to change situations they perceived as hopeless weighed on her. As did the anger of the men who came to stand against the temperance movement and challenge its message. One way or another, those men were ensnared. If not by the need for strong drink itself, then by the money they made providing it to those who had such a need. Her heart ached for them.

A long sigh escaped her. "Blessed Lord, You alone have the power to free all of those who are entangled by the webs woven by strong drink. Help them to seek You, Lord, that You might break the bonds that hold them prisoner, for Your Word declares, 'If the Son therefore shall make you free, ye shall be free indeed.'"

The tent flap rustled. She closed her eyes, feigned sleep as Clarice prepared for bed. Grant had come to her lecture, but when she had glanced his way the second time he was gone. A woman had stood in his place by the post. Had he been offended by her message? Was he a drinker and thus opposed to the temperance movement? She drew a breath against a sudden, hollow feeling in her stomach, let it out quietly. Her budding relationship with Grant was one more thing strong drink had stolen from her. She would never know what might have been.

Tears stung her eyes. How she hated wine! It had cost her everything she held dear—her happy family life, her brother and any chance for love. She lay unmoving, wishing Clarice would go to sleep so she could rise and get her Bible to hold. Clutching God's Word close to her heart always helped to stave off the bitter loneliness.

The door whispered open. Grant pulled his shoulder away from where it rested against the porch post and turned. His mother lifted the cup in her hand, gave him a tentative smile and stepped out onto the back porch.

"Our bedroom window is open and I smelled the coffee. I thought I'd come and join you—unless you prefer to be alone?"

He pasted on a smile and shook his head. "Not at

all. It's a lovely night, though there's a breeze quickening and the smell of rain in the air."

The hem of her dressing gown brushed against the painted floorboards as she came to join him by the railing. "Are you concerned a rain will harm the grapes this close to harvest?"

"No. It would take a real cloud buster to hurt them now." He took a sip of his strong black coffee and gazed out over the fields of vines. *How would Marissa feel about them?*

"Well, something has you restive." Moonlight fell on her face as she tipped her head back to look up at him. "You're not usually up making coffee during the wee hours of the night."

"Um…" Odd how that look made him want to spill out the truth like when he was a five-year-old. "Do you know about the Temperance Movement, Mother?"

"I've heard of it. Why?" Her gaze narrowed on his. "Was that lecture on temperance at the assembly you told us about this evening? Is that what has you unsettled?"

The lecture, and the lecturer. He ignored her comment about his condition. "I've been pondering what the speaker said, and I wondered if you agreed with their message is all."

"I'm not familiar with their message."

He swirled his coffee around in the cup, watched it settle. "They stand against the use of all strong drink—including wine. Mari— The speaker quoted a warning against wine from the Bible."

"And that's what disturbed you?"

He ignored the niggling unease that had kept him from sleep and tugged his lips into a grin. "No reason why it should. I don't drink wine." A gust of wind blew a fine mist against his face. "Looks like we'd best finish our coffee inside. The rain is on its way." He opened the kitchen door for his mother, swept another glance over the vines with their heavy burden of grapes then followed her inside.

Chapter Five

There were two bidders left. Grant looked at the vintner on his right and held his face impassive, though it wasn't easy. The offers were already above what his father had hoped for. "Have you a counteroffer, Mr. Hardon?"

The elderly man frowned and shook his head. "These are excellent grapes, and I hate to lose the advantage of first harvest, but the bid's gone too high for me, Winston." The owner of the Hickory Hill Winery tossed the concords he held to the ground. "I'll take my chances on the good weather holding long enough to ripen the grapes at the other vineyards. Besides, I'm not eager to be the first one to face those protesting women." The vintner brushed his hands together, gave his rival a grim smile. "I'll leave that pleasure to you, Douglas. Maybe by the time the grapes I buy are ready for harvest, some of the zeal will have worn off and the women will be content to stay at home the way they always have. Good afternoon, gentlemen."

Protesting women? Unease pricked him. Grant watched Thomas Hardon climb into his buggy and start his horse moving, shook off the disquiet and offered his hand to Dillon Douglas. "You have bought yourself an excellent yield of grapes, Mr. Douglas."

The owner of Oakwood Winery nodded, released his handshake and smiled. "Thanks to Hardon's love of a penny and lack of stomach for a bit of trouble. Not that I expect anything to come of the rumor."

"Are you referring to the women Mr. Hardon spoke of? I've not heard anything."

"None of us had until this morning when Hardon told us." Dillon Douglas's smile turned to a frown. "Seems as if this temperance stuff going on at the Chautauqua Assembly has stirred up some of the local women. Hardon's wife overheard some talk that a few of them were going to try and form some sort of protest march against the wineries in the area and she got all upset." The vintner snorted, shook his head. "A lot of nonsense. I don't know how a handful of women think they can stop us from making wine. They can march around in front of our buildings carrying signs and singing and praying till they all have blisters the size of toadstools on their feet and it won't do them a whit of good. Our men will come to work same as always—and we've got no customers for them to scare off the way I've heard they do at taverns. Now, about the grapes..." Dillon Douglas popped one in his mouth, split another with his thumbnail and peered at the seeds. "I'll send out notice to my pickers tomorrow, have them here with the wagons the next day."

"I'll be waiting." Grant stepped back as the older man climbed into his buggy. "They need to start with the vines that face south. The grapes there ripen a few days earlier than the rest."

"They'll follow your directions as to the picking." The owner of Oakwood Winery looked back as the horse started forward. "Tell your father I'll be here so we can sign the contract the day the pickers start. That should get him over this bad spell he's taken."

"I'll do that." He watched the buggy traveling down the length of the vineyard's access road, turned and headed for the house.

Seems as if this temperance stuff going on at Chautauqua has stirred up some of the local women. He frowned and climbed the steps of the back porch. Dillon Douglas could be more right than he knew. Grant opened the door and stepped into the kitchen thinking of Sarah Swan seated on a bench at Marissa's lecture clutching her handkerchief and slowly nodding. Was Sarah Swan one of that handful of women?

"How did the bidding go? Did you make a sale?"

He glanced at his mother standing by the stove wearing her apron and an expectant expression, and smiled. "I did. And for more than Father hoped."

"Oh, Grant, that's wonderful!" She laid the wooden spoon she held on a plate, skirted her worktable and went on tiptoe to kiss his cheek. "Your father will be so pleased!" The shadow of worry in her eyes lessened. "I'm sure the good news will make him feel better. You'll find him in the den going over some papers. I couldn't make him stay in bed as Dr. Fletcher ordered." Frustration flitted across her face; the shadow returned to her eyes.

He pulled her into a hug. "Please don't worry. He's strong and—"

"Stubborn isn't strong, Grant. It's merely…stubborn…" She pulled back, snatched up her spoon and stirred the contents of a pot. "Now look what you've done. I got so excited over your good news I almost burned the pudding!" She waved her hand toward the door. "Shoo! Go tell your father the good news and leave me to my cooking."

The *Colonel Phillips*, gleaming white in the sun, floated to a stop at the end of the dock and blasted its whistle. Shouts rang out. Marissa left the shade of the trees and walked to the dock while the crew snubbed the steamer fast and the gangway was put in place. The disturbed lake water swirled around the posts of the dock and lapped at the shoreline. She lifted her hand to shield her eyes against the brightness and watched for Mrs. Swan and the women she was bringing with her to disembark. She'd found a small canopy with a few benches nestled among the trees close to the shore they could use for their meeting—if no one had claimed it by the time they reached it.

The figure of a tall man moved through the shadows in the recessed area of the steamer deck, and her stomach fluttered. Was Grant aboard? A wish to see him stride down the dock and smile when he spotted her rose unbidden. She smoothed back a curl, glanced down at her dark gray day dress so somber in the sunlight and wished she were wearing one of her regular gowns. Her mother said she looked her prettiest in blue or yellow.

Well, what did that matter? She wanted no part of a romantic involvement. But Grant's friendship was… strengthening…rewarding. And withdrawn. Her face tightened. The flutters in her stomach turned to knots. His friendship had survived her attempt to rid herself of his company, but not her lecture. There was little doubt but that her temperance advocacy had offended him. He had left her lecture before she was through speaking—before the *Colonel Phillips* had blown its first warning whistle. He was most likely an imbiber. How foolish was she to stand there and hope— Nothing! She didn't *want* to see Grant Winston again.

Mrs. Swan and four other women crossed over the gangway to the dock, walked to the gatehouse and filed past the window showing their passes. A quick glance at the short line behind them and the empty steamer deck confirmed that there were no more passengers waiting to disembark. Grant hadn't come. Her wish had been granted. She would probably never see him again. She took a breath, tried to rub away the sinking feeling in her chest. *Hope deferred maketh the heart sick…* She jerked her hand down and forced the scripture verse from her mind. She was *not* hoping. It was good Grant hadn't come. She was glad.

The women coming toward her looked nervous. And guilty. It was a feeling she knew well. She smiled to put them at ease and stepped forward. "Good morning, Mrs. Swan…ladies. If you will come with me, I've found a tent we may use."

They followed her in silence, only the rustle of their skirt hems brushing over the grass giving testimony to their continued presence. She led them into the shade beneath the canopy and turned to face them. "Please have a seat, ladies. And let me say, before we start discussing the reason for our meeting, that I admire your courage in coming." Her gaze trailed over their determined faces and clenched hands. "I know what your decision has cost you. The battles you have fought with yourself over feelings of guilt, betrayal…shame. And I know that only frustration and a desperate hope to find a way to help your loved one has brought you here."

"And hatred." The woman sitting beside Mrs. Swan looked up at her. "A pure hatred for the wine that turned my Henry from a good husband and father into a useless drunk is why I'm here." The woman's eyes glistened with anger. "We lost our farm and all we had because of wine. And then it killed Henry. If my sister and her husband hadn't taken us in, I don't know how I'd have fed and sheltered my children. I'm married again now, but I haven't forgotten all that was stolen from me. I'm here because I hate wine."

"We all do, Miss Bradley." Mrs. Swan squared her shoulders. "I've read in newspaper articles from different towns that you have led protests that have closed some taverns and bars. But my husband does not go to the taverns or bars. He—he imbibes wine secretly at home and becomes…unpleasant."

Like Father. Anger and sorrow welled. She clenched

her hands, dug her fingernails into her palms to keep from being distracted by memories.

"That's why I wrote asking you to lead us in a protest against the local wineries and vineyards. Will you help us, Miss Bradley?"

She pushed her emotions aside and cleared her throat. "I have given this a good deal of thought since receiving your letter, Mrs. Swan. And while I am pleased at being given the opportunity to lead you ladies on your quest, I must be honest and tell you that I believe it doubtful that staging a protest at a winery will stop their production of wine, or even harm their profits, as there are no patrons to be turned away as there are at taverns. The same is true of a vineyard. Therefore, if that is your goal, I believe such a protest would be useless."

"I see." Mrs. Swan rose, her face a stiff mask of disappointment and frustration. "Thank you for giving us your time, Miss Bradley." The older woman faced her friends. "Well, it seems if we are to make our message known, we must do this on our own, ladies. Who—"

"You mistake me, Mrs. Swan."

The leader of the women turned back to face her, a tentative hope in her eyes. Marissa smiled reassurance and swept her gaze over the small group. "I was not declining to lead your protest, ladies. I was merely pointing out its limitations, lest you were hoping to financially hurt the wineries or vineyards and force their closure. I believe that the best result a small group like ours—" relief flickered across the women's faces as she aligned herself with them "—can hope to achieve with such a protest is to call the public's attention to the pain and destruction the wine produced by the vineyards and wineries can bring to men and families and hope that message will save others from the pain you have suffered."

She took a breath and searched the women's faces. "Temperance marches are growing in importance. Have you considered that word of your protest will spread? That, if we are successful, it may even be reported in the newspapers? That is how you learned my name. Before we go forward, you must each decide if you are willing to face that possibility."

Mrs. Swan firmed her lips and nodded. "I am. I have lived hiding the truth long enough."

"And me."

One by one the ladies gave their affirmation.

"Very well, then." She brushed back a curl tickling her cheek and searched her memory. "Every temperance protest I'm aware of has been made with the intention of closing down taverns and bars and other places where strong drink is sold. I cannot recall any temperance march against those who *produce* the strong drink. But I believe there will be many such protests to follow this one. You are pioneers leading the way, ladies! Now, my time here at Chautauqua is short, so let's discuss the matter and plan the protest in detail. I am unfamiliar with the workings of a winery, so please offer any suggestions you might have for the group's consideration. And when you speak, please tell me your name." She nibbled at her lower lip, ordered her thoughts. "Our goal will be to disrupt and trouble the

business and thus draw attention to the wine they produce and its debilitating effects. I see no possibility of
that with a vineyard, short of uprooting their grapevines which, of course, we would not do. Perhaps we
should focus on the wineries—"

"If I may?"

She glanced at the blonde woman seated on the second bench. "Yes, Mrs...."

"Jefferson. But please call me Ina." The woman
moistened her lips with the tip of her tongue. "As you
were speaking about the goal being to disrupt business,
it occurred to me that there is a way to do that to both
a winery and a vineyard at the same time."

"Both of them at once? That would be wonderful!"
She smiled encouragement. "How would we do that,
Ina?"

The women on the front bench shifted around to
look at their friend.

"Well, harvest season is beginning. That means the
vintners will soon be buying grapes and sending their
pickers and wagons out to the vineyards to gather them
and bring them back to the winery. If we were to go to
the vineyard when the winery wagons were there—"

"My stars!"

"If we could stop those loaded wagons—"

The excitement was catching. She hated to quench
the women's enthusiasm, but there was one obvious
flaw. "I agree it would be the perfect plan, ladies. But
we would need to know when a winery's wagons would
be at a particular vineyard."

"I can tell you that." The young woman sitting at

the end of the front bench scooted to the edge and all but bounced with excitement. "I'm Judith Moore. And my sister is being courted by a man who works for the Oakwood Winery. He told her that tomorrow night would be the last night he could call on her for a while, as they were going to start harvesting at the Twin Eagle Vineyard the next day and he will be driving one of the wagons."

"That vineyard is close enough to town we could walk there."

"Should we carry signs?"

"Everyone in town would see us."

"Which is the purpose of a temperance march." Marissa studied the women who had gone suddenly silent. "This sounds perfect for our purposes, ladies. Unless you have changed your minds about holding a protest?"

Mrs. Swan shook her head. "I haven't changed my mind. It's sobering to think of all that might befall, is all." The older woman squared her shoulders. "I'll make signs on wrapping paper from the store. And there's some wood from crates out back we can use to hold them."

"There's some paint left from when Carl painted the barn we can use. I'll help you, Sarah."

"And me."

Marissa frowned and stepped in with a warning. "You must keep the protest a secret, ladies. So we catch our target unaware."

Sarah Swan nodded, then glanced at her friends. "Come to my house tomorrow night. And bring your sewing so we're not discovered."

"Well, it seems most of the details of the march are taken care of, save one important one." Marissa smiled to hide her trepidation at the thought of getting on the steamer for the trip to Mayville. "When and where shall we gather to begin our march, ladies?"

The heated temperance debate had stopped. The crowd was thinning fast, drawn away by the singing group that was the night's entertainment if the bits of conversation swirling around him were any indication. Grant fastened his gaze on Marissa and moved forward against the flow, holding his stride in check, lest his eagerness cause him to bump into someone. He'd missed being with her. Ridiculous after knowing her for so short a time, but there it was.

The women she was talking with nodded and walked away. "Marissa…"

Her body stiffened. He braced himself and prepared to apologize for his faux pas the last time they'd been together, unwilling to accept rejection. She turned and looked up at him. His pulse kicked. He drank in the warmth in her eyes, puzzled over her tentative smile.

"Good evening, Grant. Was there something you wanted?"

Her posture was stiff, almost…defensive, her tone polite. But the warmth, the gladness in her eyes when she'd turned and seen him gave the lie to it all. "Yes. To apologize again for my lack of manners the other night—"

She shook her head. "My fault entirely. I should not have—"

"Marissa—" He reached for her arm, stopped, dropped his hand to his side and rushed to get out his apology before she interrupted him again. "I have never thought of you as anything but a proper young lady who was kind enough to bend the rules of propriety a little because of the special circumstances of the Chautauqua Assembly in order to accommodate the wishes of this young man who thoroughly enjoys your company and hopes you will not deny him that pleasure. Which brings me to my second purpose." He stretched his right leg out behind him and made her a deep, sweeping bow, ending with his hand over his heart. *Please let the humor work, Lord.* He raised his voice to a normal level again. "Would you do me the honor of accompanying me on a stroll along the shore?"

"Get up before someone sees you!" Her cheeks flamed.

"Not until you agree, my lady." He faked a wobble, flailed his arms.

"Stop! I'll walk with you." She huffed the words, but her lips were twitching.

He grinned, straightened and offered her his arm. She caught at her lower lip with her teeth, worried it a moment then took her place beside him.

"Do you always resort to blackmail to win your way, Grant?"

"Never before, Marissa." He guided her onto the main path and headed down the hill. "You test my ingenuity."

"Is that what you call it?"

He chuckled, sucked in air when she gave him a

sidewise glance. "I came to your lecture the other night." Her hand stiffened on his arm.

"I know. I saw you standing by the post."

Something was wrong. She'd gone all distant and defensive on him again. Had she not liked his being there? "You made a strong argument."

"It's not an argument to me. It's my life."

The quiet words carried bitterness, a burden of grief and sorrow. Her hand twitched. He tightened his arm against his side lest she try and pull her hand away. "You mentioned your brother again tonight during your lecture. I'm sorry for your loss, Marissa. Is your brother the reason you joined the Temperance Movement? I know it's hard when—"

"A man's death is unnecessary? When you learn your brother has been drinking and you run to the tavern to get him, to beg him to stop, and—" Her voice broke. She pressed her lips together, shook her head.

He pulled her off the crowded path into a small cleared area with a bench, halted and looked down at her. "What happened, Marissa? I'm not merely being curious. I'd like to understand—if it's not too painful for you to talk about."

She stared up at him for a moment, then nodded, stepped to the bench and took hold of the back rail. "I didn't know Lincoln had taken to drink. When I was told, I ran to the inn to stop him, to remind him of our father. I was too late. Lincoln came staggering out of the inn, fell off the walkway in front of a passing carriage and the life was crushed from him by the horse's hoofs." She blinked, gulped in air. "He was my brother. And I couldn't save him."

The pain in her voice was like a live thing he could feel. "And so you joined the Temperance Movement to try and save others like him."

"Yes. But not for Lincoln alone. For my father and my mother and all those like them, as well." She glanced up, met his gaze and looked back down at the bench. "The innkeeper took me home, and I went to my parents' room to tell them about Lincoln. My father was…asleep from the wine he'd been drinking all evening, and my mother was huddled in her rocker crying from the black eye he'd given her." Her grip on the bench tightened. He stepped close and placed his hand over hers, longing to take her in his arms and hold her until her sorrow and grief eased.

"Mother's eye was still swollen and discolored when she stood by Lincoln's grave. But she wore a mourning hat with a black veil that hid it. She's clever at doing that. Wearing clothes to hide her bruises and pretending there's nothing wrong, I mean. So was I. But I don't do that any longer."

Her father beat her? Anger soared. "Marissa…"

She jerked her hand away, grabbed a handful of her long black skirt then thrust it from her. "I hate wine, and I hate this gown. Every time I wear it I remember Lincoln, and my father and mother and all that wine has cost me."

Wine. That niggling unease he'd experienced since her lecture returned. How would she feel about his family owning a vineyard?

"But I'm not hiding the truth any longer. It's worth the discomfort if I can save someone else from—from what my family has endured." She drew a breath, looked up at him. "And now you know about me. But I know little about you—what you do apart from attending science classes here at Chautauqua, and swimming in your pond." She smiled, smoothed back a curl the way his mother patted at her hair when she was nervous, or wanted to change the topic of conversation. "Have you a family, Grant?"

"My parents. I'm an only child." She winced, and he could have bit off his tongue for reminding her that she no longer had a sibling. He glanced down at the lovely enamel watch pinned to her bodice. Time was growing short; the *Colonel Phillips* would be blasting its whistle soon and there was so much he needed to tell her. *Lord, please make her understand my situation.* "That's the reason I'm only able to come to Chautauqua in the evenings. You see, when I was fifteen, my father had an accident that left him crippled and unable to run the…family business." Interest flickered in her eyes. "The responsibility fell on me, so I gave up my plan to study to become a scientist and took over the physical work. Father, though he suffers from spells of ill health, still manages the business."

"You wanted to be a scientist?" Curiosity shone in her beautiful blue eyes.

He nodded, slanted his lips into a grin. "I'm a man who likes to find answers to problems."

"Your parents must be very proud and thankful to

have a son willing to forgo his dream to provide for their needs. I hope your father doesn't suffer unduly."

"The spells are coming more frequently of late." A frisson of concern drew his eyebrows down into a frown. "That's why I was unable to come to Chautauqua yesterday. My father had one of his spells and I had to keep his business appointment."

She nodded understanding. "Your fascination with science must come second to your responsibilities."

The steamer blew its first warning.

He was beginning to hate that whistle.

"It's time for you to go." She looked disappointed. His pulse quickened. "Marissa, I need to—"

She shook her head. A smile played at the corners of her lips. "I shall find my own way to my tent. It's not far."

"That's not what I was going to say." He pulled in a breath, held her gaze with his. "Marissa, I'm the caretaker of my father's vineyard."

She went perfectly still, stared at him. "A *vineyard*…" She took a step back.

He followed, took hold of her upper arms. "Marissa, please…my time is fleeting and I've so much more I want to say. But I can't come to see you for the next few days. The pickers are coming to start tomorrow and I have to be there to oversee the harvesting of the grapes. Father is unwell, and it's my responsibility." He looked down at her pale face, the shock in her eyes, and pressed his case. "I hope you will allow me to call on you when I am able, to give me a chance to explain—"

The steamer blew its second warning. He had no

more time to convince her with words. He pulled her close, slid his hands down her arms and grasped her hands, hoping she would believe him sincere. "I'll be back in a few days, Marissa. And we'll talk more."

He ran for the path, glanced back. Marissa was staring after him, her face stiff with shock, one hand pressed to her chest and the other gripping the rail of the bench. "I'll be back!" He turned and charged downhill.

Chapter Six

Today's lecture had gone well. And she hadn't felt nearly as uneasy riding the steamer this time. Now, if the protest march would go as well...

Marissa gripped the rail and watched the people making their way toward the dock, summoned by the blast of the *Colonel Phillips*'s whistle. Sunlight sparkled on the water, but its warmth was waning and it would be dusk when she made her return trip to Chautauqua. She should have thought to bring a wrap. The steamer lurched, slowed and slipped alongside the Mayville dock, lake water slapping at its sides.

I'm the caretaker of my father's vineyard.

She caught her breath and glanced at the road that passed between the railroad station and a hotel, followed its wide curve into a sloping climb to the top of the low hill. *I live in Mayville and our home is not on Chautauqua Lake, though our land borders it.* Her stomach churned. She took a firmer grip on the rail and searched the shoreline for grapevines. Grant was a *vineyard* owner. And he'd had to stay home today to oversee the harvest of his grapes. She swallowed hard and closed her eyes, hoped for the hundredth time that Grant's vineyard wasn't the one Judith Moore had been talking about yesterday. It was a selfish wish. Grapes were grapes no matter who grew them. And grapes made wine. She'd reminded herself of that fact every time she relived Grant's words through her long, sleepless night.

"All ashore for Mayville!"

The call settled like a rock in her stomach. How could someone be reluctant and eager at the same time? She frowned and pushed back her windblown curls, ran her hand down the front of the skirt of her plum-colored day dress and joined the passengers gathering into a loose cluster at the head of the gangway. A young gentleman doffed his hat and smiled. "After you, miss."

She stepped cautiously, kept her gaze fastened on the plank at her feet and released her breath when she stepped onto the dock. The short, ruffle-trimmed train of her gown slipped off the white-painted gangplank and whispered over the weathered wood as she made her way forward. A dozen or so canoes and rowboats tied to the long dock bobbed gently on the waves splashing against the pilings and rolling under the dock on their way to the shore. She moved closer to the center and wished the two women in front of her would walk faster.

"Miss Bradley!"

Ina Jefferson stood apart from the people waiting to board the steamer. Marissa hurried to her side and smiled. "Thank you for coming to meet me. Is everything ready?"

"Yes, indeed. Lily and Judith were already at the store shopping and visiting with Sarah when I passed by on my way here. Susan will be there when we arrive. It's a bit of a walk…all uphill once we reach the curve in the road."

"Yes, I noticed that." She shoved all thought of Grant from her mind and focused on the coming protest. "I'm ready. Shall we be on our way?"

"The harvest is going well." Grant took a swallow of lemonade, eyed his father over the top of his glass. He looked…frail. Not a word associated with Andrew Winston. "The wagons should be on their way to the winery in less than an hour. I figure the concords should all be picked in another two days."

"The catawbas be ready by then?"

Something was wrong. His father was trying to hide it, but there was worry in his eyes. He glanced over at his mother and swallowed back the questions he wanted to ask. There was no sense in adding to her concern for his father. He drained his glass and set it on the table. Perhaps his news would ease his father's mind. "No. The vines on the east slope will be ready in about a week, perhaps a day or two earlier if the weather holds. They'll have a decent yield. But the other vines—those that survived but were damaged by the killing cold—have a limited yield. Mr. Douglas looked at the catawbas again after your meeting this morning. He'll buy them, but for a lower price because of the difficulty in picking."

"I expected that. Dillon Douglas likes to squeeze a nickel tight as the next man." His father looked down, swirled the lemonade in his glass. "Best we can do, I guess. It'll help."

Help? With what? He needed to have a private talk with his father. "Well, I only came in to let you know the harvest is going well. And to tell you Douglas will stop by with another contract for the catawbas. I've got to get back to work. It'll be dusk soon and they'll start loading the wagons." He stepped out onto the back porch, shrugged off his unease and trotted down the steps. He'd confront his father about what was wrong tonight, after the pickers had gone.

The lowering sun warmed his shoulders, threw his shadow before him as he strode down the stone walk to the bottom of the hill where the pickers were working.

"Winston!"

He pivoted, stared at the vintner striding down the path between the concords and the old vines. The man was scowling. Grant started up the slope to meet him. "I didn't expect to see you again until tomorrow, Mr. Douglas. Is there a problem?"

"Not yet. But it looks as if one is on the way." Dillon Douglas shifted his gaze toward the access road. "Those wagons loaded?"

"No. The filled baskets are sitting in the rows waiting to be carried to the wagons when there's enough for a full load—the same as always. They should have enough baskets filled by dusk. It's been a good day." He glanced at the sky. There wasn't a rain cloud in sight. "What's the problem, Mr. Douglas?"

"Them women!" Dillon Douglas snorted. "Hardon's wife was right. There's six of them marching through town on their way here. All carrying signs and singing hymns! Riling up the whole town! Everybody's going out on the street to watch them."

"Here? Why would the women come here? Your winery is—"

"Useless without *grapes*." The vintner narrowed his eyes and leaned toward him. "Your grapes, at the moment, Winston. Sitting in those baskets—" Dillon Douglas shot out his hand and pointed "—waiting to be hauled to my winery. It seems it's not only the wineries they're after. They're marching against vineyards, too. And they're on their way."

Suspicion reared. "You said six women, Douglas. Is Sarah Swan among them?"

"She's marching in the lead beside some young woman I don't know. And you can be sure Toby doesn't know it! Why, he'd—" Dillon Douglas chopped his hand through the air and started back up the hill. "You build a fire under those pickers and get those wagons loaded, Winston. I want them out of here! There's no telling what those women have in mind." The vintner pulled the contract for the concords from his pocket and waved it in the air. "And remember, no grapes, no payment!"

He clenched his hands to keep from grabbing hold and shaking Douglas. That money had to keep them through the next year. And his father was already worried about something. Likely that demand note he'd taken out last year. He pivoted on his heel and started toward the pickers. He had to think of something. And quick.

She's marching in the lead beside some young woman I don't know.

The memory of Sarah Swan at the temperance lecture turned his suspicion to certainty. It was Marissa. It had to be. But what could—

"Douglas!" The vintner halted, turned toward him. He closed the distance between them at a run. "I've an idea. You said Toby wouldn't know about Sarah marching. And I agree. He'd never stand for it. It would be bad for business."

"What of it? You're wasting time, Winston. Get those pickers—"

"Hear me out! I doubt the other husbands would know or approve, either. Why don't you go tell them and arrange a little march of your own…" He nodded as understanding broke across Dillon Douglas's face.

"It just might work, Winston. Good thinking!" The vintner grinned and thumped him on his shoulder. "You get those wagons loaded and I'll get the husbands. But there's one woman I don't know."

I do. "You leave her to me."

"Fair enough. I'll be back as soon as I gather up all the husbands!"

He nodded and ran toward the pickers, anger spurring him on. He hoped he was wrong, but his gut told him he wasn't. Marissa had to have had this march planned last night when he'd told her about his fam-

ily owning a vineyard. And she'd never said a word…
Yes, she had.

I hate wine. Her soft, choked voice echoed in his
head.

And, evidently, vineyard owners, too. Including
him. How could he have been so wrong about her?
His face tightened. "You men!" The pickers straightened, their heads and shoulders appearing above the
lush green vines. He raised his voice so the men in the
far rows would hear him. "Start loading the wagons!
Mr. Douglas wants them out of here now!"

"Onward, Christian Soldiers, marching as to war…"
Marissa glanced at Sarah Swan singing and marching
beside her. The woman's hands were white with strain
from holding the sign she carried so tightly. It was the
perfect slogan for their purpose. Grapes Make Wine
and Wine Makes Trouble and Sorrow. But it was obvious from the older woman's grim expression that it
was more than a slogan to her.

She glanced up at her placard and wished again that
she'd been given a different one to carry. Lips That
Touch Wine Shall Never Touch Mine. She winced in-
wardly. She understood the sentiment, but it was too…
personal. Especially after last night. Grant owned a
vineyard; he would surely drink wine. And he— No!
No more dwelling on foolish romantic dreams about
Grant Winston. She had to forget him.

A house stood on their right, square and solid and
somehow proud. She focused her attention on the home
to drive out the unwelcome thoughts. It had a vine-

draped front porch, ocher-painted clapboard siding
and a deep overhang on the tin-covered hip roof that
shaded the second-story windows. No one came out
of the house to watch them as they passed. Were they
standing back out of sight and watching them march
by with tight-pressed lips or smiles?

"We're almost there. That is the access road to the
vineyard just ahead."

Sarah Swan's grim tone drew her back to their purpose. She looked forward. A dirt path led off to the
right, guarded by a carved wooden sign declaring the
land belonged to the Twin Eagle Vineyard. She stiffened her back and squared her shoulders, sang with
more fervor.

The path parted fields of trellised grapevines, laden
with bunches of light pink fruit that flowed over the
brink of a hill. Over top of the abundant vines she
could see the sparkling water of Chautauqua Lake at
a short distance.

*Our home is not on Chautauqua Lake, though our
land borders it.*

Her stomach knotted. Did these vines go all the
way to the lake? She tightened her grip on her sign
and walked toward the crest of the hill. Dust swirled
up from the path, settled like powder on the bottom of
her long plum-colored skirt. She looked down, came
to an abrupt stop.

"Oh, look! We're right on time! There are the Oakwood Winery wagons. Over there—at the bottom of the
hill." Lily Edmunds dipped her sign in that direction.

The sign bearing the words Help Us Save Our Children. Stop Making Wine flashed in front of her, blocking her view. It didn't matter. She'd already seen the loaded wagons—and the tall, broad-shouldered man waving them forward. She closed her eyes, hoped... prayed. *Let me be wrong, Lord. Please let me be wrong.*

"They're starting up the hill!"

"What shall we do?"

There was panic in the women's voices. She clamped a firm hold on her emotions and faced them. "We shall do what we came to do, ladies. Come with me to where we can't be seen." She led them to a spot a short distance from the road entrance. "This is where we will make our stand. We are going to place ourselves in a line across this road and keep those wagons from leaving. Those grapes will not make wine!"

Wagons creaked. Horses' hoofs thudded against dirt. The wagons were getting close.

"Sarah, you stand with me in the middle." She grabbed the older woman's hand and pulled her into place, took two steps to her right. "Lily and Ina, you take up places on the other side of Sarah." She waved her hand to the left. "Judith and Susan, you do the same on my right."

She watched the women hurry into place, then swept her gaze over each of them. "Perfect, ladies. Now, remember—don't move!"

"But the horses!"

Lily Edmunds gave a most unladylike snort. "You'd do better to worry about the driver, Ina. The horses won't hurt you."

Hoofs thudded. The bobbing heads of a team of horses showed over the crown of the hill.

"Ready, ladies?" Marissa drew herself to her full height, squared her shoulders and lifted her sign high as the horses came plodding over the crest dragging the loaded wagon behind them. "Onward, Christian Soldiers, marching as to war…" Her voice rang out clear. The other women followed her lead and burst into song.

"Whoa!" The wagon driver hauled back on the reins, gaped down at them.

Grant came striding over the crest looking different than she'd ever seen him. He was wearing a blue work shirt, brown twill pants, boots and a frown. Her heart lurched. She forgot to sing. The other women fell silent.

"Good day, ladies." Grant dipped his head in their direction. He swept his gaze over them, met hers for a second then looked up at the signs they held. His face went taut.

Hers flamed. It took all of her discipline and determination not to thrust her sign behind her back.

Grant stepped to the horse's head, grabbed the cheek strap and walked forward to within a few feet of them. "Get that other wagon up here, Joe!"

"Hup! Hup!" The team of horses came into view, followed by the wagon. The driver halted the horses and looked their way. "What's all this?" He scanned their signs and grinned.

"You find this amusing, Joe?"

Grant's voice sent a shiver down her spine. He was angry. Very angry. She braced herself as he turned from the sobered driver and walked toward their line.

"I'm surprised to see you here, ladies. I've never known any of you to turn on a neighbor before." He flicked a look in her direction.

Her heart sank. Clearly, he blamed her.

Ina Jefferson gasped and lowered her sign. "That's not what we're doing!"

"It's not personal against you or your father, Grant. It's the grapes."

Marissa glanced at Sarah Swan. The older woman looked uncomfortable but determined.

"These grapes provide our livelihood, Mrs. Swan. That's personal. The same as it would be if I tried to shut down your husband's store." Grant's gaze traveled from woman to woman. "Or Noah's farm...or Carl's tanning business...Albert's barbershop...or John's office." His gaze skipped over her, settled again on Sarah Swan. "I'll ask you to step aside now and let the wagons pass."

The older woman drew a deep breath and shook her head. "I can't do it, Grant. I'm just too tired of the abuse."

"Mind your tongue, woman!"

Sarah Swan stiffened.

Marissa spun around.

A group of men strode from the road toward them. None of them looked pleased, save the one in the middle.

"John!"

"Carl!"

"Albert!"

The women dropped their signs, gaped at the men.

Their husbands, no doubt. She glanced at Grant. He didn't look surprised. Had he sent for the men? How had he known—

"Where's your pride, woman?" A portly man with a red beard strode up to Sarah Swan, snatched the sign from her hand and tossed it aside. "Heaping up shame—"

"My only shame is in hiding the bruises from your hand all these years, Tobin." Sarah looked over at her. "Thank you for your help, Miss Bradley. Our protest to stop the grapes from reaching the winery may have failed. But I will no longer have to sacrifice my self-respect to hide the truth. And in that there is victory."

The older woman's words strengthened her resolve. She tightened her hold on her sign and watched the women walk off with their husbands.

"Out of the way, young lady." The man who had led the husbands climbed into the first wagon. "I have grapes to get to my winery before dark."

She moved in front of the horses, raised her sign and her voice. "Onward, Christian Soldiers, marching as…"

"What the—" The man jerked to his feet, his face as purple as the grapes overflowing the baskets behind him. "Get her out of the way, Winston!"

"—royal Master—"

Grant stepped close, his face a closed mask. "It's over, Miss Bradley. The other women have gone home. Please step aside."

"—into battle—"

He stooped. His arms closed around her knees, lifted. She dropped her sign and grabbed for his shoulders. They felt like rocks. She pushed, glared down at him. "Put me down!"

"Will you stay out of the path and let the wagons pass?"

"Never!"

He heaved.

She flopped over his shoulder, gasped and kicked her feet, pushing against his back, but she couldn't get enough purchase to push herself erect. His hard shoulder pressed into her abdomen, drove her breath from her with his every stride across a stretch of grass. She tried to crane her head around to see where he was taking her but couldn't manage.

"Grant Winston! Whatever are you doing? Put that young woman down and mind your manners!"

"Ooof!" She bounced against him as he stepped onto a stone walk then trotted up a set of steps. He released the death wrap he had around her knees, gripped her waist and lifted her off his shoulder. She shoved against his chest and almost toppled backward when he let go of her.

"Grant!"

"I'm sorry, Mother. I had to get her out of the way of the wagons. It'll be dark soon."

"Well, I'm sure you could have done so in a more gentlemanly fashion. Now, if you know her name, introduce me to this young woman."

He looked chagrined. It did her heart good. She wanted to stick her tongue out at him the way she had at Lincoln when they were children, but she straightened her hat that had been knocked askew and turned to face Grant's mother instead. The serene look on the older woman's face made her feel completely undone. She jabbed at the curls falling free around her face.

"Mother, this is Miss Bradley. Miss Bradley, my mother, Mrs. Winston." The anger in Grant's deep voice didn't help matters. She drew in a calming breath and made an effort to regain her composure.

"How do you do, Miss Bradley? I'm certain you must be warm after your...exertions. May I interest you in a glass of lemonade?"

The winery wagons rolled by out on the main road. Heat climbed into her cheeks at the woman's graciousness in the face of her recent activity. "How kind of you, Mrs. Winston. But I must take the *Colonel Phillips* back to Chautauqua tonight, and I don't care to make the long walk back to the lake in the dark." She turned toward the steps.

"There's time enough." Grant shot her a look and leaned against the post at the top of the porch steps.

Obviously, he didn't trust her. Did he think she would run after the wagons?

"Oh, good. I'll be right back with our drinks." Mrs. Winston disappeared inside.

"I'll walk you to the dock and see you safe back to Chautauqua."

Grant's tone said it was only good manners that prompted the offer. She swallowed the hurt of his lost friendship and shook her head, which promptly undid all the good her poking and jabbing at her hair had done. "Please don't bother. I remember the way." She lifted her chin and started by him. He shot out his arm and blocked her access to the steps.

"I *said* I'll see you safe to Chautauqua. My mother will be upset if I don't. I won't bother you after that. You have my word."

"Very well." She stared at his tight mouth and set jaw, turned away and shoved the hair that had fallen forward away from her eyes.

The door opened and Mrs. Winston stepped onto the porch. "Grant, would you please come and get the lemonade for our guest? Your father is a little tired and needs me to help him retire."

Grant gave her a warning look and stepped to his mother's side.

"I was going to see Miss Bradley safe back to Chautauqua, Mother. But I'll see her onto the steamer and then return." A frown creased his brow. "Do you want me to stop on our way to the dock and send the doctor back?"

"No, that's not necessary, Grant. Your father's only tired. And he would be ashamed of you if you didn't see Miss Bradley safely home." Mrs. Winston looked her way and smiled. "Please come again, Miss Bradley. I was looking forward to getting to know you. Good evening."

"Good evening, Mrs. Winston."

"Wait here." Grant growled the words and disappeared into the house.

She looked out at the fading light then glanced back at the door. Grant didn't want to be with her, and her emotions were too…unsettled to be with him. It would be better, less hurtful if she simply left. But she couldn't go looking so disheveled. She reached up to tuck more of the escaped curls into her still-confined hair.

The door opened and Grant came onto the porch, a shawl dangling from his hand. He glanced at her, sucked in a breath and held out the wool wrap. "I thought you might need this for the ride back on the steamer. There's most always a breeze on the lake at night."

He was so nice, even in his anger. She stared at the shawl, swallowed hard and shook her head. "That's very thoughtful of you, Grant, but I think it best if—"

"Just take it." His jaw twitched. "You can give it back when we say goodbye."

His tone left no doubt that he would accompany her to Fair Point whether she agreed or not. And that the goodbye they said then would be final. She blinked away a sting of tears and nodded. It was for the best.

Chapter Seven

Grant leaned his shoulder against a post and stared out over the lake, irritated beyond reason by Marissa's attempts to keep her hairdo tidy. Why didn't she just allow the unruly curls to blow free? What did a few curls around her face hurt? Except they made him want to— He broke off the thought and jammed his hands into his pockets. That was over. Along with all he'd been considering and planning since the night of her first lecture.

"I'm sorry your father is feeling unwell, Grant. I hope he's better tomorrow."

The sympathy in her voice rankled. Where was her concern when she'd decided to try and destroy their livelihood? Had she even considered that before she'd hatched her protest scheme against them?

"He's burdened with worry. He'll be better when the harvest is over and he can settle his debts and set aside money enough to keep us through the next harvest." He glanced at her then looked back out over the water. "That's what was in those baskets in the wagons you tried to stop, Marissa. Our living for the coming year, and my father's peace of mind." *And my chance to have a business of my own.* Which had seemed more pressing of late. He held back a snort of disgust for his idiocy in thinking she'd felt the same depth of attraction as he.

Nothing but silence. Evidently, she felt no need to answer. Or had none. He watched the red rays of the setting sun being swallowed by the encroaching night and listened to the rush of the water along the steamer as the reflected red glow was erased from the lake. The trip to Fair Point had never seemed so long.

"I only saw the grapes in those baskets, Grant. And what the grapes represented."

Did she not see the flaw in her justification? He turned and fastened his gaze on hers. "No, you saw *one* side of what they represented, Marissa. I'm sorry for all you've suffered—truly sorry—but I grow grapes for a living, not wine."

"They make wine."

He pulled in a breath. "Dillon Douglas uses them to make wine, yes. That's how he makes the living that takes care of his family. And John Hirsch sells the wine at his tavern. That's how he makes his living and cares for his wife and seven children. And I grow grapes for my family, to make our living. There are *two* sides to this temperance issue, Marissa. You've opened my eyes to yours—to the pain overindulgence in wine or liquor can cause. I was unaware of that. I guess because women like Sarah Swan and the others with her today keep it hidden."

"What else can they do?" She lifted her chin. "It's shaming and painful for others to know that your husband or father—" Her voice broke. She faced out over the water and blinked hard.

Her pain tore at him, but he pressed his point. "They can do what you are doing, Marissa. They can stop hiding. I think what you are doing in bringing the truth out into the open as you do with your lectures will help to get rid of that shame. And, also, as you point out in your lectures, strengthen and help those who are suffering by learning that they are not alone in their despair. I hope that it does. No woman should have to endure what you and your mother suffer, Marissa. What Sarah Swan bears. But causing others pain and suffering by taking away their means of livelihood will not help you and your mother, or Sarah Swan and the others."

She turned back and looked up at him.

"I don't want to cause anyone pain or suffering, Grant. Certainly not your family. I didn't even know—" She stopped, drew in a long breath. "Mrs. Swan wrote me a letter asking me to come and lead a small group of women in protest against the local wineries and vineyards. And it seemed an excellent way to spread the temperance message. I met Sarah Swan after my first lecture then held a meeting with her and the others yesterday to plan our march. That's when Judith Moore said the Oakwood Winery would be harvesting grapes at the Twin Eagle Vineyard today and wouldn't it be a good idea if we could stop the wagons? I didn't know you owned— But then I thought maybe— And I hoped and prayed you didn't— And— Oh, I'm so confused!" She choked on a sob, hid her face with her hands. "I don't want to hurt anyone. I want to help— Oh, I just *hate* wine!"

She hadn't known it was his vineyard. His pulse raced. "Marissa, we—"

The whistle blew. If he could have reached it, he would have ripped it off and thrown it in the lake. The steamer lurched, slowed. He grabbed Marissa's hand and tugged her toward the gangway. "We have to hurry. I only have time to walk you to your tent and run back before the steamer starts its return trip. I'll tell you what I want to say on the way."

"No." She pulled her hand out of his and stepped back. "You haven't enough time, Grant. And…and you were right. It's best we say goodbye right now. I— It's our…situation." Her shoulders drew back. Her chin lifted. "I listened to what you said, and I agree now that it's harmful for me to try and destroy someone's means of making a living, no matter how much harm I think it might do. But I can't stop protesting strong drink. And you— It's hopeless."

He might have believed her but for the shimmer of tears in her eyes. "No, it's not." He glanced at the people boarding for the return trip to Mayville, took hold of her elbow and led her to a secluded spot by the side wheel. "I want to continue to see you, Marissa. And I think you feel the same about me."

"Yes, but—"

Yes. His pulse leaped. The "but" didn't matter in the face of that yes. He pulled her closer. "There's no time for argument. I realize my running the vineyard goes against all that you believe, Marissa. But I told you running the vineyard was not my choice. If not for my father's accident, I would be a scientist or have a business of my own. And now, with the concords growing well and the money from the harvest, I'll be able to hire someone to care for the vineyard in my place."

"Oh, Grant…truly?" Hope flickered in her eyes.

"Truly. That way my parents will keep their home and livelihood, and I'll be free to find another way to make a living. It's too late to pursue a science career, but I've thought of buying a steamer. I've money set aside, and I know a captain that's moving away and wants to sell his boat and his house." His throat thickened. He closed his hands around her narrow waist, took a breath and plunged ahead into uncharted waters. "With my share of this year's profits I should have enough to make an offer to the captain. Do you think you could get used to riding on a steamer?"

Her smile took his breath. "Would you be beside me to keep me safe when the deck is slick?"

"I would. And one more thing, Marissa…"

"Yes?"

The word was little more than a whisper. His heart thundered at the look in her eyes. "I read your sign. And…I don't drink wine." He leaned down and brushed her soft lips with his, then stepped back, took her hand and led her to the gangplank before he gave in to the temptation to capture her lips in a real kiss.

* * *

The torches sputtered flickering light onto the path. Small twigs and the few early fallen leaves crackled beneath her feet.

I'll be free to find another way to make a living... Do you think you could get used to riding on a steamer? Her heart was singing the words over and over again. How strange that no one walking on the path heard it. She smiled at the whimsical thought and pulled the wool shawl more closely around her shoulders against the evening chill that had settled among the trees.

I read your sign. And...I don't drink wine.

A tingle ran down her spine, spread out in a delicious warmth. Her steps faltered at the memory of the moment when Grant had brushed her lips with his. Only the presence of the others walking on the path kept her from spreading her arms and whirling about in happiness. Nothing she had ever known came even close to the emotion that had rushed through her when he'd pulled her close.

She sighed and stepped into the large clearing at the top of the hill, walked toward her tent and stopped. Clarice was home. Observant, inquisitive Clarice. Her tent mate's shadowy form showed clearly between the canvas wall of the tent and the oil lamp on the desk where she sat working—no doubt adding substance to the notes she'd taken today for her "Chautauqua Experience" article.

Reticence moved her forward to the wooden bench beneath the trees at the end of the clearing. She was too honest to lie, too happy to dissemble and too shy to want to share this new, confusing but wonderful emotion with anyone. A smile touched her lips. She raised her hand to smooth back a curl tickling her temple, and her wrist brushed against something cold and hard. She winced and stared down at her mother's enameled watch—her father's apology. Reality burst upon her euphoria. People changed over time. Her father hadn't drunk wine until they moved to town. How could she be sure that Grant—

No. She would not doubt. She would not let the hurtful memories intrude on the joy of the moment. It might be all she would ever have. She would keep the memory unsullied by the ugliness in her life. She lifted the side of Grant's mother's shawl that had slipped from her shoulder and covered the watch.

Grant whistled his way up the porch steps and into the house. "Mother…" He stepped into the sitting room. Empty. A chair scraped on the upstairs floor. Ah, she was in the bedroom with his father. Good! He could tell them both he'd finally found a woman he was interested in courting in a serious way—a temperance advocate. Well, maybe he'd withhold that bit of information from his father until after he'd met Marissa.

He grinned, ignored the banister and took the stairs two at a time, halted at the top. A strange sort of heaviness weighted the air. Silence pressed upon him. He fastened his gaze on his parents' partially open bedroom door and started forward.

Light spilled into the hallway. A lanky man in a

dark suit stepped out of the bedroom and pulled the door closed behind him. "I thought I heard you, Grant."

"Good evening, Dr. Richards." He shot another glance toward the bedroom. "Is Father having another spell?"

The doctor shook his head and placed a consoling hand on his shoulder. "I'm sorry, son. Your father's heart finally gave out."

Denial stiffened his back. "But that can't be. He always—" He stared into the doctor's eyes and the truth slammed into his heart. He fisted his hands, swallowed back the useless protest. "He wasn't feeling well when I left for Fair Point. I should have stopped then and asked you to come to see him."

"It wouldn't have changed anything, Grant. There's nothing more I could have done. This has been coming for some time. It's only your father's determination that kept him alive this long."

Stubborn isn't strong, Grant. It's merely...stubborn...

His chest tightened. He cleared his throat. "Is Mother all right?"

"Yes. She's with him."

He nodded and reached for the bedroom door.

The doctor put out his hand and stopped him. "I'm on my way to get Porter."

The funeral director. He took a breath, stared down at the floor.

"It was your father's request. He said it would be easier on your mother. And he told me to tell you the best thing you could do for him and your mother now was to get the harvest in and tend the vines."

That was his father. Was. The word left him breathless. He nodded and grabbed the doorknob, fought for
control as the doctor patted his shoulder, then walked
down the stairs.

The front door opened and closed. Silence settled—
pressed in on him. "I need Your help, Lord. I need You
to give me strength and wisdom that I might be all that
my mother needs me to be for her now." The whispered
prayer rose from his heart, rasped from his constricted
throat. He pulled in another breath, squared his shoulders and turned the knob.

Marissa dumped her wash water into the bucket,
rubbed cream on her face and hands and glanced
around the tent. It had seemed spacious before. Now
it seemed much too confining. The happiness bubbling inside her demanded expression. But there was
no place she could be alone to release it. She glanced
at Clarice, sleeping soundly in spite of the snores and
occasional snorts coming from the surrounding tents.
Perhaps, if she were quiet...

She lifted her plum dress from her cot, hummed
softly while she shook it out and draped it across her
trunk, then folded Grant's mother's scarf.

I want to continue to see you, Marissa...

She placed the scarf on top of her dress, her fingers
lingering on the softness. They had been so focused
on each other when they said good-night that they had
forgotten about the scarf. At least she had. A thrill ran
through her. Grant had told her he would be too busy
overseeing the harvest to come to Chautauqua for the

next few days. Had he left the scarf on purpose? So she would have to return it? Good manners dictated that.

She laughed softly, draped the scarf around her shoulders and dipped and whirled about in the small space.

"Oft in the twilight I'm dreaming… Dreaming of joys that may be…"

The long skirt of her nightgown billowed, fluttered down around her legs and billowed out again.

"Longing for eyes that are beaming… Patiently watching for me…"

Clarice's cot creaked.

She froze, choked off the song.

Clarice yawned, opened her eyes and rolled up onto her elbow. "Is something wrong, Marissa? Are you ill?"

"No. I couldn't sleep is all."

"Are you dreaming, too?" Her tent mate's lips curved in a tired smile and she rolled down onto her back. "I dreamed I…heard…singing…"

She watched Clarice's eyelids drift closed and breathed a sigh of relief. The last thing she wanted was a barrage of questions about her unusual behavior. These new feelings Grant brought forth in her were not to be fodder for Clarice's article. She could see it now— "Miss Practical finds love at Chautauqua!" What if her mother— Oh, no! She hadn't kept her promise to write!

The small box of stationery supplies her mother had insisted she bring with her was at the bottom of her trunk. She carried them to the small desk and set Clarice's writing box on the floor. A twirl of the knob raised the wick in the oil lamp and spilled golden light over the desktop. She settled in the chair, dipped her pen in her ink and leaned forward over the flower-decorated stationery paper.

Dearest Mother,
Please forgive me. I am sorry I have been so long in writing. I am very busy. The Chautauqua Assembly is very well attended. There are thousands of people here, not the hundreds I expected. As you may suppose, my lectures have drawn a good deal of attention. The debates held after I speak are heated but, for the most part, well-mannered. You need not fret for my safety, Mother.

I have a most interesting tent mate. Her name is Clarice Gordon. She is a young reporter who is incessantly taking notes for an article she is writing for the Sunday School Journal, *one in which I make an anonymous appearance. I shall attempt to obtain a copy for you.*

She stopped writing and stared down at the letter. Should she mention Grant? Could she keep what was in her heart from overflowing onto the paper? She longed to tell her mother how wonderful he was, and how much she liked him. But— No. That information would be better shared in person. She sighed and dipped her pen.

Your worry over my journey was all for naught, Mother. It was not at all troublesome. I detrained at the Mayville Station, which is located on the lake only a few feet from the dock

where the Colonel Phillips *is moored. I confess
riding on the steamer made me nervous. It was
dark, and raining, and the deck was slick. A very
kind young man assisted me. Mr. Winston also
helped allay my nervousness when we disem-
barked at the campgrounds here at Fair Point.
I was most appreciative.*

*Living in a tent is not as burdensome as you
supposed, Mother. It is certainly not as comfortable as home, but it answers the need for
shelter quite well. So, Mother, you need not be
concerned for me. I am well. I pray this letter
finds you the same. My best to Father.*
Your loving daughter,
Marissa

Was her mother well? Or was she bruised and bat-
tered? Concern welled, knotted her stomach. Memories stole her joy. Was she making a mistake? Was she
being foolish to even consider placing her heart at a
man's mercy? Many men were kind and loving husbands and fathers. She knew that. And Grant seemed
so wonderful, so kind and caring. But how could she
know? Strong drink changed men, eroded their mor-
als and self-control.

She folded the letter, sealed and addressed it, turned
down the wick and put her things away. She would post
the letter when she went to Mayville to return the scarf.
Tears stung her eyes. The happiness that had filled her
at that thought earlier was gone—stolen by the memory
of her drunken father's hand striking her.

She stared at the folded length of soft gray wool. Mrs. Winston had seemed so…serene when she met her. There'd been no fear or shame lurking in the woman's eyes. No hesitance in her warm and welcoming smile. It was impossible to think Grant's mother had ever been struck by her husband.

You've opened my eyes to yours—to the pain over-indulgence in wine or liquor can cause. I was unaware of that... No woman should have to endure what you and your mother suffer.

Her breath caught. Her impression was right. There was no abuse or drunkenness in Grant's family or he would surely know. Grant *was* kind and caring. But if—

I don't drink wine.

Her pulse quickened. She pulled back the covers, slipped into bed and rested her head on her feather pillow. He was a vineyard owner. Surely if Grant were going to drink wine, he would already do so. The problem was hers. She blinked tears from her eyes and stared at the canvas stretched above. *Blessed Lord, please help me to learn to trust again.*

Grant leaned his forearms on the porch railing and stared at the wisp of steam rising from the cup of coffee clutched between his hands. How was he going to cope? He had his father's funeral and burial to plan and attend, his mother to care for through it all, and the business end of the vineyard to manage as well as continuing to oversee the harvest.

He straightened and looked out over the vines trailing away down the slope to the lake. It would help if there were someone who could step into his place. But every time he had suggested they hire a man to help him, his father had insisted that they managed well enough by hiring temporary help during pruning and other pressing times.

That uneasiness he'd been suppressing for months rose. He should have insisted that they discuss the vineyard finances in spite of his father's ill health. He'd known that his father was worried. Maybe he could have helped...

"It will be all right, Grant."

Some care he was giving his mother. She was reassuring him. He looked over at her sitting on the porch swing, her lovely features gilded by the light of the oil lamps hanging on either side of the kitchen door. She looked tired. And sad. The shadow of grief in her eyes ripped at his heart. "I know."

He put aside the concerns weighing on him, sat down beside her and pushed against the porch floor with his feet. The swing swooped back and forth. "And you're going to be all right, too." He slanted his mouth into a grin. "When I gwow up, I'm going to take bewy good cawe of you." It worked. Her lips curved into a smile at his resort to his oft-repeated promise as a child.

"This is nice. It puts me in mind of when you were little and *I* would swing *you*." She looked over at him, her eyes warm with love and memories. "I could heal all of your hurts with a kiss or a cookie then."

"Or both."

"Yes. Or both." She looked down at the cup she held

and took a breath. "I'm afraid I don't have a cookie big enough to heal this one."

He cleared his throat, leaned toward her and pushed his cheek forward. "A kiss will make it better." Surprisingly, it did. There was something special in his mother's touch.

"There's something your father wanted me to tell you, Grant." She looked at him then leaned against the swing back. "He told me to tell you that he was very proud of you. And that he considered himself blessed to have you for a son." Her voice choked. She wiped the tears from her eyes then fastened her gaze on him again. "I can't tell you the countless times, since the accident crippled him, that Andrew said to me, 'I'm blessed to have a son willing to lay down his dream and pick up mine, Ruth. And the boy's a worker! He's got a real touch for the vines. They'll prosper under his hand, and so will we. Yes, sir. I'm blessed!' And so am I, son. You are such a comfort to me." She gave him a wobbly smile. "Now…let's talk about something else—like that young lady you…er…brought to the house this afternoon."

"Marissa?" He blurted out her name, caught off guard by the change of subject.

His mother's eyebrows rose. "*Marissa?* How long have you known this zealous young temperance advocate?"

"I met her on the *Colonel Phillips* on the way to Fair Point the night before the assembly began."

"A vineyard owner and a temperance lady? That must have been quite a meeting." She took a sip of her coffee, peered at him over the top of her cup. "It's odd that you haven't mentioned this young woman until now."

Speculation flickered through the sadness in his mother's eyes. Her undying hope was that he would marry and give her grandchildren. Perhaps telling her about Marissa was the perfect way to comfort her now, to give her hope for the future and take her mind from her sorrow. "Well, let me remedy that right now." He gave another push with his feet to keep the swing in motion. "It was raining that night and the deck was slick…"

Chapter Eight

The long, sloping uphill climb was both too long and too short. Marissa stopped in front of the Winston house, her heart pounding. Would Grant be pleased to see her? Or had his expressed desire to continue to see her changed now that he'd had time to think about their situation? He had said it would be a few days before he would be able to come back to Chautauqua. It had been five. And she had been too busy with lectures and meetings with women who wanted advice on starting temperance groups and meetings for teachers and speakers called by the Chautauqua leaders to make the trip to Mayville. And now...well, now here she was, doubts, nerves and all.

She looked down at the folded scarf in her hands, adjusted the small "thank you" sachet on the top and hoped again that Mrs. Winston liked lavender. A pat of her curls and a quick smooth of the long skirt of her dark gray day dress gave her a bit more confidence. She straightened her back and shoulders and walked up the stone path to the inviting, vine-covered porch, trepidation in every step. When they'd met, Mrs. Winston had been very gracious and kind to her in spite of the protest she'd led against their vineyard and Grant all but dumping her on their back porch. But what of Mr. Winston? He might not take as kindly a view of her attempt to stop their grapes from reaching the winery.

Our living for the coming year, and my father's peace of mind...

Her stomach knotted. Why did things have to be so complicated? She drew a breath and reached for the brass knocker on the white-painted front door. Three sharp raps and her fate was sealed. She would have to face Mr. and Mrs. Winston, Grant and whatever was to be. There was no turning back now.

The latch clicked.

She lifted her chin and smiled.

"Marissa!"

The sight of Grant, the glad surprise in his voice and eyes sent her doubts flying and her heart soaring.

He stretched out his arm and took hold of her free hand. "Come in here."

Her breath caught at his soft, husky tone. She moved forward, then stopped, jarred by the sight of a black band on the sleeve of his shirt. She swept her gaze up to his face. "Grant, what—"

He pulled her inside and closed the door. "My father passed away the evening I took you back to Fair Point, Marissa. I learned of his death when I came home that night." He cleared his throat. "That's why I haven't been able to come to Chautauqua to see you. We…buried him yesterday."

"Oh, Grant, I'm so sorry." Tears welled in her eyes. "So very sorry."

He nodded, pulled her into his arms and laid his cheek against her curls. She rested against him, at one with him in his grief.

"I'm glad you came." He cleared his throat again, leaned back and looked down at her. "I couldn't leave to come and explain why I couldn't come to see you. And I couldn't think of any way to get word to you. I'm sorry."

"Oh, Grant, don't apologize. I understand. I only wish there were something I could do to ease your pain. But I've learned that only time will do that." She blinked the moisture from her eyes and wiggled her hand holding the scarf that was trapped between them. "I came to return your mother's wrap, but I don't want to disturb her now." She looked up and met his gaze. Warmth spread through her, settling in her heart. "Will you please give it to her along with the small thank-you gift and—"

"You're not leaving." His arms tightened around her. "Seeing you is exactly what I need right now."

"And I'm here."

Mrs. Winston! She shoved against Grant's chest and spun about. The sachet fell. She stooped and snatched it up, faced Grant's mother and held out her hands, staring down at the small lace-edged sachet pillow atop the soft gray wool scarf. She would likely be ordered from the woman's house. Exactly what she deserved for— Her cheeks burned. She took a breath and lifted her head, looked at Grant's mother pale in her black mourning clothes. "I came to return your wrap, Mrs. Winston. Thank you so much for the use of it. And may I offer my deep sympathy for your loss."

"Thank you, Miss Bradley." Mrs. Winston blinked, looked down and lifted the sachet. "What is this?" She lifted it to her nose. "Mmm, lavender."

"It's a small token to show my appreciation. I hope you will find it useful." She drew a calming breath. Perhaps she could leave gracefully after all. "Now, if you will excuse me…"

"I'm afraid not, Miss Bradley."

She braced herself for the chastisement she deserved for being found in the woman's son's embrace.

Mrs. Winston gave her a wan smile. "I owe you a glass of lemonade."

She stared at Mrs. Winston's smile, taken aback by the woman's graciousness. She knew the effort that smile cost her in her grief. "You're most kind, Mrs. Winston. But I don't want to intrude on your grief. I know how—" Memories flashed. Her voice broke. Grant's hands closed around her waist, and everything in her longed to lean back against him.

Mrs. Winston reached out and touched her arm. "Grant told me of your brother's recent passing, Miss Bradley. I'm sorry for your loss. Perhaps we can comfort one another. I'm sure you will understand that I find myself at…a loss. Our friends have returned to their homes for the evening, and you do owe me a visit." Grant's mother drew a breath, gave her another smile. "Now…If *you* will excuse *me*, I will go and get our lemonade. The weather is so pleasant I believe we'll have our visit on the back porch." Her gaze lifted to her son. "Grant…"

"May I escort you to the back porch, Marissa?" He stepped from behind her and made a slight bow.

She looked after Mrs. Winston remembering her own mother's collapse when Lincoln died. "Your mother is amazing, Grant. There's a…a strength and a serenity about her I noticed the other day that's still there, even in her grief."

He nodded and took hold of her elbow. "My mother is very strong. It's her faith." He led her through the sitting room and opened the door onto the back porch. "She misses my father dreadfully. But she knows they will be together again in Heaven one day and that comforts her. And she firmly believes that when you have given your heart to the Lord and become His child, He watches over you and will work a blessing for you into every situation." He held a chair for her at a small round table. "That's you."

The look in his eyes stole her concentration. "What… is me?"

"Mother's blessing. And mine…" He leaned down. Her pulse leaped.

"Mr. Winston."

She jumped and jerked back against the chair, heat flooding into her cheeks at sight of the man striding up the stone path.

"Can't a man have any privacy?" Grant growled the words under his breath then glanced out over the railing. "Coming, Joe!" A frown creased his forehead. "It looks as if I have some business to take care of in the vineyard. I'll be back as soon as possible, Marissa." He touched her shoulder, turned and trotted down the porch steps.

She rose, stepped to the railing and watched him hurry down the walk. The man spoke and gestured down the slope. Grant nodded and both men disappeared downhill. Her stomach tightened. She turned away from the sight of the lush trellised grapevines. Thankfully, Grant would not be managing the vineyard much longer—only until he found a man to replace him. And when that situation was resolved, perhaps—

"Grant, will you get the door please?"

The muffled words pulled her from her dreaming. She rushed to the door on the other side of the table and pulled it open. "Grant was called away by a man from the vineyard. He said he would return as soon as possible. May I carry that tray for you, Mrs. Winston?"

"Thank you, dear. But the table is only a few steps. And I find it helps if I do things."

"Yes…" Her mind flashed back to those first days after Lincoln's death when her mother had taken to her bed and refused to get up. Was it Mrs. Winston's faith that gave her strength, as Grant had said? It was anger that had motivated her. It still did. She moved to the chair she'd vacated and sat while his mother set out three small plates then poured lemonade into two of the three glasses filled with bits of ice.

"I'm sorry Grant had to leave us, Miss Bradley, but I'm afraid the grapes take precedence over everything during harvest—even a guest." His Mother smiled and handed her one of the cool, filled glasses. "But I'm not sorry you are here to keep me company while he works. It will give us a chance to become better acquainted. I hope you don't mind, but my curiosity was aroused by the…er…unusual way we met, and, as it was obvious that you two knew each other, I asked Grant about you. He said your family lives in Fredonia?"

"Yes." *How much had Grant told his mother?* "We lived on a farm until we moved into town five years ago, so I understand about the demands of a harvest." She sipped her lemonade, thankful to be off the subject of grapes, but leery of what was to come. "Mmm, this is delicious."

"I brought out sugar in case it is a bit too tart for your taste. Grant prefers his lemonade on the sour side the same as—the way his father liked it." Mrs. Winston lowered her gaze a moment, then drew in a breath and looked back up. "Forgive me, Miss Bradley. Andrew and I sat here often, especially after his accident. He loved to look out over the vines. They become a part of your life…" Her smile trembled. "Are you enjoying your Chautauqua experience, Miss Bradley? You seem young to be giving lectures."

She lifted a cookie from the plate Mrs. Winston held out to her and smiled her thanks. "I am younger than the other teachers and speakers I've met at Chautauqua. But there are times when experience supersedes age." She winced at the bitterness in her voice. "Please forgive me, Mrs. Winston. I didn't mean to sound terse or—"

"You are going through a difficult time, Miss Bradley." Mrs. Winston's hand covered hers. "I admire your loyalty to your brother."

So Grant had told her the circumstance of Lincoln's death. She swallowed hard, fighting the tears stinging the backs of her eyes at Mrs. Winston's comforting touch. It was what she had needed so desperately and never received from her own mother. But she couldn't accept what she didn't deserve. "Even though that loyalty brought me here to try and stop the harvest of your grapes?"

"Even though." Mrs. Winston squeezed her hand, then released it and sat back in her chair. "But, in the interest of truth, I must admit I'm thankful your effort failed. I don't know how we would manage without the profit from the grapes. Especially…now."

She nodded, broke off a bite-size piece of cookie. "I didn't know this was Grant's—your family's—vineyard when we came. I—I hoped it wasn't." The admission brought warmth flowing into her cheeks again. She hastened on. "But I couldn't let it make any difference." *Oh, no! Lord, please don't let her ask what I meant by "it."* She put the bite of cookie in her mouth to quell her nervous urge to explain and glanced up at the dusky sky. Where was Grant? She would have to leave for the dock soon and she wanted to say goodbye. *Goodbye.* The thought wrenched at her heart.

"You care for my son. I can see it in your eyes."

She stiffened, drew her gaze back to Mrs. Winston and looked into her calm, steady gaze. There was no censure, only acknowledgment. Her nerves steadied.

"Grant cares for you also. But, of course, you're aware of that."

There was no sense in trying to deny it. The woman had seen her in Grant's arms. She inhaled, blew out the breath and nodded. "Yes. But…it's…difficult."

Mrs. Winston's lips twitched. "A temperance advocate and a vineyard owner attracted to one another? I should think so."

A vineyard *owner*? She looked out at the lush vines and her stomach churned. Did Grant now own the vineyard? Would that make things easier or harder? Or did it remove all chance—all hope of their budding relationship growing into something more?

"Fortunately, there is nothing too difficult for the Lord."

It was a firm statement, not merely a cliché spoken to glide over an uncomfortable moment. How wonderful it would be if it were true. The plod of hoofs and the creak of wheels stopped the wish. She rose and went to the railing, looked toward the vineyard access road and watched the horses appear pulling wagons loaded with overflowing baskets of grapes. Her stomach knotted. *How much wine would all of those grapes make? How much misery would they cause?* She turned her back and resumed her seat, took a swallow of lemonade to get rid of the bitter taste in her mouth.

"You will see, Miss Bradley."

The woman sounded so certain. But the doubt in her heart and the knots in her stomach told her otherwise. "Please, call me Marissa." Mrs. Winston's answering smile was so lovely it added to the sadness in her heart. How wonderful it would be to have this woman in her life if only—

"Grant told me how the two of you met aboard the *Colonel Phillips* while you were on your way to the Chautauqua Assembly, Marissa. And I believe God's blessing was on that meeting. And on those that have followed." A small smile touched Mrs. Winston's mouth. "It will be interesting to see how the Lord works things out."

If only He could. She reached for her glass and swallowed the unspoken doubt along with the lemonade.

The sinking sun's last rays shimmered on the water, cast their golden hue over the *Colonel Phillips* floating at the end of the long dock. Grant skimmed his gaze over the people waiting to board and placed his hand over Marissa's holding to his arm. "Let's stop here a moment." He led her away from the light cast by the lanterns under the wide overhang of the railroad station roof to a darker area beneath a tree. "I wish I could escort you all the way back to Fair Point, Marissa. But—"

"Please, don't feel you have to explain, Grant. Your place is with your mother." Her hand tightened on his arm. "She is a strong woman, but she still needs the comfort of her son. And I would expect no less of you."

The kindness and understanding in her eyes soothed his concern. He nodded, took hold of her hands and pulled her around to face him. "Thank you for understanding about Mother, Marissa, but there's more." He heard her quick intake of breath, hated what he had to tell her. "The pickers are coming daily, and I have to manage the harvest. And now, since I've inherited Father's estate, handling the business and the finances for the vineyard and for the house and Mother has also fallen to me."

Her gaze slid away from his. "So much responsibility will take a good deal of your time."

She understood! "Yes. My days are taken up with the vineyard and my evenings with going over my father's records to familiarize myself with the finances. And that means I have no time to try and find a man qualified to take my place managing the vineyard— or to inquire about buying the *Jamestown.* That's the steamer I told you was for sale." He took a breath, laid it out clear. "My plans for the future have to be delayed. And I'm afraid I won't be able to come to Chautauqua to see you any longer."

"I see. Well, then—"

The *Colonel Phillips*'s whistle blew.

She pulled her hands from his grasp and stepped back, lifted her chin. The sunset glow piercing through the leafy canopy overhead fell on her taut features. His heart lurched. "Marissa, what—"

"Please don't say anything more, Grant. I understand that your situation has changed and—and I wish you well." Her smile looked forced. She glanced at the water, squared her shoulders and looked back at him. "Please tell your mother goodbye for me."

"Goodbye?" He stared at her, dumbfounded. "What are you saying? That you're unwilling to give me more time? That you're through with me?"

Her eyes widened. "I thought you were saying you no longer had time for me."

"What? No." He stepped forward and drew her into his arms. "I was going to ask if you would give me until the harvest is over and I've had time to straighten out the finances to start working on my plan for the future. And if, in the meantime, you would mind making the trip here to Mayville to see me. I know you don't like to ride the steamer."

"You're not saying goodbye?"

"I'd sooner cut off my arm. Well...maybe not my arm..." He smiled and tightened his embrace.

She stared up at him, blinked, then fastened her gaze on his and nodded. "I could get used to riding the steamer."

Marissa shunned the cabin and stood by the railing to watch the lights of the railroad station fade into the distance. The flesh over her ribs was still warm from Grant's arms holding her close.

She sighed and drew her gaze toward the dock, now merely a dark smudge on the water at the edge of the lake. Was Grant still standing there watching the *Colonel Phillips* growing smaller as it steamed away? Did men even do that sort of thing? And what did it matter? Grant had too great a demand on his time to stand idle and watch a steamer disappear.

The thought sobered her. Grant now owned the vineyard and the house. They went together. Her stomach curled. He had said his plans for the future were delayed—and she didn't doubt that he meant it...now.

But what about after the shock of his father's death had passed, and he'd had time to think about everything? The Winston house was beautiful and comfortable and his mother's home. How could he move away and leave his mother in that large house alone? That would be cruel. And it would be foolish and wasteful and…and selfish of him to sell it and buy another, even if he moved his mother in with him. And Grant was not a selfish man. She wouldn't admire and respect him if he were.

It will be interesting to see how the Lord works things out.

If only God could. She had never cared for a man the way she cared for Grant. And when he took her into his arms… The memory brought forth a sigh. Grant Winston made her forget her determination to never fall in love or marry.

The steamer headed around the outcropping and the lights of Mayville disappeared. So did her romantic dreams. It would be lovely if she could believe there might be a future to the relationship, the…*attraction* she shared with Grant, but it was impossible. She admired Mrs. Winston's faith and Grant's determination but, try as she might, she couldn't rid herself of her doubts. *Almighty God, forgive me my unbelief, I pray. And let me be wrong, O Lord. Please let me be wrong.*

Her face tightened. It was foolishness to pray such a thing. There was no possible way of overcoming all of the obstacles that stood in the way of her having a serious relationship with Grant no matter how she might want that to happen. Those lush vines would soon wrap around her heart and choke off any love that might grow there. And there was no way to stop that from happening. No possible way.

Chapter Nine

A bright yellow leaf drifted down and landed on her open Bible. Marissa admired its color, brilliant in the sunshine, then lifted her head and looked up at the branches overhanging the bench where she sat. The leaves were all green except one small cluster of bright yellow reminders that summer was passing.

The doubts she'd been trying to quench with her Bible reading surfaced again. The assembly would soon be over. Would Grant's grape harvest be finished before it was time for her to go home? Did that even matter now? Everything had become more complicated by his father's death. How could Grant manage all of his new responsibilities *and* find a way to pursue their complex relationship on top of his grief? It was better, less hurtful, to simply let it go. Why couldn't she do that? Why couldn't she stop thinking of Grant and longing to see him?

She picked the leaf up by its stem and twisted it back and forth between her thumb and finger wishing she could know the serenity she'd observed in Grant's mother instead of the constant sense of unease she'd lived with for the five years since her father had begun drinking wine. He'd turned from her protector to the one she most feared and made their home a place of tension and apprehension instead of a sanctuary of love and safety. And Lincoln had died. How could she hope to find serenity? It all made her furious!

She threw the leaf to the ground and reached to close the Bible, pausing when a verse caught her eye. *The Lord is my rock, and my fortress, and my deliverer; my God, my strength, in whom I will trust...*

Trust? How could she trust? Everyone had betrayed her. Her father struck her. Her mother stood by and did nothing but cry and plead with him to stop. And Lincoln, whom she'd thought she knew so well, had secretly taken to strong drink. How could she trust anyone?

Tears flooded her eyes. She blinked them away and stared down at the verse. She wanted to trust God. She wanted to trust Grant. And she was trying. She was truly trying, but deep in her heart—

"It's impossible! Do you hear me, God?" She looked up at the sky, battling the tears that were pushing into her eyes. "It's like the situation at home—instead of getting better, things have gotten worse. Grant *owns* that vineyard now. And he has to take care of his mother and that's her home and I *want* him to care for her, and I don't want her to have to leave but—" she clenched her hands into fists "—but every time I see those vines it makes me *ill*. And angry. I—I care about Grant, I truly do. But I can't go against my convictions!" She swiped the tears from her eyes, flipped the Bible closed and surged to her feet. "Our…relationship…cannot grow into something more. It's impossible!"

It will be interesting to see how the Lord works things out.

She caught her breath, hugged the Bible to her chest and closed her eyes, wished Mrs. Winston had never said that to her. She liked Grant's mother so much. She didn't want to disappoint her, to be the cause of her losing faith when things didn't work out with Grant. "Mrs. Winston trusts You, Lord. She is serenely confident that You can do the impossible, that You can make a way where there is no way and bring a blessing where there is no blessing. I pray she is right."

The plan Grant had offered as their solution flooded into her head along with a dozen others she'd thought of, all flawed. She pressed her lips together and headed for the tent to put away her Bible and prepare for her afternoon lecture. She had a few more days. It would be better…easier…if she told Grant goodbye now, but she wouldn't, *couldn't*. There was a stubborn, *foolish* part of her heart that clung to the hope that Mrs. Winston was right—even if she couldn't believe it.

"Would you like more meat and gravy, Grant? Or potatoes?"

Grant looked across the table and shook his head. "I'm sorry to have to leave you alone, Mother. But I've got to get back to the vineyard." He frowned and laid his fork on his plate. "The catawbas are somewhat sparse on the frost-damaged vines, and the pickers tend to slow down. I want to keep them working at their best speed."

"You don't have to apologize or explain, Grant. This isn't the first harvest I've been through." She smiled and rose, gathered their dirty plates and flatware. "I'll get your cake."

He shoved back from the table and dropped his arm around her shoulders. "I'm sorry, Mother, I know you're a veteran at this. It's only...well...never mind." He gave her a peck on the cheek and straightened. "I'll have the cake later, with supper, after the pickers have gone. This good weather won't hold forever and I want the harvest finished."

"You sound like your father." The smile she gave him trembled a little. "He was always worrying about the weather holding during harvest. He always asked me to pray..."

He nodded, wishing he could take away her sorrow, thankful the work of the harvest helped hold his grief at bay. "You'd better pray, Mother! I need your help. We're in this together."

He stepped to the door and pulled it open, glanced back over his shoulder. "If Marissa comes—"

"I'll entertain her until you come in."

This time his mother's smile was steady and reached her eyes. "I'm certain you will." He grinned, gave her a wink and closed the door, then paused a moment and listened to be sure she was all right. He didn't want her crying alone. The soft tap of her shoes against the wood floor moved toward the sink cupboard. Her voice floated out the window.

"Thank You, Abba, Father, for the sunshine and warmth of this beautiful day. Please make the good weather continue until the grapes are all picked and the harvest is over. And thank You, Lord, for bringing Marissa into Grant's life. She is a true blessing to him, and to me, during this sorrowful time. I only wish Andrew had met her."

The words floating out of the open window had become shaky. He turned and reached for the doorknob. Dishes clinked against the wood cupboard.

"But I'm sure Andrew knows all about her. More even than I do. Oh, Father God, a beautiful, fiery *temperance* advocate and my Grant? They care for each other. I know they do. I can see it in the way they look at one another." A fork scraped against plates. "And, I confess, the situation between them seems rife with insurmountable problems I see no answer for. But I know with You all things are possible, Lord. You already know the answer. Oh, my! I can't *wait* to see how You work this out!" A soft little laugh and the splashing of water accompanied the end of the prayer.

Grant tiptoed across the porch and down the steps, careful to not let his boots thump, then hurried down the stone path, his heart a little lighter from the sound of his mother's laughter. She believed that God had brought Marissa into his life, and was happy about it. And she believed that things would work out for them to be together. That was encouraging.

A beautiful, fiery temperance advocate and my Grant…

A smile tugged at his lips. His mother would be praying for them now. And that was more encouraging yet.

The lowering sun warmed him, glinted off the flashing blades of the pickers' knives. Grant moved between the trellised rows, letting his presence urge the pickers to greater speed while he counted baskets. It was taking much longer to accumulate two wagonloads because of the damaged or dead vines. He frowned, stepped to one of the gray canes and examined it. There was no sign of returning life. He would dig up the severely frost-damaged catawbas and replace them with concords next spring.

He lifted his head and swept his gaze over the trellises he could see, frowned at the sight of the many gaps. The damage was especially extensive in this part of the vineyard. It would take a lot of time and work. He'd need help. No. He wouldn't be here.

The thought brought him up short. He rubbed his hand over the sun-warmed flesh at the back of his neck, frowned down at the ground and considered his plan in the light of his father's passing. He couldn't leave his mother to live alone in their big house. And he couldn't make her leave the house she'd called home for all of her married years—especially not so soon after her husband's death.

He sucked in a breath and looked at the grapevines stretching out for acres around him. He couldn't stay—

not and court Marissa with an eye to making her his
bride, which he'd been thinking about more and more.
The strong connection, the attraction he'd felt for her
right from the first day, grew stronger every time he
was with her. But he'd seen the way she reacted when
she looked at the vines. He'd told her his plan. Promised her. And it was no small measure of her growing...
regard...for him that she had agreed to wait, to give
him time to work things out.

But I know with You all things are possible, Lord.

He grasped on to his mother's favorite quote, let it
settle the churning unrest. Buying that steamer had to
be the first stop. He'd figure out the rest when that was
done. But he could do nothing without the money due
him. And that meant getting this harvest in. He scowled
up at the sun sinking toward the western horizon and
started for the next row to count the filled baskets.
Seven more and they could start loading the wagons.

Marissa scanned the crowded benches, lifted her
gaze to those standing at the sides of the canvas canopy. "As I have said before, the use of alcoholic beverages is more prevalent now than it has ever been in
our country. And I urge you to lend your voices and
your support to those in your towns and cities who are
protesting the sale of strong drink."

She waited for the stirring that plea always brought
to quiet, then took a breath and followed the urging
deep within that would not be quenched. "Every sale
of strong drink that is stopped is a victory! But I know
from my experiences that it's impossible to stop all

sales, to close all of the taverns and inns and clubs and other places where men can procure alcoholic beverages. Therefore, before I close my lecture tonight, I would like to suggest that there is something more that you can do, something that will be helpful to those who fall victim to the abuses inflicted upon them by family members who overindulge in wine or other strong drink."

Reflex raised her hand to the enameled pendant watch pinned to her bodice. Her face tightened. She pushed back the memories and stepped to the edge of the platform. "The first step is one we have already discussed—stop hiding the truth. I know how hard that is—and how necessary." She squared her shoulders and lifted her chin. "I joined my voice to those speaking out for temperance because my brother's imbibing of strong drink caused his tragic, accidental and unnecessary death. I started a temperance group in my town. I traveled to other towns and led protest marches and spoke to those who wished to form temperance groups. And I am lecturing here at Chautauqua to spread the message of the danger inherent in strong drink. What I have *not* done is what I am about to encourage you to do."

The silence was so deep she could feel it. She took a breath and plunged ahead. "I became so focused on stopping the sale of alcoholic drink, I forgot about the needs of those who are suffering the abuses caused by it. I let my anger rule me…and I forgot about mercy." She drifted her gaze over the faces of the people looking up at her. "If a woman or a child in your town suffers abuse at the hands of an imbiber, where do they go for help? Is there someone in your town who would welcome and care for them? Or do they suffer alone in silence because of their shame?"

There was a quiet stirring.

"It's my experience that most people who want to start temperance groups are interested in doing so because they have either experienced the abuse caused by wine and other strong drink or known someone who has. And if you are planning on starting such a group, I strongly encourage you to do so. But I now encourage you to not only speak out and protest against strong drink, but to also provide a place where those who suffer the abuse caused by it can come when a hand is raised against them." She reached for her mother's watch, felt the metal dig into her grasping fingertips. "Women and children who are abused need a place where they can shelter and be safe until the imbiber sobers and the danger passes. They need a place where they know they will receive understanding instead of judgment and not be made to feel shame. I am going to work to establish such a place when I return home. I hope you will consider doing the same."

She released the watch and took a breath, easier now that she had obeyed the urging and the tightness in her chest had eased. "Thank you all for coming and listening to my message. This concludes my lecture, but I will be happy to answer any questions you might have."

Applause broke out. The sound of a steamer whistle rose over the chatter and rustle and bustle of the people rising from the benches and skirting around support posts to make their way from beneath the canopy.

Was that the *Colonel Phillips*? She gazed out at the surrounding clearing. She'd spoken too long. It was dusk. Her heart sank at the thought of missing the steamer. Her head told her it was for the best. She lifted her hems and descended the steps to talk with the group of women coming forward.

Grant opened the door and entered the den, stopped short at the sight of the empty Windsor chair at the long stretcher table his father had used for his desk. A floorboard creaked beneath his weight. It always had, but the sound was loud and obtrusive in the silence. He stepped onto the oval braided rug to muffle his footsteps, remembered the night his mother had recruited him to place the rug beneath the table—after his father had retired and could not object. She'd wanted to be certain her husband's feet and legs were warm after the accident that crippled him.

He glanced through the open door into the sitting room rich with an oriental rug, damask-covered settees, pillows and curtains, pictures and chalk figurines. His father had not denied his mother any comfort, but his austere nature showed in this room. There was no padded furniture, only wood chairs, the large stretcher table, a wood settle that sat at a right angle to the stone fireplace and a bookshelf along the far wall. Folding wood shutters, installed on all the windows in the house by his father, who had lived through a few fights with Indians in his early years, were the only thing the two rooms held in common. A long rifle, another reminder of those early years, rested on cast-iron pegs driven into the mortar between the stones above the wood beam mantel of the den fireplace.

A band of tightness circled his chest. His father's presence seemed so strong in the room he felt like an intruder. He hadn't come in here often. His father had never talked with him about finances. He'd always muttered, "We're doing fine" and changed the subject whenever he inquired—except last year when his father had to tell him about taking out the demand note to carry them through when the frost had ruined their grapes before harvest. He frowned and moved around the table to the chair. His gut told him he should have insisted on discussing the vineyard finances in spite of the doctor's warning to not upset his father and overstress his weak heart. It was too late now.

He lit the oil lamp, adjusted the wick, pulled a ledger from the drawer and placed it on the table. His father's bold slanted writing stared up at him from the top of the first page. *Twin Eagle Vineyard, 1874.* He flipped the page and stared at the headings written in the same bold hand. The date at the top, *January 1*, and listed in a precisely aligned column beneath: *Weather, Purchases, Hired labor, Work done*, all followed by cryptic notes that told him nothing about the vineyard's financial record, save money paid out.

He thumbed forward through the pages until he came to the present month of August. There were three additional entries to the column on that page: *Yield*, followed by *Concords-G, Catawbas-F-P. Price*, followed by *Concords-H, Catawbas-L*. And last, *Vintner*, followed by *D. Douglas*.

What did it mean? He scrubbed at the back of his neck and studied the letters *G* and *F-P*...they could mean "good" and "fair to poor." That would make sense. And the *H* and *L* could mean "high" and "low." There were no figures, of course. It would be up to him to fill those in when the harvest was over and the bank draft was in his hand. A harvest was a chancy thing, with nothing for certain, as they'd found out last year.

Where was the information about the demand note? How much had his father borrowed? He flipped backward through the pages but could find no mention of the note. He pushed back the chair, opened the drawer and searched through it. Nothing.

The ledgers from past years were on the bookshelf. He found the one for last year and turned to the month of August, stared at the pitiful numbers that recorded the frost-damaged harvest. There was no record of a demand note. He flipped to September, then on through the pages to December with the same result. He'd have to wait until he took Dillon Douglas's payment draft to the bank to find out. Thankfully, the concords had produced an abundant crop that had brought a top price. The money for the harvest should be enough...

He ignored the frisson of worry worming its way into his thoughts, placed the ledger back on the shelf, snuffed the lamp then left the room. He'd know in a few days. But that didn't help him plan—

"Well, I've finished the supper dishes and put the kitchen to rights." His mother stopped by the settee and stared up at him. "Does that scowl on your face mean you found bad news in—there?"

He noted the way her eyes skittered away from the door to the den, shook his head and smiled. "No. It means I'm not as smart as you've always thought me to be. I couldn't make much sense of things on a first quick look. I'll try again when the harvest is over and I have some time to spend on figuring things out."

"I hope it's not too difficult, Grant." She lifted her hand and smoothed back her hair, brushed at the front of her black gown. "Andrew should have taken you into his confidence. Especially…lately. But he didn't like to talk about his business with anyone."

"I know. It's all right, Mother." He glanced at her overbright eyes, shifted his gaze to the window. "It's nice outside. And I'm not ready to go to bed yet. What do you say we go out on the porch and sit on the swing?" He slanted his lips in a crooked grin. "I can eat another piece of that chocolate cake you made, and you can ask me more questions about Marissa."

"That sounds lovely. I'll get the cake." His mother headed for the kitchen, tossed him a look over her shoulder and smiled. "But don't think you are fooling me, young man. I know you only want an excuse to talk about your young woman."

His young woman. His. He liked the sound of that. *Work it out, Lord. In spite of all the obstacles, work it out, I pray.*

Chapter Ten

She shouldn't have come. The rapid beating of her heart told her that. Marissa glanced at the Winston house and hurried up the path, crossed the cool ivy-shaded porch and knocked on the door. Her pulse jumped. Foolish of her. Grant was most likely working in the vineyard. Still...

She smoothed the front of her plum-colored gown then reached up and checked to make certain the bow of the wide ribbon confining her curls was straight.

The door opened.

She smiled and lowered her hands, ignored the warmth crawling into her cheeks at having been caught primping. "Good afternoon, Mrs. Winston. I hope I haven't come at a bad time?"

"Oh, my dear, no. Come in. You are a gift, Marissa." Mrs. Winston smiled and pulled the door wide, closed it again when she stepped inside. "I am finding it difficult to find things to do. How does one clean an already clean house?"

She glanced at the dark blue apron covering Mrs. Winston's black dress, lifted her head and sniffed the spice-scented air. "I think one bakes instead?" She gave another delicate sniff. "Something smells delicious."

"I'm making hermits. They're Grant's favorite cookie. And this batch is about done. Come in the sitting room and have a seat while—" Mrs. Winston stopped, turned and looked at her. "Unless you would like to come to the kitchen and visit while I finish baking the cookies?"

How wonderfully welcome and comfortable Mrs. Winston made her feel—to *her home*. She shoved away all the thoughts connected to that one and curved her mouth into a smile. "Do I get to eat one warm from the oven?"

"If you like walnuts. I add them for Grant." Mrs. Winston gave a little laugh and motioned her to follow. "Anyway, you needn't stand on manners. Grant simply snatches cookies off the tin. And you can be sure he takes more than one. See?" She smiled and gestured toward the bottom shelf on a long table in the center of the large kitchen. "That worn spot on the edge of the shelf is from him standing on it before he was tall enough to reach the top of the table. His hands were so small then he could only take the cookies one at a time."

What a lovely memory. She closed her eyes, tried to imagine Grant as a child too small to reach the tabletop.

"Andrew used to stand him on the sink cupboard so he could 'help' him pump the water when he washed up after coming in from tending the vines. It was Grant's favorite time of day. He would climb up onto the wood box there under the window and watch for his father."

There was a mixture of pain and happiness in Mrs. Winston's voice. She glanced over at the wood box. The edge of the hinged top was worn.

"Forgive me, Marissa. I seem to be caught up in memories since…Andrew's passing. But they're everywhere I look. It's a comfort. Please, have a seat." Mrs. Winston gestured toward a round table and four chairs, then hurried to the stove and peeked in the oven. "Oh, my, here I am, chatting about memories, and these are done and the other tin isn't ready to go in."

A cloud of mouthwatering aroma rose from the tin of hot cookies Mrs. Winston placed on the table. She glanced at the puffy brown orbs lumpy with raisins and nuts, and was tempted to follow Grant's example. Good manners kept her hands at her sides. She shifted her gaze to the crockery bowl sitting beside a tin partially covered with mounds of raw dough at the other end of the long worktable. "Is there something I can do to help?"

Mrs. Winston looked across the table at her, and an odd expression, almost a look of yearning, swept over her face for the space of a blink. "Well…if you would be so kind, you can lift the cookies off the tin onto the table to cool."

She gave a loud sniff and smiled. "I shall be delighted."

Grant's mother laughed, pulled an apron from a drawer and handed it to her, then picked up the wood spoon in the bowl and dropped mounds of dough on the unfinished tin. "I'm so glad for your company, Marissa. And Grant will be delighted. He had thought you would come last night."

He had missed her. A little thrill of pleasure chased down her spine. "There was a meeting for teachers and lecturers I had to attend in the late afternoon, so my lecture was late beginning." She picked up a turner, slipped it under a cookie and lifted it to the table. "And then I got carried away and spoke over-long." She snatched a crumb off the tin and popped it in her mouth.

"Grant says your lectures are attended by hundreds of people. I confess, I would be most uncomfortable in your position."

"As am I." She scooped up another cookie and slid it off onto the table. "I had no idea when I was invited to speak at Chautauqua how many people there would be in attendance." She shook her head. "I had thought perhaps a few hundred, but there are thousands!"

"Well, I admire your courage. There! That's the last of them." Mrs. Winston slipped the tin of cookies into the oven, picked up the bowl and spoon and carried it to the sink cupboard beneath the window. "Is your temperance message well received?"

"By some. Others strenuously object to what I say, of course—which leads to lively debates." A sudden thought hit her. "Though not last night."

Mrs. Winston poured hot water into the dishpan, placed the teakettle back on the stove and glanced at her. "What was different about last night?"

"I'm not certain. I spoke out against strong drink as

I always do. But then…" She removed the last cookie and carried the still-warm tin over to the sink cupboard. "…I felt…*compelled*…to speak about the women and children who are abused by those men who turn mean and even violent when they drink wine or other strong drink." She picked up a towel and began drying the washed bowl Mrs. Winston placed on the wood drain board. "I explained that those women and children are victims of society as well as of their husbands or fathers."

Mrs. Winston's hands stilled. "I don't understand. How are they victims of society, Marissa?"

She looked at the frown on Mrs. Winston's face and her heart sank. Had she ruined her welcome in the Winston home? "They suffer in silence because they have no place to go for shelter or help until their husband or father sobers and—" She stopped, sniffed. "Are the cookies done?"

"Oh, my! I got so interested in what you were saying, I forgot all about them!" Mrs. Winston dipped her soapy hands in the rinse pan, snatched up a towel and hurried to the stove.

"I'm sorry I didn't have time to spend with you tonight, Marissa." Grant covered her hand with his, smiled down at her. "But that's soon to be over. The pickers will start on the last portion of the vineyard in the morning, and by dusk tomorrow the harvest will be over."

"Truly? I'm happy for you, Grant. And for your mother. You've been working so hard. And she's… lonely." She smiled, blinked and looked down.

He stopped walking, turned her to face him. "That's

not the reaction I was expecting, Marissa. What's wrong?"

She took a breath, gave a little shrug. "It's... everything." She pulled out of his grip, turned away and stared out over the water. "I—I think it's best if we say goodbye, Grant."

The words took him like a punch to the gut. He stiffened, stared at her rigid back. "You mean, for us to go our separate ways?"

She flinched, nodded.

"Then turn around and look at me and tell me that's what you want."

She shook her head. Her hand, pale against her dark gown, clenched. "I can't."

His heart jolted. He sucked in air. "Why not? It should be easy enough if it's what you want."

"But it's not!" She whipped around, her eyes anguished, wet tracks of tears glistening on her cheeks. "It's what has to be. And I'm not—not strong enough to do what I must, when you—when I'm—I have to go. Goodbye." She spun back around toward the dock.

He caught her hand, took her into his arms. She pushed against him, then grabbed fistfuls of his shirt, buried her face against his chest and burst into tears.

"Marissa, what—"

She shook her head, pressed her face tighter against him. "I l-love your m-mother."

His mother? What did that mean? He pulled in another breath, took a chance. "She loves you, too."

"Ohhh..." Tears soaked through his shirt.

Definitely not the right answer. He lowered his head

and pressed his cheek against her curls, helpless in the face of her distress. "Marissa, you have to help me. I don't know what's wrong, and—"

"Y-your h-house."

His house? He tried to make the mental leap and failed.

"It's b-beautiful. And your mother l-loves it. It comforts h-her. But she can't live there a-l-lone." She drew a long, shuddering breath and lifted her head. "You have to stay, Grant. And I can't—the vineyard. It's all…impossible."

"Marissa, it's not. Mother believes God brought us together, and so do I. She will do nothing to keep us apart. And I won't do anything to hurt her. We have to give us a chance, Marissa." He lifted his hands and cupped her face, wiped the tears from her cheeks with his thumbs. "Granted, my father's death has changed things, and I'll have to alter my plans. But I'll find a way. I haven't had time to work things out thus far, but the harvest will be over tomorrow night. And the next day I'll go to the bank to take care of all the financial needs. And then—"

The *Colonel Phillips* blew its warning whistle.

He smiled and brushed a light kiss across her lips. "And then I'll make an offer on the *Jamestown*. Trust me to work things out, Marissa. Wait a few more days."

She sighed, squared her shoulders and nodded. "All right, Grant. I'll wait."

Moonlight sparkled on the crest of waves rolling off the side of the *Colonel Phillips* to slap against the pilings of the dock and flow on to caress the shore. Marissa walked down the gangway and through the pool of light thrown by the lamps atop the posts at the end of the dock. Her shoes clicked on the weathered boards as she walked to the small gatehouse.

"Good evening, Miss Bradley. Go on through."

"Thank you." She smiled and stepped onto the shore, stopped at the sight of her tent mate standing by the nearby boating dock, then took a breath and moved forward again. "Have you been taking notes on the people out rowing or canoeing, Clarice? Are they going to be in your 'Chautauqua Experience' article?"

"Perhaps." Clarice hitched her writing box higher under her arm and fell into step beside her. "Actually, I have been for a canoe ride. A most enjoyable experience, though a little breath-catching before one is seated. The footing in a small canoe is chancy at best and I quite feared for my writing case until my guide got me settled and we began gliding across the water. I understand the attraction now for wooing couples. You feel quite alone with only the whisper of the water and the dip of the paddle to disturb the silence. Most romantic. I shall write it that way. Yes, and I shall make 'Miss Practical' the heroine." A smile curved her mouth, but her eyes were watchful. "Have you a suggestion for a hero?"

"Hmm, let me think…" Marissa lifted her hems and stepped onto the main path, grateful for the trees that shut out most of the moonlight. Clarice was far too observant for comfort and she was afraid of what her face might show. "I suppose 'Canoe Man' would be too obvious—and the same would be true for 'Lake Man.'"

"I had something more romantic in mind."

"Romantic…" She thrust all thought of Grant from her mind lest she blurt out his name by accident. "I have it! 'Chautauqua Beau.'"

Clarice paused, lifted her hand and swept it through the air above her head as if she were reading a banner. "'Miss Practical meets her Chautauqua Beau.' I like it. It could start any young lady dreaming."

"Then you may use the name with my compliments." She skirted around a man lighting one of the post torches and hurried her steps to pass a group of people on the path ahead of them. Clarice would work on her notes when they got to their tent.

"And what did you do in Mayville that was interesting, 'Miss Practical'?"

Thank you, Mrs. Winston, for my answer. She looked Clarice straight in the eye and smiled. "I made cookies."

The sounds from outside filtered through the tent's canvas walls, laughter, coughs, snores, low-pitched, muffled voices. The only sound inside the tent was the scratch of Clarice's pen against paper at the other end of the small desk.

Marissa turned to the beginning of the fifth chapter of the book of Isaiah and skimmed over the words. The verse was here… Ah! Yes. This was the verse she wanted to use in her new lecture on helping the victims of those who became mean and abusive when they overindulged in wine and other strong drink.

She placed her Bible so the light from the oil lamp in the center of the desk would fall on the page, pulled her lecture note paper close and dipped her pen in her inkwell. Isaiah 5:11. "Woe unto them that rise up early in the morning, that they may follow strong drink; that continue until night, till wine inflame them!"

Inflame. Her face tightened. *Inflamed* was the exact word to describe her father when he'd been drinking his wine and become abusive. It described the look in his eyes when he raised his hand—

"Marissa."

She jolted out of her thoughts, looked over the top of the oil lamp at Clarice. "Yes?"

"I wanted to tell you that I attended your lecture yesterday."

She studied Clarice's face then lifted her chin. "I remember when you told me you would be writing about me and my lectures. You warned me then to make them good for if they weren't, you wouldn't hesitate to say so. Are you warning me now that your report will be unfavorable?"

"No, quite the contrary. I was very moved by your plea on behalf of those who must bear abuse in silence because society has, heretofore, ignored this problem. I think, as you stated so eloquently, that it is time that was changed."

Clarice corked her inkwell, put it in the wood box with her other writing supplies and hooked the latch. "The editor of the *Sunday School Journal* asked me to do a feature piece on one of the lectures or classes here at Chautauqua. I've chosen yours. I've titled it 'Mercy and Sacrifice.' And I included your plea for those who are interested in starting a temperance group to also provide a place where those women and children who suffer the abuse caused by the overindulgence in wine and other alcoholic beverages can shelter and be safe until the imbiber sobers and the danger passes. As you said, 'a place where they will receive understanding instead of judgment and not be made to feel shame.'"

"Clarice..." She pressed her hand to her chest, shook her head in disbelief. "I—I'm stunned. I don't know what to say."

Her tent mate smiled. "Perhaps this will help you think of something. I added a plea for the churches who receive the *Journal* to rise to the call of mercy and meet the need." Her smile faded away. "The *Sunday School Journal* has a monthly circulation of over one hundred thousand. Hopefully, many of them will answer the call."

"Clarice!" The squeal was out before she could stop it. She clapped her hands over her mouth.

Clarice burst into laughter. "Well, that should wake all of our neighbors."

"I don't care! *One hundred thousand!* Oh, Clarice, thank you!" She surged from her chair, whirled across the small space and enveloped Clarice in a huge hug.

Chapter Eleven

"And you've been living in a *tent* this whole time?"

Marissa couldn't hold back her smile. Mrs. Winston looked appalled. "It's truly not as bad as it sounds. The tent is quite spacious with tall walls, a high sloped ceiling and a wood floor. My tent mate and I each have a cot and our trunks, a chair and an oil lamp. We share a small desk, a washstand and a large clean tree root system on which we hang our coats and some clothes."

"A root system!" Mrs. Winston shook her head and went back to dicing carrots.

"It works quite well." She sliced the rutabaga she'd peeled in half, then cut each half into thick slices.

"And you have a—what did you call her?"

"A tent mate." She lined up the slices for dicing, paused at the sound of boots thudding against the porch floor.

"Oh, dear!" Mrs. Winston dropped her knife, wiped her hands on a towel and hurried to a cupboard across the room.

The door was shoved open and Grant burst into the kitchen. "Mother, Charlie cut himself. I need a cloth to bind his hand until I can get him to the doctor."

"Here it is." Mrs. Winston hurried toward him, a narrow roll of white cotton in her hand. "Do you need me to come wrap his hand?"

"No. I'll do it." He backed toward the door, glanced her way. "I can't stay, Marissa. I have to take Charlie's place to get…" His boots pounded against the porch.

She stared at the door, her heart pounding. "I hope the man will be all right."

"He will be." Mrs. Winston resumed dicing the carrots. "Dr. Fletcher is good at sewing them up."

Her stomach objected to the idea. She looked down, wielded the knife in her hand with new respect. "What did Grant mean, he'll have to take Charlie's place? I couldn't hear the last of what he said."

"Grant is determined to finish this harvest today. The overcast skies do not look promising, and if it rains they will have to stop picking and wait for the fruit and vines to dry. That can cause mildew, or the grapes can get overripe and spoil, which means no sale." Mrs. Winston tossed the diced carrots in a bowl and started peeling potatoes. "Now Grant has lost one of the pickers. He'll step in and pick in Charlie's place as well as direct the harvest so he can be done before the rain comes."

"I see." She tossed the diced rutabaga in the bowl and glanced out the window at the gray cloudy day, torn between wanting the rain to come and ruin the grapes and the weather to hold so Grant could finish the harvest. Nothing was clear-cut anymore. She held back the sigh that wanted expression and began dicing the peeled potatoes.

"I wonder if you would do me a favor, Marissa."

She glanced over at Mrs. Winston, who had carried away the vegetable peelings in a small bucket and was now preparing wash water for the dishes. "Of course, if I'm able. What is it?"

"I've been praying about what you said the other day about women and children who are treated badly by their spouse or parent who overindulge, and about Sarah Swan and the other women who came here to protest our growing grapes."

Mrs. Winston came toward the table, a wet, soapy rag in her hand. "Would you add those vegetables to the soup stock please, Marissa?"

She carried the bowl to the stove wondering what was coming.

The table was cleaned with a few vigorous swipes of the soapy rag. "And I think the Lord would be pleased if I did something to help."

Her breath caught. She stirred the vegetables into the stock and waited while Mrs. Winston rinsed the soap from the cloth and returned.

"So…" The rinsed cloth swished over the table. Mrs. Winston gave it a last swipe then stepped over beside her and picked up the empty bowl. "When we get these dishes done, will you go with me to Swan's store to talk with Sarah? The soup can sit and simmer unattended, and I don't want those women suffering alone anymore, Marissa. Not while I've got this big empty house."

Her jaw dropped. She stood there with the spoon in her hand, too shocked to speak.

"You're dripping."

She gathered her wits, put the spoon down and smiled. "I'd be honored to accompany you to the store, Mrs. Winston." She couldn't stop herself, didn't want to. She loved Grant's mother. She threw her arms around Mrs. Winston and hugged, squeezed words past the lump in her constricted throat. "May God bless you for your warm, caring heart."

The bowl clattered against the stove. Mrs. Winston's arms closed around her and returned her hug. "He already has, Marissa. He already has."

"It's over, Marissa. The harvest is finished!" Grant whooped, grasped her by her small waist, lifted her into the air and spun in circles.

She grabbed his shoulders to brace herself, laughing down at him. "You'd better hush and put me down or our secret spot won't be a secret any longer."

"Hmm, we can't have that." He lowered her until her face was level with his, then, unable to resist, claimed her lips. Her arms slipped around his neck and her lips parted, trembled against his. His heart thudded, knocked against his chest wall in a wild hammering that stole his breath. *Help me, Lord. I don't want to let her go. Not now. Not ever.*

He crushed her to him, lowered his forehead to her hair, closed his eyes and breathed in the soft, feminine scent that clung to her. "I'll be going to the bank tomorrow to straighten out the finances for the vineyard, my mother's living and my own plans, Marissa. After that I'll be free to—"

"Don't, Grant. Please don't say any more."

He watched the tears in her eyes pool, tremble and slide down her cheeks, and made an effort to get control of his emotions. "I'm sorry, Marissa, I misunderstood. I thought you would welcome my—" Her fingertip touched his lips, soft, warm… He fought the desire to kiss it.

"You didn't misunderstand, Grant. I don't want you to say anything until everything is resolved. And— and I don't s-see how it can be." Her lips quivered. Her whole body trembled in his arms. "I try. I truly try, Grant. But every time I look at those grapevines I see my father's hand poised to strike. I see Lincoln, and all the hurt and misery and waste—" Her lips pressed together. Her eyes closed, hiding her pain from him.

He tightened his arms and held her.

The rain clattered against the porch roof, splattered on the stone walk and pattered against the wind-whipped leaves of the vines. Grant leaned against the porch post, his mind's eye seeing the destruction such a storm would wreak on grapes waiting to be picked. *Thank You, Lord, that the harvest is finished.*

He shifted his weight and scrubbed his free hand over the back of his neck. It was odd to think he'd never have to worry about another harvest. Truth be told, after all these years, the vines had almost become a part of him. He'd miss walking among the sloping trellises checking for mildew and rot, pruning vines and watching the fruit develop until their dark purple clusters gave off the rich, robust aroma that hovered like a cloud beneath the concords' leafy canopy.

Of course, he'd always liked riding the steamers. But he wasn't sure how he'd like doing it all day long. It didn't seem as if there'd be much to keep a man occupied. But there was no use speculating about it. He'd find out soon enough. He'd have the Oakwood Winery bank draft tomorrow.

He frowned, wiped misty moisture from his face and shoved a damp lock of hair off his forehead. That was another odd thing, him taking care of the finances. Why, he didn't even know how much money had accumulated in the bank from his share of the harvests profits they'd earned since he'd been managing the care of the vineyard. He only knew it would be sizable. His father had never been forthcoming about finances, and he'd never pressed him.

That little curl of worry twisted in his gut. He shifted his position to lean on the other shoulder and shoved his hands in his pockets. He'd be rid of that annoyance tomorrow.

The kitchen door creaked and the aroma of coffee wafted through the rain-washed air. He turned and smiled at his mother, not much more than a shadow in the dark. The oil lamps by the door proved of little use against the black stormy night. She walked to his side, held out a heavy stoneware cup. A pang pricked his heart. *Don't give me one of those fancy, flimsy china things. If I'm gonna have a cup of coffee, I want a real cup.* "Dad's cup?" He slipped his two middle fingers through the handle and curled his hand around the cup the way he'd learned from watching his father.

"You're the man of the house now. Not that you haven't been carrying a man's weight around here for several years. It's a…symbolic thing." She gave him a wobbly little smile, patted his arm then moved to stand by the railing. "This porch was your father's favorite place. He said he did his best thinking out here."

He watched his mother's hand glide back and forth on the railing, lifted his gaze to her face soft with memories. He could never ask her to leave this house. And she couldn't live here without him. He glanced out at the vines, clenched his fingers around the cup. *Lord, I need an answer.*

"Are you standing out here contemplating your good fortune in having the harvest finished before this storm hits?"

He pulled his gaze back to his mother. "Something like that."

She gave a little nod. "You're a good deal like your father, Grant."

There was a thickness to her voice. Time to change the tone of the conversation. "It's learned behavior." He grinned and took a sip of the hot brew.

She nodded, took a breath and straightened. "This is a real downpour. I hope Marissa is warm and dry. I can't *imagine* living in a tent in this weather."

Her name stuck in his heart like a dagger. He'd been trying to hold thoughts of her at bay, to not remember her deep pain that might keep them apart. No. He'd have the money tomorrow. He'd work it out. Somehow he'd work it all out. He pulled in a breath of coffee-scented air. "It sounds like you've gotten spoiled, Mother. I remember hearing tales of some pretty sparse living conditions in your early years as a bride." He forced another grin. "At least Marissa's tent has a roof."

"That big old harvest table sheltered us well enough until your father got the roof put on the house."

His mother giggled like a young girl.

The teasing banter was doing them both good. He took another stab at it. "So I've heard. But then I've seen that table, and it's pretty narrow." He waggled his eyebrows.

"Grant Zephaniah Winston!"

He laughed and tapped her cheek. "Is that a blush I see, Mother?"

She jerked back and shoved his hand away. "You behave yourself, Grant. You know full well you can't see anything in this dark, and so do I."

All the same, her hand lifted and touched her cheek. He chuckled and took another swallow of coffee.

The rain increased, fell like a gray curtain on the other side of the railing. Closed them in. It was a good night for talking. Sharing...

"I like Marissa, Grant. I've tried to guard my heart around her, but she's so...so..."

He took a breath and spoke it out. "Lovable?"

She gave him one of her looks. "Your description?"

He took a last swallow and tossed the rest of the suddenly tasteless coffee out into the night. "Yes. Almost from the first meeting."

"I thought so." She lifted her hands from the railing,

brushed the spattering of rain from them and cupped his face. "Marissa loves you, too. Though I'm not certain she knows it."

His heart clenched. Not even his mother's touch could make this all better. "There are…challenges."

She stepped back and looked up, studied his face. "I've never known you to run from a challenge."

"Who says I'm running?"

A slow smile curved her lips. She gave a small, satisfied nod and touched his arm. "I'll pray."

The drumming of the rain on the tent roof was so loud she couldn't even hear the corn husks crackle when she moved. Marissa rose, shivered at the touch of the damp, cool air and groped around the foot of her cot in the inky darkness searching for her dressing gown and slippers. Her little toe bumped against the corner of her trunk.

"Ow!… Ow!… Ow!…" She plopped down on the cot and grabbed her toe, rocking back and forth. The back of her hand bumped her slippers. She pulled them on, fumbled around and found her dressing gown, tugged it on and lifted the domed lid of her trunk. Her fingers found what she was seeking. She carried the stationery box to the desk guided by the tiny glow of the oil lamp's lowered wick, then twisted the knob until the light fell in a golden circle on the table.

There was no need for quiet. She sat and arranged her stationery paper, uncorked her inkwell and dipped her pen.

Dearest Mother,

It is raining. A veritable deluge! The drumming of the raindrops on the tent is so loud I find sleep impossible. To my amazement there is not a single leak! The night air has taken on a decided chill, but my dressing gown and slippers keep me warm.

In my last letter I shared the information about my tent mate, Miss Clarice Gordon. I am writing now to give you further news. Miss Gordon has been assigned the task of writing a feature article for the Sunday School Journal *on a subject or lecture, of her choosing, given here at Chautauqua. Miss Gordon has chosen my most recent lecture for this honor.*

She paused and stared into the darkness, considering how to continue. It was almost certain that her mother would not be pleased with the content of her lecture. And it was positively certain that her father would not. She sighed and dipped her pen.

The subject of my chosen lecture is the abused victims of those who overindulge in wine or other strong drink. In it I explain how the women and children who are abused need a place where they can shelter and be safe until the imbiber sobers and the danger passes. And I urge those interested in starting temperance groups in their towns to provide such a place. I am going to work

*to establish such a place when I return home,
Mother. I hope you will join with me in this work.*

*In her article, Miss Gordon also asks the
churches who receive the* Journal *to "rise to the
call" and establish safe shelters such as I have
described above. And now, Mother, for the exciting news. The* Sunday School Journal *has a
circulation of over one hundred thousand! Oh,
Mother, only think of the many women and children who will be helped if a mere portion of the
churches receiving the* Journal *become involved.*

She put down her pen and rubbed her arms. The
mere thought of all the women and children who might
be helped because of this one article set her nerves a-
tingle. She only hoped her mother would be one of
them. That she would not let her pride stand in the way
of getting needed help.

*I know you worry that I may be harmed doing
temperance work, Mother. But I am quite safe.
Shortly after my arrival, I led a small march on
a local vineyard to protest their growing grapes.
Unfortunately, we were unsuccessful in stopping
the wagons that carried the grapes to the winery. But there is a wonderful sequel to that story.
I met the vineyard owner's mother, and she is a
truly lovely woman. I told her of Miss Gordon's
article, and she is opening her home as a place
of shelter and safety to the women and children
of Mayville who are abused. She is a woman*

*of strong faith, and I feel it is, indeed, the Lord
who has guided her to do this. I can think of no
other reason why the mother of a vineyard owner
would provide shelter for the abused.*

*I pray this letter finds you well, Mother. My
best to Father.*
Your loving daughter,
Marissa

She stared down at the letter, remembering how surprised Sarah Swan had been when she and Mrs. Winston entered the Swans' store together. And Sarah had
been dumbfounded when Mrs. Winston explained her
purpose. She shook her head, still a little dazed and
disbelieving herself. But it was true. Sarah Swan was
going to tell the other women, and they were all going
to Mrs. Winston's home to work out the details of establishing a shelter.

The abused women were going to have a shelter at
the very vineyard where they had protested. It was…
unbelievable.

*Fortunately, there is nothing too difficult for the
Lord.*

Mrs. Winston's words. Mrs. Winston's faith.

She took the letter into her hands and read what she
had written. It was all unbelievable. And it was only
part of what had happened.

Grant. Perhaps…

The doubts pounced. All of the reasons why Grant's
plan would never work tumbled through her mind. Her
heart wanted to believe. Her head called her a fool.

She sealed and addressed the letter, left it on the desk to be posted when she went to Mayville and put her stationery box in the trunk.

Rain beat against the canvas. Wind slapped against the walls, bulging them in and sucking them out again. She returned to the desk, lowered the wick in the lamp and made her way back to her cot in the dark. A quick shrug removed her dressing gown. She stepped out of her slippers and climbed beneath the covers blinded by the black night. She turned her head toward the desk and stared at the tiny spot of light in the darkness.

Thoughts of Grant's kiss washed over her, would not be denied. Warmth crawled into her heart, then into her cheeks at the memory of her response. What had come over her? She had slapped the only other man who had tried to kiss her. And they had been courting a few months at the time. But it was so…different. She *wanted* Grant to kiss her. She wanted to be in his arms. How was it possible that she felt safe in his strong embrace?

Fortunately, there is nothing too difficult for the Lord.

She turned onto her back, closed her eyes and shrugged off Mrs. Winston's words. Even if they were true, why would the Lord be interested in her relationship with Grant?

Chapter Twelve

A shadow flowed across the faces of the buildings that lined the street. Grant paused on the side of the walkway to let a wagon pass by and glanced up at the sky. The sun was playing hide-and-seek with another dark cloud. But that was all right. He didn't have to worry about those rain clouds anymore.

He grinned and patted the pocket over his heart. An apt place for the Oakwood Winery's bank draft to be, since it was the ticket to his heart's desire. His grin broadened.

"You look like a cat that's cornered a mouse, Winston."

He turned his head in the direction of the voice. A tall, thin man with a limp was coming up the walk toward him. "I haven't got it cornered yet, Fleming. But I'm working on it."

Harold Fleming chuckled and tipped his hat. "Well, keep up the fight."

Grant lifted his hand in farewell and strode across

the street, impatience driving him. Dillon Douglas had kept him talking for an hour, telling him how good the concords were—as if he didn't already know. He was the one who had brought them into the vineyard.

"Good afternoon, Grant Winston."

Oh, no. He halted, doffed his hat to the town chatterbox. "Good afternoon, Mrs. Chesterson."

The plump woman stood in the middle of the walkway and looked up him. "I was so sorry to hear about your father's passing, Grant. My sincere condolences."

"That's very kind of you. Thank you." He glanced over her shoulder hoping she would take the hint and let him pass.

"And to your dear mother, of course."

He dipped his head. *Perhaps if he didn't talk—*

"How is Ruth holding up?" She tipped her head to the side, straightened her hat. "I hope her grief isn't making her ill."

That's not what her eyes said. Her eyes said she hoped there was a good story she could pass along. "Not at all." He fixed a steady gaze on her. "Mother's faith gives her strength."

"Yes. Yes, of course it does. Well, I must be going. Tilda Forrest is unwell, and I want to drop by and see if there's anything I can do to help her." She pulled a penny candy from her purse and popped it into her mouth. "Remember me to your dear mother."

He dipped his head in acknowledgment and stepped to the side of the walkway. "My greetings to Carl."

She sailed by and he dodged around a sleeping dog waiting outside the barbershop for its owner, trotted up the four steps to the bank's entrance and opened the door. Fred Gardner peered at him from behind his barred window.

"May I help you, Mr. Winston?"

He shook his head, too focused on his quest to tease his old friend about the formality. "I need to see Mr. Taylor. Is he in?"

"If you'll wait here, I'll—"

"Fred." He shot him a look.

"He's in. Go on back."

He strode through the archway at the back of the room into the hallway and knocked on the door on his left.

"Come in."

The banker's office was large and sober with oak-paneled walls and a high domed ceiling. A five-lamp chandelier dangled by a chain from the highest point. He removed his hat, hung it on the rack that stood beside the door and moved forward, his steps muffled by a red-patterned oriental rug.

"Ah, Grant. I've been expecting you to come in to see me." Walter Taylor rose and came around his desk, his hand outstretched in welcome. "I'm sorry about your loss, Grant. Your father was a fine, upright man. I enjoyed doing business with him."

"Thank you, sir." Grant shook the banker's hand, calloused from the whittling he enjoyed doing in the evening.

"I assume this visit means that your grapes have all been harvested in spite of that little bit of trouble you had. Most interesting watching Sarah Swan and the other women march through town holding their signs and singing. I sympathize with their cause, having seen some of the damage imbibing can do to a man's good sense. But I find their methods ineffective." Walter Taylor waved a hand toward a chair and stepped back behind his desk. "I admired your solution. I imagine it saved a lot of hurt feelings."

"Perhaps. But I disagree that the women were ineffective." It might not have been the wisest thing to do, but he couldn't ignore the urge to speak out in Marissa's defense. "The women may have failed in their initial aim of preventing our grapes from reaching Douglas's winery, but they have succeeded in calling attention to their plight." He dropped down into the leather-padded chair indicated and answered the question that was put to him. "We finished picking at dusk yesterday."

"You were fortunate. Bringing in those concords was a smart move, Grant." The banker gave him an approving look. "Most of the grapes in the other vineyards in the area are only beginning to ripen. I'm afraid that storm last night will cost most of those vineyard owners a pretty penny. Now, what can I do for you?"

"Well, I'm a little at a loss as to actual numbers here. My father didn't like to discuss finances. But I know he took out a demand note last year to carry us through until this year's harvest." He reached into his pocket and pulled out the bank draft, then leaned forward and placed it on the desk. "I'll pay that note off, of course. And then we'll handle the rest of the profits the usual way. My percentage and the remainder will go into the vineyard account."

Walter Taylor picked up the bank draft, studied it a moment then looked at him over the top of his glasses. "What about the other payment?"

That curl of worry he'd been carrying around in his stomach until the harvest was over turned into a tight knot. "What other payment?"

"The annual payment on the mortgage your father carried on the house and vineyard is due."

"A mortgage! On the house and vineyard?"

"I'm afraid so."

Best we can do, I guess. It'll help.

So this was what his father had been worrying about. "I had no idea." His face tightened. He rose and walked about the room, came back and sat. "Is there enough money in the draft to cover both payments?"

"Oh, yes." The banker nodded, tapped the draft against his palm. "And with enough left over to comfortably carry both household and vineyard through to next year's harvest. Barring any unforeseen problems or expenses, of course."

Which meant there was no money to hire a man to take his place managing the vineyard. The knot in his stomach tightened. "And my percentage?"

Walter Taylor shook his head. "There'll be nothing left to pay your percentage, I'm afraid."

His year's wages, gone. He'd been counting on that money to buy the *Jamestown*.

Marissa...

He jerked his mind from the thought of her. He had

to concentrate, to think of what to do. He took another turn around the room trying to assimilate the information he'd been given and to figure out what questions he should ask. He had to know what he was facing. "How much longer does the mortgage have to run?"

"Next year's payment will be the last."

He nodded, scrubbed his hand over his neck. It wasn't unmanageable. The newest concords he'd planted would be producing in the coming year, and that would increase next year's yield at harvest. The vineyard could survive, though he wouldn't be able to hire anyone to help him run it this coming year. He'd thought he'd be free. He'd promised Marissa...

He pushed that problem aside for the moment and focused on his own finances. He'd never withdrawn any money from his share of the account. His father had told him just to come to him for any money or need... Yes. His plan might still work out with a little altering. He would have to forget about buying the steamer, but there should be more than enough to buy a house and furnishings. That would allow him to live away from the vineyard while he courted Marissa. And with his wages from the vineyard to provide a living... He would explain it was only for one year... Yes. His plan was salvageable.

The knot loosened a little. His breath came easier. "One more question, Mr. Taylor. I would like to know the amount of my share of the account."

The banker looked up at him, took off his glasses and rubbed the bridge of his nose. "I'm afraid that's more bad news, Grant. There is no money in the account." He settled his glasses back on his nose then rested his hands on his desk. "Your father used your share of the money to pay off a few notes when profits were low. He meant to pay you back, of course, but the money was never there…"

He had nothing. It took him like the kick of an angry horse, drove the breath from his lungs. He rose and strode to the door, lifted his hat from the rack and walked out of the room.

Marissa closed the front door and led Judith Moore into the sitting room, the way a daughter of the house would. Her heart warmed at the thought and her imagination took flight.

"Judith, come in."

Mrs. Winston's voice brought her back to earth. She left Judith to seat herself on the settee next to Sarah Swan and moved to stand beside the door that led to the dining room and kitchen.

"Welcome, everyone."

She looked at Mrs. Winston standing in front of the stone fireplace then swept her gaze over the women in the room. They looked—

"My, my, ladies, I must say you all look a bit stiff and uncomfortable, and I can't imagine why. You've all been here before."

Her gasp was lost among those of the other women. She darted a look at Grant's mother, noted the glint of humor in her eyes and understood. "Not by invitation."

"Too true!" Mrs. Winston laughed and after a moment of shocked silence the others joined in.

"That's better." Mrs. Winston stepped closer to the group. "Ladies, this feels far too formal and…well… stodgy for our purposes. Let's hold our meeting over tea and cookies on the back porch. It's this way."

She watched the women following Mrs. Winston to the door, then hurried to the kitchen for the tea tray and carried it outside.

"Thank you, Marissa." Mrs. Winston smiled and touched her arm. "We are discussing possible ways of reaching women and children in the area who we aren't acquainted with, but who may need our help, with the news of our shelter. When we have worked out all of the details of course."

Our shelter. How gracious of Mrs. Winston to include the others in her idea. She grew more fond of the woman every day. "I've passed the newspaper building on my way to and from the dock." She placed the tray in front of Mrs. Winston so she could pour the tea. "I should think news of such a shelter would be of interest to the editor. I'm certain he would write up an editorial piece about it. And he might be willing to print copies announcing the founding of the shelter that you could distribute."

"Posters announcing the shelter. That's exactly what we need." Mrs. Winston beamed approval at her.

"We could ask the different churches to display them."

"Ina, that's a wonderful idea!" Lily smiled, lifted a cookie from the tray and passed it on. "Perhaps some of the women would join us in caring for those who need help. Not everyone lives here in town."

"I'll post a notice in the store."

"Oh, Sarah. Will Mr. Swan allow you to do that?"

The suggestions and comments went on and on. Marissa studied the faces of the women gathered around the table. They looked so different than they had on the day of the march. They'd been so grim that day. Now there was purpose and dignity and…hope in their expressions. They were no longer alone.

"Ladies, these are all wonderful ideas! But before we approach anyone about spreading news of our shelter, we must decide what we will say in the announcements. Why, we haven't even got a name." Mrs. Winston swept her gaze around the table. "What shall we call our shelter, ladies? Any suggestions?"

The women looked at each other, nodded and in one voice said, "The Twin Eagle Vineyard Shelter for the Abused."

Impossible. Marissa bit back the word.

Sarah Swan squared her shoulders. "Unless you prefer not, Ruth."

"Why, I would be honored, Sarah."

A vineyard that shelters the abused? Marissa left the women discussing the wording of the announcement and stepped to the porch railing. Sunlight and cloud shadow moved across the lush vines toward the access road where they had tried to stop the winery wagons and failed. Or had they? Perhaps their protest had been more successful than they knew.

Fortunately, there is nothing too difficult for the Lord.

A quiet she had never before experienced washed over her. It wasn't quite serenity. But still… A smile touched her lips and her heart. She was truly starting to believe.

There had to be a way. Grant stood pitching stones into the pond and watching the ripples grow larger and larger. There had to be a way. But there wasn't. Not any he could see. He was trapped.

No money.

No steamer.

No house.

He brushed his hands together, shoved them into his pockets and stared at the water. His situation was like those ripples, an encompassing circle that only got bigger and bigger. There was no way out.

Marissa.

The knots in his stomach twisted. How was he to tell her?

Pain ripped through him. He yanked his hands from his pockets, crossed them at the nape of his neck, bowed his head and closed his eyes.

Your father used the money to pay off a few notes when profits were low. He meant to pay you back, of course, but the money was never there…

"God, I promised her! I *promised* her!"

He had to find a way.

He raised his head, tightened his hands holding the back of his neck and pressed his elbows together in front of him, trying to stop his churning thoughts.

The same thoughts tumbled over and over through his mind, like those heinous ripples!

I try. I truly try, Grant. But every time I look at those grapevines I see my father's hand poised to strike. I see Lincoln, and all the hurt and misery and waste...

He lowered his hands and stared at the lush grapevines that surrounded him, let out a sound that was half moan, half growl. He couldn't bear the sight of them. He pivoted and headed down the hill, his boot heels striking the path with jarring impact.

No money...

No steamer...

No house...

I don't want you to say anything until everything is resolved. And I don't see how it can be...

He reached the bottom of the hill, turned left and ran along the path that followed the edge of the lake, away from town, away from the railroad station and the dock. He might not be able to outrun his thoughts and problems, but he could exhaust himself so they didn't hurt as much. He lengthened his stride, pumped his elbows and dragged air into his lungs.

He'd had it all planned, all figured out to the last detail—except one. There was no money. All those years he'd worked to improve the vineyard, to increase the yield, to grow hardier vines that would withstand the cold, to build his father's dream...

He ducked beneath the low-hanging limb of a maple tree and ran on.

And his wages...his share of the profits...nonexistent.

Gone. What he had for eleven years of hard work was a mortgage. A *debt* hanging over his head. He was ensnared. Caught in a circle of circumstance that was not of his doing but that left him no way out. No matter which direction he turned in, he was blocked. Marissa had been right. There was no way to resolve the situation.

He ignored the agony of his straining lungs and pushed on, driven by frustration and anger. He couldn't sell the house and vineyard. That would clear the debt, but it would leave him and his mother without a home. They would have nothing. And with no money he couldn't buy a steamer or any other business. And because of his father's accident, he'd had to forgo his education and work the vineyard. He had no other skill… no other way to earn a living. No. He had no choice. He was shackled. Entangled by the vines. He had to keep the house and vineyard to provide for his mother, and to make his own living.

He broke through a band of trees into the small clearing where he had come as a child to dream his small-boy dreams and staggered to a stop, dropped to his knees and gasped for air.

Two years.

He could work his way free in two years. One year to pay off the mortgage and clear the house and vineyard of debt for his mother. And one year to earn enough to give him a good start in a new business. Barring any unforeseen problems or expenses, of course.

He flopped to his back on the ground, watched the sunlight war against the darting shadows of the clouds, then draped his arm over his eyes and let the question he'd been holding off come.

Would Marissa continue to see him while he managed the vineyard for two more years?

Chapter Thirteen

The sun was losing its battle with the cloud shadows. The landscape was turning dark. Marissa shoved her thoughts, as dark as the clouds, away and shifted in her chair so she could not see the grapevines. The fabric of her black gown rustled softly. She glared down at it, wishing she could rip it off and throw it away. She was so tired of all the somberness that constantly reminded her of her loss and grief. How could she forget it?

The kitchen door opened and she pushed at the curls that dangled on her forehead and smiled.

"They are all gone home." Grant's mother smiled and took a chair. "You must be feeling very pleased about your fledgling group, Marissa. Your idea has borne fruit, though we are still trying to find our way."

"This group was your idea, Mrs. Winston. But I thought the first meeting of the Twin Eagle Vineyard Shelter for the Abused went well."

"Yes. Very well. The Twin Eagle Vineyard Shelter for the Abused. My, oh, my…" Mrs. Winston shook her head. A smile curved her lips. "I certainly did not expect the women to choose that name. Our Abba, Father, has a rather droll sense of humor."

It was a notion foreign to her. "You think God has a sense of humor?" The idea was intriguing. She rather liked it.

"Of course. He made man, didn't He?"

Mrs. Winston's laughter was contagious. Her own bubbled up to join it, though she wasn't sure the subject matter was appropriate. God was treated with somber reverence, like a rather cruel, all-powerful entity simply waiting for the opportunity to punish someone for disobeying His commands in her home. "And you think that God is, in some 'mysterious' way, responsible for the ladies selecting that particular name?"

"I do. Though there is nothing 'mysterious' about it. The Bible says God will guide us continually and that He will 'establish our thoughts.' And besides—" Mrs. Winston's eyes twinkled at her "—have you ever known five women to agree on anything that quickly?"

The laughter burst free. A paroxysm of amusement that made her sides ache and her eyes water. It felt wonderful.

"You should do that more often, Marissa. Your laughter is like music."

She wiped her cheeks and eyes with her fingertips, fought against a rush of sadness at the thought of returning to her home where there was no laughter… none at all since Lincoln had died.

"What is it, dear?"

Her throat constricted, ached at Mrs. Winston's caring touch. She looked down at Grant's mother's hand on hers, at the black fabric that encased both of their arms. *Both* of them. Yet Mrs. Winston somehow found joy, and the love and strength to care about another's hurt in the midst of her mourning. *She* got angry. Oh, she had joined the temperance movement because she wanted to prevent others from suffering the pain and shame and grief she had known, but it was anger and a strange sort of selfishness that motivated her, not love. She simply wanted the abuse, the waste of lives, to stop so she didn't have to think about it and remember anymore. That was why she so hated those vines on the other side of that railing. Why she couldn't bear to look at them. They made her remember.

"Marissa…"

Such concern in Mrs. Winston's voice and eyes. "I'm sorry. I was remembering my brother. And that there's been no laughter in our house for a very long time."

"I'm sorry, dear." Mrs. Winston's hand squeezed hers. "I can see your pain at having lost your brother. And I know the grief one bears at the loss of a child. But time will ease the grief, Marissa. You and your parents will all laugh again."

The love and serenity in Grant's mother's eyes caused the desire, the *hunger* to know it for her own to rise in an overwhelming wave. She took a breath and braced herself for the shocked reaction her revelation of the truth would bring. "I know what you say about grief is true, Mrs. Winston. But it's not Lincoln's death that stole the laughter from our house. It's the fear and abuse. You see, my father is a secret imbiber. To the members of the community he is seen as a kind, upright and honorable man who is a loving husband and father, and a faithful Christian man who never misses a church service." She hated the bitterness that spilled out in her voice but was helpless to stop it. "The truth is, when he's at home he drinks wine to excess and turns into another person altogether. He shouts and rages and pushes and strikes my mother or me without cause. Then, when his ire is spent, he goes to their room and collapses on their bed." *Oh, the pain of speaking those words!*

The metal of her mother's watch she'd clasped without thought dug into her fingers. Her face tightened. "Father's always remorseful, of course—once the wine leaves him and he wakes. This is my mother's watch—an 'apology' gift to her from my father after a particularly bad beating. She was too bruised to leave the house for two weeks, but she had a costly watch for others to admire and then exclaim over her husband's generosity, when she was able to rejoin society."

She pressed her lips together to stop from saying more, from letting the anger ruin this day as it did so many. Her breath caught as Mrs. Winston lifted her hand and slipped her fingers between the dangling pendant of the enameled watch and the black fabric of the mourning gown that covered her hurting heart.

"I don't believe you and your mother are the only ones who suffer pain from those blows, Marissa. Whenever I see this watch, I will pray for you and your mother, and for your father. He must be in terrible torment."

It was not the response she had expected. Her father suffering torment? It was a possibility she had never considered. She rose, crossed to the railing and stared out at the trellised vines. Vines that could have produced the grapes that made the wine that had destroyed their family. "Grant once told me that you believe that God watches over His children, and that He will work a blessing for them into every situation. Is that true?"

"Yes, it is."

So calm...so sure. She wrapped her arms around herself, trying to stop the turmoil raging within. "Even in loss and mourning?"

"Even then."

There was a rustle of fabric. The whisper of the hems of a gown against the porch floorboards mingled with soft footfalls. Mrs. Winston gently clasped her shoulders and turned her around.

"Look at us, Marissa. We stand here together, each dressed in black, each mourning the loss of a dearly loved one, yet blessed, because in the midst of our grief and sorrow we have found each other, and you have found the gift of love in my son. How can I not believe?" Mrs. Winston reached up and her soft, warm hands cupped her face in a loving touch. "The Bible says, 'Weeping may endure for a night, but joy cometh in the morning.' Trust Him, Marissa. Trust the Lord. He'll work it all out."

Grant pushed to his feet, the back of his shirt and pants damp from the still-moist ground. His head hurt. He grimaced and rubbed at his temples. The ache was all he had to show for the hours of intense thinking. It was for sure he didn't have an answer. At least, not one he wanted.

He brushed his pants legs and shirt free of bits of twigs and grasses and weeds, then straightened, looked around the small clearing and tugged his lips into a slanted grin. "Not a very manly reaction, Grant, running to your boyhood 'hidey-hole.' Still, it's better than punching a hole in a wall, or ripping up the vines by their roots." He slapped the flimsy branch of a sapling aside and left the clearing. "Nope, we can't have that. The house and those vines are all you've got. Well, them and the debt."

He glanced toward the sun hanging low in the sky and broke into a ground-eating lope, left the path along the lake and started up the long, sloping hill. The trellised vines flowed by him on both sides, denuded now of their fruit. His trained eye picked out the signs of the damage done by last night's storm as he passed: a torn leaf, a cane ripped free of the wire support. He sucked air into his lungs and slowed to a trot to catch his breath and better assess the harm done. "Count your…blessings, Winston! If that storm had…hit a few hours earlier…"

Bits of green shredded leaves were everywhere. He trotted on up the slope studying the ground and frowned. It could as easily have been bits of grapes littering the straw spread beneath the rows to keep away weeds that would compete for the nutrients in the soil. If he hadn't pushed the pickers and gotten the harvest finished before the storm hit, he wouldn't have had money enough to pay off the note and this year's mortgage payment and have money left for operating and living expenses in the coming year. He would have had to go further into debt with another demand note. "Thank You, Lord, for…the blessings of good… weather and a completed…harvest."

He jogged down a cross path to his left and then, again, turned uphill. The stone chimneys and the cedar shingles of the house roof showed above the vines on the crest of the hill. His stomach tightened. He slowed to a walk. The ocher-painted siding and upstairs window came into view. The shingled porch roof. They were there—shadow figures sitting on chairs in the darker depth of the porch. One with blond curls not even the darkness could hide.

Please, Lord…

He took a breath, combed his fingers through his hair and moved on. The click of his shoe's heels against the stone walk alerted them. Marissa rose and looked his way. Her eager smile took the breath he had left.

Help me, Lord…

He tugged his mouth into a smile and trotted up the steps. "Well, look at you two, all cozy and relaxed, drinking lemonade on the porch while a man works." He shot a look at his mother, locked his gaze on hers. *Don't challenge me, Mother. Don't ask…*

"I thought your work was over. Now that the harvest is in, I mean."

He hadn't expected the question from Marissa. Her eyes widened as he moved closer. That was a mistake. She could see the condition of his clothes even in the darkness under the roof. "That storm last night was a bad one. I was checking to see how much damage was done and I got a little wet and messed up."

"There must be quite a bit of damage since it took you this long, son. We had a bite earlier, but your dinner is in the warming oven. I'll go and—"

"Not now, Mother. I'll eat later. I have to get cleaned up." He shot her a look of gratitude for not asking all those questions that were in her eyes. "It's almost time for the *Colonel Phillips* to make its last run, and I'm going to take Marissa home." He managed another smile. "All the way to Chautauqua."

The dark clouds that had spread over the sky all day stacked up in the west and erased the sunset. Marissa gripped the rail and smiled, safe and secure with Grant beside her, though the lake water was a churning black whisper below them.

"I am learning so much from your mother, Grant. She was absolutely wonderful with those women this afternoon. When they came to your house they were all tense and uneasy. And in a matter of minutes she had everyone relaxed and talking about starting a shelter for abused women and children as if they did it every day."

"Mother has a way about her that puts people at ease."

"She truly does. I sensed it the first time I met her, though I was so embarrassed I could hardly bring myself to look at her."

The grin she loved slanted his mouth. "Why? Because I carried you up on the porch like a sack of grain and all but dumped you at Mother's feet?"

"*And* mussed my hair in the doing so badly I couldn't fix it!"

"I thought you looked pretty." He slid closer along the rail. "No, more than pretty...beautiful." His hand covered hers. His thumb slipped beneath the hem of her sleeve and drew slow little circles on the tender inside of her wrist.

"You did?" She drew a shaky breath, tried to will her pulse to stop skipping.

"Um-hmm. I like your hair sort of mussed up, with some of the curls hanging here..." He brushed the back of his index finger from her temple to her ear. "And here..."

The same warm, tender touch whispered along the skin from the hairline behind her ear to the top of her high collar at the nape of her neck. She forgot how to breathe. His fingers tightened and drew her forward, and his lips moved over hers. She melted against him, wanting their kiss to last forever.

When he lifted his head, she opened her eyes, took a breath and stepped back, gripping the railing for support. "Tell me what's wrong, Grant."

He nodded and moved to stand at the railing beside her. The oil lantern hanging from the upper deck swayed back and forth challenging the darkness. The edge of its pool of yellow light gleamed on the sun streaks in Grant's hair with each pass. Her hand itched to touch them.

"I got some unexpected news when I went to the

bank today. But let me tell you from the beginning. At least as far as I know it." He leaned his shoulder against a support post and turned to face her. "Late this morning Dillon Douglas came to the house and gave me a bank draft to pay for the grapes he'd bought from us—me." He glanced down at the black band on his arm then looked back up at her. "I keep forgetting."

"I know. I do, too." Her heart hurt for him. She knew that first raw grief.

"We had a harsh winter last year that ruined most of the catawbas and the harvest profits were small. My father took out a demand note for enough to see us through to this year's harvest. I knew I had to pay off that note, but the draft was for a sizable amount and I was still fairly well 'set up' by it. My father and I had an agreement. Instead of earning wages, I managed the vineyard for a percentage of the profits. That money was determined at harvest and put into the account at the bank. It worked out well. If I had a need, my father would give me the money. I never touched the account, though I had a rough idea of the total amount due me."

His gaze fastened on hers. Her stomach tensed.

"That money, plus my percentage from this year, would have been enough to buy the *Jamestown* and a house and furnishings."

Would have been. She looked out into the darkness lest he read of the sudden fear in her eyes.

"What I *didn't* know was that the bank carried a large mortgage my father took out against the house and vineyard some years ago. And that a payment was due."

The fear swelled. From the corner of her eye she saw him shift his weight and scrub his hand over the back of his neck.

"I feel the fool, being caught unaware. But my father didn't like to talk about his finances. Whenever I questioned him, he'd say, 'We're doing fine' and, with his ill health and the doctor's warning not to upset him and stress his weak heart, I never pressed him further."

There was disgust and self-condemnation in his voice. She shook her head and reached over to touch his hand. "You were doing what was best for your father, Grant. There's no blame to be found in that."

"Thank you for that." He turned his hand over and grasped hers, lifted it, kissed her palm, then let it go.

She curled her fingers over the warmth from his lips and braced herself, knowing there was more to come.

"After paying the note and the mortgage payment and setting aside money enough to provide living and operating expenses for this coming year—my percentage of the profits was swallowed by the debts. And then Mr. Taylor told me there was no money in the account. That my father had used my money to meet various emergencies and situations over the years. That he had meant to pay me back, but there had never been an opportunity…"

Her heart sank. She stared down at the dark water, fought back tears. *Why had she ever allowed herself to hope…* Grant's hands closed on her upper arms. She lifted her head.

"I made you a promise I can't keep, Marissa."

"You didn't...know..." She forced out the words. He had to know that she didn't blame him.

The *Colonel Phillips* blew its whistle. The steamer lurched. The deck quivered beneath her feet.

"I've spent every minute since I left the bank trying to find an answer, to figure a way to make things work out. But the truth is I have no money, Marissa. I cannot buy the *Jamestown*. I cannot buy a house. And I cannot hire a man to manage the vineyard."

The steamer slipped into place beside the dock as silently as her foolish dream of a future with Grant slipped away. Light from the lamps on the posts at the end of the dock fell on Grant's face and she read the same disappointment, the same sense of loss in his eyes.

"I thought of selling the house and vineyard, but that is not possible. There is still the mortgage. Another large payment is due next year. If I sell the property now, I have to clear that debt. And that will leave Mother and me without a home, and no way for me to make a living to provide for her. I *have* to manage the vineyard for the next two years."

Her last vestige of hope died. *It was over.* A horrible emptiness swept over her. The gangplank banged into place. "All ashore for Fair Point and Chautauqua!"

"I know it's not what I promised. But it will be in two years, three at the most. Will you continue to see me, to find out where our feelings for each other will take us during those two years, Marissa?"

God will work a blessing into every situation.

She never would have thought this horrible emptiness would be a blessing. But as long as she didn't think or feel, she could get through this moment. She drew a breath and shook her head. "No, Grant. I want to. With all my heart I want to. But I cannot. Not as long as you have a part in making the wine that has destroyed my family and killed my brother." A shaking took her. Her throat and chest tightened. "Every time I see those vines I see Lincoln and my mother and father. Every time I think of those wagonloads of grapes you raised, I wonder how much suffering and misery they will cause." She stopped, swallowed and blinked. The pain was swelling. She had to hurry. "I agreed to continue to see you these past few days because I thought you would be severing your ties to the vineyard, but that hope is gone. I'm sorry, Grant. I'm so very sorry. I care for you…but I cannot be a part of that."

His hands tightened on her arms. "I'm not giving you up, Marissa. I'll come tomorrow and—"

"No, Grant. Don't come to see me again. Chautauqua is over in two days and I'll be going home." She gathered all of her strength and looked up at him. "Let me go, please." *No, don't! Hold me, Grant. Don't let me go.* "The gangway is in place and it's time for me to leave." She waited until he'd released her, choked out, "Please tell your mother I said goodbye" and walked away.

Chapter Fourteen

Marissa slipped her hand through the cord of her purse, picked up her Bible and stepped outside. The tent flap flopped closed behind her. She waited a moment for her dry, burning eyes to adjust to the sunshine then walked from the tent to the main downhill path. The storm promised by the massing of last night's dark clouds had been blown away. But the storm that had raged in her heart all through the long night was still roiling and churning.

Weeping may endure for a night, but joy cometh in the morning.

She closed her mind to the memory. If she allowed herself to think about her personal life, she would fall apart. And that wasn't acceptable. She had work to do, and a schedule to uphold for two more days.

Two more years. At the most three.

Grant's voice echoed in her thoughts. Her heart twisted into a knot of pain that would never untangle.

Not in two years. Not ever. She had only two more days and then she would leave Chautauqua and—

She took as deep a breath as her constricted chest would allow and hurried to the empty bench in the small clearing she had claimed for her study place. The thin pages of her Bible fluttered in the slight breeze. She flipped through them reading the names of the books at the top, hoping the name of one might trigger her memory. Nothing came to her. Obviously, Mrs. Winston's assertion that God "establishes our thoughts" didn't pertain to her or her temperance lectures.

Pain flashed. Had Grant told his mother she had refused to see him again? What would Mrs. Winston think of her now? The stinging started again in the backs of her eyes. She blinked hard and yanked her mind to the business at hand. There had to be a pertinent verse somewhere. She slipped the twisted silk carry cord off her wrist, put her purse on the bench and withdrew a pencil and a folded piece of paper. The three short lines she'd written in the midst of her sleepless night stared up at her.

The abused are not the only ones who suffer pain
from the slap of a drunkard's hand.
    The imbiber may be in a torment of guilt.
(Hurting the ones he loves.)
    Pray for the abused and the abuser.

That odd feeling swept through her again as she read. The one she had experienced when she thought of asking people to not only start their temperance groups for the purpose of standing against the use of strong drink, but also use their groups to establish a place of help and safety and understanding for the abused of those who turned mean or violent when they overindulged.

She sat very still, afraid the feeling would disappear if she moved. It was a *quietness*, a sort of *knowing* deep within that brought her certainty that this was the right thing to do. She would end her temperance lectures by encouraging people to consider and pray for all of those involved in the situation—those who made and provided the strong drink, those who suffered abuse because of it and the abusers.

Her father.

Her face tightened. Her cheek tingled at the memory of his hand striking her. She opened the Bible, tucked the paper inside to keep it from blowing away and rose. The peaceful feeling was gone, replaced by the anger and turmoil she'd endured for five years. She glanced at the people passing by the clearing on the main path and curtailed her desire to pace lest she draw someone's attention. She was in no condition or mood to have a casual conversation.

The short train on her plum gown dragged across the weeds and grasses, became ensnarled with a piece of dead branch. She stopped and freed her hem, then walked on, fighting the painful memories. How could she bear to go home? She dreaded the very thought of it. But how could she not return? Fear for her mother's safety foamed to the top of her churning emotions. She was not strong enough to stop her father when he became inflamed with wine and raised his hands against her mother, but she could step in and take some of the blows herself. Her mother was too frightened, too cowed to do the same when her father turned his ire on her.

Her head throbbed. She closed her eyes and rubbed her temples, refused to allow the memories of Grant's love, the safety she felt in his arms, to surface. It would be her undoing. She blinked away the tears stinging her red, swollen eyes and set her plan. She would approach the churches in Fredonia about starting a place of safety where her mother and others like her could flee to receive help and understanding, and then she would be free to leave. Of course, nothing would truly be changed in any of them. If only that could be. A foolish wish. She breathed out a long sigh and glanced back at the bench. She had a lecture to prepare, and feeling sorry for herself was not going to get her work done.

The effectual fervent prayer of a righteous man availeth much.

She froze, then glanced around, which was silly of her. She knew full well that verse was only a thought. But it had been so clear it was as if it had been spoken. "'The effectual fervent prayer of a righteous man availeth much…'" Conviction came as she spoke the verse aloud.

I will pray for you and your mother, and for your father. He must be in terrible torment.

She smoothed the front of her gown and shook dust from her hem, struggling against what she felt prompted to do. The urge grew stronger. She returned to the bench, sat and picked up her Bible, clutched it to her chest and bowed her head. "Almighty God, I'm sorry for coming to You with anger in my heart. But it's all I've felt toward my father in a very long time. He hits and pushes my mother, and he hits and pushes me. And I don't understand, because he wasn't that way. He still isn't…until he drinks wine. But he does so more and more frequently, and he gets meaner and meaner."

She heaved a sigh at the futility of it all. "I don't even know what to pray, Lord. I do so want things to change. I want my father to be the way he was. I want him to stop drinking wine and to be a loving husband and father again. And I'm sorry if that sounds self-ish, as if it's all about me. But—but—" She faltered, gripped by a sudden surge of childhood memories. "—I remember how he was. He *never* struck us. He hugged us, and—"

She opened her eyes and looked down at the watch pinned to her bodice. "And he seems remorseful. That did not occur to me until Mrs. Winston mentioned it. But Father must be suffering torment at the pain he is inflicting on the people he loves. I don't know why he doesn't stop, but—" She drew a breath then plunged ahead. "Mrs. Winston said You continually lead us. So I am asking You to lead us…to lead *me*. If there is a way I can help my father, please show me. And please lead my father. Please help him to stop drinking that hateful *wine*! I so wish my mother and my father could be happy again. I confess, I don't know how that can be. But I'm asking You to make a way. Please, Lord, make a way for them to be happy again. Amen."

She lowered the Bible to her lap and leaned back against the bench. It took her a moment to realize that the anger that had driven her for five years was gone. There was a sorrow, a deep sorrow in its place. And love. Her love for her father had returned. A sob caught in her throat, burst out with an accompanying rush of tears. She buried her face in her hands and rocked to and fro, unable to stop her crying.

Grant examined the cane the wind had blown off the trellis, cut off the damaged end and tossed it into the cart, then wound the cane loosely along the supporting wire. The storm damage was not as extensive as he had thought at first glance. The leaves of the canopy had taken the brunt of the damage.

He grabbed the handle of the cart and tugged it behind him to the end of the row, turned and started down the cross path to check on the concords. They had fared well. Even the grape clusters he had saved for observation were still intact. The thick canopy had done a good job of protecting them.

He swept his glance along the trellises as he walked, thankful he'd brought in the concords over his father's objections. They had produced an abundant harvest. Without them, there would not have been enough money to pay the debts. And this field of two-year-old plants would bear fruit next year. They would add a considerable amount to the yield. And that meant greater profit. Maybe it would be enough to hire someone to help him. But that wasn't important now. He could handle the work, and Marissa would be gone.

Tomorrow.

The word was a dagger to his heart. If only there were an enemy he could fight! If only he could go and throw her over his shoulder and carry her back here to the house the way he had done the day of the protest. But it was her heart he needed to capture, and he'd failed. He emptied the cart on the compost pile then dragged it to its place in the barn. The sharpness of the pain of losing her would dull over time; he'd get over that. But the memory of her, the budding love for her in his heart would be there forever.

He looked around the barn, kicked the base of the straw pile into a neater edge, then brushed off his clothes and started for the house. He could only stall so long. He might as well go in and face her. His mother already knew there was something wrong. She'd known when he came dragging himself home last night. She was only giving him time. But if he didn't come in for supper, she'd come looking for him.

A wry smile tugged at his lips. Sometimes it wasn't so good having an intelligent, intuitive mother. But there were some things she didn't need to know. And the financial situation he faced was one of them. What it had cost him was another. He understood his father's keeping quiet about the mortgage now.

He squared his shoulders, trotted up the steps and strode across the porch to open the kitchen door. He pulled his lips into a smile. It wouldn't fool her, but a man had to soothe his pride. "Something smells good in here."

"Roast beef with potatoes and carrots, slaw and jelly tarts for dessert."

His favorite meal. She knew all right. His smile turned genuine. He draped his arm around her shoulders and dropped a kiss on top of her head. "You're kind of amazing, Ma."

She smiled at his use of his childhood name for her and patted his arm. "Only a mother." Her gaze fastened on his. "The storm damage under control now?"

She wasn't talking about the vines. His smile slipped a little. "Yep, amazing."

"Well?"

She wasn't going to let him get away with that. He quit pretending. "Not all of it." He moved to the sink to wash, splashed refreshing cool water on his face and reached for the soap. "I'm still working on it." Spoons scraped against pans as she dished up the food.

"Which part don't you want to tell me?"

He choked, coughed when the soap got in his mouth and scooped in a handful of water to rinse it out.

"That's what'll happen if you don't tell the truth."

His mother's laughter lightened his heart. He rinsed and toweled off, joined her at the table and said grace. The first bite of his roast beef encouraged him to take another in spite of his knotted stomach. He added a bite of carrot then reached for the gravy.

"You looked pretty rough when you came in from the vineyard last night." His mother cut off a bite of her beef, looked up and caught him staring at her. "I've never known you to work in the fields in your suit."

"I didn't plan to. I just walked out to the pond and then noticed the storm damage…" He busied himself ladling the gravy onto his potatoes.

"You're skating fairly close to that soap, Grant."

He looked up.

"Did I ever tell you I went to school with Walter Taylor?"

The bite of potato and gravy scraped down his gullet and hit his stomach like a stone.

"He was sweet on me at one time. He wanted to court me when we got older, but I'd met your father by then…" She smiled, then gave her head a quick little shake and looked over at him. "Anyway, when you were busy in the vineyard this afternoon, I went to town and paid a call on Walter at his office."

So much for protecting her. Could nothing he planned work out? "Mother—"

She reached over and placed her hand on his arm. "Don't fret, Grant. We'll take our cold tea out on the porch after supper and talk about it. Have some slaw. It's just the thing on a warm day." She handed him the bowl, then resumed eating.

Well, maybe nothing he planned worked out the way he figured, but he was smart enough to know when he was beaten. He scooped a spoonful of the shredded cabbage onto his plate.

The shore was teeming with people. Children ran squealing and laughing and splashing along the water's edge, obviously too excited by the promise of a fireworks display to settle in one place or pay heed to the admonitions of their calling parents.

"There's a spot there, beside that tree, Clarice." Marissa gave her tent mate a hopeful look. She did not want to get into that writhing maelstrom. "Will that do?"

"Anywhere will do!" Clarice hugged her writing box and crowded closer. "Mercy, what a moil!"

"I quite agree." Marissa clutched Clarice's arm and tugged her through the stream of people coming off the hill to the tree. "Oh, look. Here's a large rock you can stand on for a better advantage."

"Perfect." Clarice set her writing box down, hefted her skirt hems and climbed onto the rock. "Oh, my. I shall never be able to describe this scene with justice. There aren't words… Come up here, Marissa."

She started to refuse, then set her mind to enjoy this celebration even if Grant wasn't beside her…holding her hand…taking her in his arms… Tears threatened. She blinked them away, lifted her hems with one hand and took hold of Clarice's offered hand with the other. "One…two…three!"

She lunged and Clarice tugged. It was too much momentum. "Ohhh…!" She perched atop the rock, fighting for balance. Toes…heels…toes…heels.

Clarice laughed and grabbed her arm. "Steady. The top of this stone looks a lot bigger from on the ground."

"It certainly does." Her voice trembled as much as her hands. She grabbed her skirt and shook her hems into place then brushed back her fallen curls. "Oh, my." Red and gold streaks from the setting sun shot their brilliance through the dusk settling over the dark, placid lake. A steamer, pristine white against the sweeping line of the dark tree-covered hills that formed the far shore, floated in regal splendor at the center point, and dozens of canoes and rowboats, holding gaily dressed ladies and their beaus, bobbed gently on the water between. She had a sudden, fervent wish that she and Grant were part of that beauty. Her heart swelled with a yearning ache that stole all pleasure from the moment. She sat, stretched her feet to the ground and moved to stand beside the tree, trying not to remember.

The streaks of red and gold were swallowed by the night sky. Along the shore, torches flickered, then flamed to life. A loud bang sounded. A flare, trailing light, streaked skyward from the steamer then burst into a bouquet of tiny flares that drifted down toward the water. A collective gasp rose from the crowd.

"It's begun. I must record this." Clarice slipped from the rock, opened her writing case, pulled out a candle and grinned up at her. "I'm always prepared."

"So I see." She forced a smile and nodded toward the paper Clarice was placing on the lid of her writing desk. "And who are to be the hero and heroine of this 'adventure'?"

"Miss Practical and Chautauqua Beau." Clarice pulled out her pencil and started writing. "You see, Miss Practical didn't realize it would happen when they met—but the man has quite stolen her heart."

Marissa stared at Clarice, fought back a sob before it escaped, then slipped around behind the tree and let the tears fall.

The day was waning, yielding its dominance to the coming night. A quiet time that lent itself to contemplation—and conversations. Grant gazed up at the red-and-gold streaked sky, shoved his hands in his pockets and scowled. *Peacefulness was downright irritating when your heart ached.*

"I'm so thankful there was enough profit to pay the debts and still have what is needed for the coming year's expenses." The soles of his mother's shoes brushed against the porch floor as she came to stand beside him. "So very thankful you didn't have to go into further debt to see us through, Grant. It's a blessing."

The word grated. It felt like a trap to him. He pressed his lips together to keep back words that would serve no good purpose and rolled his shoulders to relax the tight muscles.

"Although I don't imagine it feels like much of a blessing to you. Not when there is another mortgage payment due next year."

He yanked his hands from his pockets and turned to look at her. "Mr. Taylor had no business telling you about that. He shouldn't have discussed the vineyard finances with you at all—I don't care if he is an old friend. I'm managing things now. The debt is mine, and I'll take care of it. He had no right to put that worry on you." He stopped, looked down at her hand on his arm.

"I'm sorry your money is gone, Grant. I know you had plans…"

Marissa. Pain shot through him. He straightened and forced his lips into a grin. He couldn't let his mother know what losing that money had cost him. "Who, me? I'm too old to be going off to college to learn to be a scientist."

She looked at him.

He did his best to maintain that phony grin and meet her steady gaze.

"You forgot about the soap, Grant. Marissa didn't come today."

"No." He looked back out over the vines, fought to keep his voice even. "She won't be coming again." He clenched his jaw, fought the ache in his heart.

Silence settled. He looked ahead into the dark space of empty years.

His mother drew a breath, went on tiptoe and kissed his cheek. "Don't lose faith, Grant. God will turn this into a blessing for both of you. You wait and see. I don't know how, but God will turn this into a blessing."

A blessing! Marissa was gone out of his life. He couldn't answer. The best he could do was nod.

Chapter Fifteen

Marissa willed her feet to go faster up the hill. It was amazing…unbelievable. But the anger was truly gone. She'd waited for it to return, certain that it was only the emotion of the prayer that had caused the deep sorrow to replace the anger and bring her love for her father back. But she still felt exactly the same when she rose this morning after her restless night. God had somehow changed her heart. It was the only answer. Five years! Five years of anger were simply *gone*. And if the Lord could do that…

It will be interesting to see how the Lord works things out.

The hollow ache inside grew. She'd made a mistake. A horrible, terrible mistake! The thought of being around those vines for two more years was still repugnant to her, but she should not have gone against her heart and cut Grant out of her life. She should have at least tried. She should have waited for the Lord to work His will as Mrs. Winston had said. Was there still a chance? She blinked her red, swollen, dry and burning eyes, fought for breath as she crested the hill. *Forgive me for my unbelief, Lord. Please forgive me, and have Your way. Oh, God, please let there be a promise of tomorrow.*

The morning sun bathed the front of the house. She rushed up the sidewalk to the vine-covered porch and knocked, made herself wait. Would Mrs. Winston turn her away? Would Grant tell her to go?

The door opened and Mrs. Winston stood there in her black gown. *Please, Lord—*

"It's about time! He's almost through with his coffee." Mrs. Winston stepped back, swept her hand through the air in a command. "He's on the back porch." Her smile conveyed her blessing.

"Thank you." She breathed the words, lifted her hems and ran through the sitting room, pulled open the door. "Grant…"

He spun around, threw the cup in his hand and lunged forward.

She made it halfway across the porch before she was crushed breathless against him, her arms around his neck, her feet dangling in the air. "Grant, I—"

"Marissa…"

She met his kiss, returned it with all of the yearning that swelled her heart.

"I thought I'd lost you…"

She opened her eyes and looked at him, at the vines that fell away down the hill behind him and shook her head. "Not if you're willing to wait for two years."

"Well, I must say, you two sound very sensible. I

find that a little surprising." Mrs. Winston touched the stoneware cup on the table, glanced at the splatter of dried coffee on the porch floor and laughed. "You seemed a bit impatient a few minutes ago."

Her cheeks flamed. "I'll mop—" She tried to move.

Grant laughed and tightened his arms around her waist. "I'll do it later, Marissa. After you've gone back to Fair Point. Until then, you're staying right where you are."

"We'll leave the coffee where it lies, for now." Mrs. Winston's eyes twinkled. "I rather like looking at that evidence of my son's happiness. And of God's blessing."

God's blessing? Yes. She rested back against Grant, who was leaning against the railing behind them, and sighed. Two years seemed a very long time. *Two years.* Would their feelings for each other survive the separation? She forced a smile to hide her aching heart.

Mrs. Winston picked up the cup. "Now, I'm going inside to wash the breakfast dishes, including this cup." She reached for the kitchen door, stopped and turned back to face them. "Marissa, I know this is your last day at Chautauqua, and I will be coming with Grant to hear your lecture. I know Andrew would want me to, and I don't care a fig about propriety—I care about you and my son. And so does our Abba, Father."

Mrs. Winston clasped the cup against her chest and closed her eyes. "Father God, I have learned of the financial situation that ties Grant to the vineyard. And I know of the pain and grief that form a barrier to Marissa being with him while he tends the vines."

Grant's arms pulled her closer. Marissa swallowed hard and closed her eyes.

"It *seems* a snare with no escape. But I know You, Father God. And I know, also, that there is a vast difference between a snare and an embrace. Both encircle you—but one to do ill, and the other to love and protect. So I ask that You, Father God, *break* the snare that keeps Marissa and Grant apart, and instead enfold them in the blessing of Your loving embrace. And, Father God, please, *do* something with those grapes!"

If only.

The kitchen door opened and closed. Marissa blinked the tears from her eyes, turned in Grant's arms and rested her head against his shoulder.

The corn husks crackled. That was a sound she would *not* miss. Marissa smiled and tugged the bottom sheet free of the cot's mattress, folded it and placed it on top of the other linens in her trunk. Her folded gowns and her waterproof filled the Saratoga to overflowing. She glanced around the tent, spotted her slippers, tucked them down the side of the trunk, stuffed her pillow in the domed lid and snapped it closed.

The tent flap flopped aside. Clarice stepped in and put her writing box down on the desk. "You're all packed and ready to go?"

"Yes." Her smile was a little shaky. She would miss Clarice and her forthright ways. "I'll be taking the steamer to Mayville to catch the train for home after I finish my short lecture summary." *Home.* Her stomach sank at the thought.

"So the 'Chautauqua Experience' is over for 'Miss Practical.'"

Yes. But she wouldn't end it on a melancholy note. She gave Clarice a wry smile. "Well, a bit of it will live on in print." The laughter chased any sadness at parting away.

"True enough. Perhaps more than you know."

"Oh, dear." She peered at Clarice's mischievous grin. "What does that mean?"

"Oh, a walk at dusk along the lake shore with 'Mr. Boat Man.'"

"Clarice!"

Her tent mate gave a delighted laugh. "Your face is so transparent, Marissa! Did you really think I wouldn't recognize Mr. Winston?"

"Well, I *hoped*!"

"Miss Bradley! Good afternoon, Miss Bradley! Is your trunk ready to be carried down?"

She spun about at the call and hurried to throw back the tent flap. "Yes, it is. That's it over there. It's to go on the *Colonel Phillips*, bound for the train station at Mayville." Her stomach flopped. Her Chautauqua experience truly was coming to an end.

"I'll see to it, miss." The man hefted the Saratoga to his shoulder and carried it out the opening.

"Well…" She swallowed the sudden lump in her throat and lifted the black wool wrap she would wear on the train off their tree root coatrack. The night air was getting cooler.

Clarice put two new pencils in her writing box, latched it and walked toward her. "I have what I came for. Let's walk down to the Goodbye Teachers Forum together."

* * *

The sun was sliding toward the hilltop when it was her turn to say goodbye. Marissa stepped to the podium and gazed out at the audience. So many people. But there were quite a few familiar faces she had seen at her lectures. Clarice, of course, sitting at the front with her writing box on her lap and her pencil poised. Mrs. Austin, who nodded and smiled. And Mrs. Austin's daughter, Rose, her face free of bruises, who gave her a shy nod. And there, smiling up at her, were Sarah Swan, and Ina, and Judith, and Lily...

And then her gaze fell on the ones she sought. Mrs. Winston, with her lovely face so calm and serene, looking dignified in her black mourning gown. And Grant, so handsome he took her breath away. She didn't dare meet his gaze, lest she forget everything but him and the wonder of their growing love.

She took a breath, grateful she had only to speak a short summary of her message and then say goodbye. "When I accepted the invitation to speak here at the Chautauqua Sunday School Assembly, it was with a great deal of trepidation. Temperance, the subject of my lectures, is a controversial one."

A murmur of agreement rippled through the crowd.

"Overindulgence in strong drink can alter a man's personality. It can make a kind man cruel and abusive to those who love him, and whom he loves, and bring senseless death to young men through their own foolish actions."

I miss you, Lincoln.

"I thought there was only one answer to the problem—

to close down all of the taverns and inns and clubs where strong drink is sold. And I still wish, with all my heart, that *all* strong drink would cease to exist. But that is an improbable hope."

Another murmur of agreement spread among her listeners.

There are two sides to this temperance issue, Marissa. She looked down at Grant, read the understanding in his eyes, and looked away before she lost control and the tears started to fall.

"So I leave Chautauqua with a different wish in my heart. I wish that all of you would extend mercy to those who are the victims of the imbibers. That you would work in your towns and communities to create a shelter for the abused, a place they can flee to when an angry hand is raised against them. A place where they and their family will receive understanding and love, instead of judgment and shame."

She lifted her hand and grasped her mother's watch, then looked down at Mrs. Winston.

"And I hope that all of you will pray for the *abusers*, and create a place where they, also, might receive help and understanding. For surely, when they sober and realize how they have hurt the ones who love them, the ones they love, they must suffer the pain of torment."

Please help my father, Lord. She lowered her hand and lifted her chin, prepared to share the verse she had found yesterday in the clearing when she had prayed for her father.

"The Bible says we are to pray for one another—

even those 'who despitefully use you.' My hope, my *prayer* is that you will answer that call. Thank you and good evening."

The house was dark in the dusk, the porch a beckoning shadow. When would she see it again? Marissa closed her mind to the thought. All afternoon and evening she had been saying goodbye, and the hardest was yet to come.

"I'll go in first and light the lamps for you, Mother."

Grant's voice drew her back to the present; his fading footsteps brought her to another moment of parting. She would miss his mother. She had learned so much from her and had grown to love her. The hems of the short trains on their black gowns brushed across the stone as they walked side by side to the house. Her throat closed around a painful lump when Mrs. Winston stopped at the base of the steps.

"I'm so thankful I came to hear you speak tonight, Marissa. I was very moved by what you said. And I know many others were, as well."

"That's very generous of you, Mrs. Winston." She picked a leaf off the vine and tucked it into her pocket to take home with her. "It was you who made me think about how my father must be suffering. I only repeated what you taught me."

"You said what was in your heart, dear. If I, in any way, helped you to recognize that, I'm very pleased."

Yellow lamplight spilled from the sitting room window and chased the shadow from the porch. *It was time*. Her eyes stung with tears.

"I shall miss you, Marissa. I've grown very fond of you."

"And I of you." The words were a painful whisper. Grant's footsteps sounded on the porch. Mrs. Winston's hand touched her arm.

"Will you write to me, dear? I shall wor—wonder about you, and how you fare with your temperance work. I'll be most interested to know how you come along with the shelter for the abused you are planning to start in your town."

Grant came off the porch, moved a few steps toward the road and waited.

She swallowed, forced out words, tried for a smile and failed. "I'll write. I'm certain I shall be asking you for advice. Your shelter will be far ahead of mine."

"*Our* shelter, Marissa." Mrs. Winston gave a soft, little laugh. "If you hadn't led Sarah and the other ladies in a protest march against the vineyard, the Twin Eagle Vineyard Shelter for the Abused would never have come into being. What a blessing that march turned out to be."

God will work a blessing for you into every situation.

She blinked and nodded.

Mrs. Winston stepped close, enfolded her in a warm hug. "And what a blessing you are to me, dear. I shall pray for you every day. And for God to work things out." Mrs. Winston laughed, turned and walked up the steps. "I know you and Grant have made plans, but I believe God has a plan, also. And I prefer His, no matter what it may be, because His way is always the best way. Now, I shall stop talking and go inside so I don't make you miss your train."

The door closed.

She looked down at the stone walk, took a deep breath and caught her lower lip with her teeth.

"Marissa…"

"Y-yes?"

"If I hold you will it make it better or worse?"

"B-both."

"Then, for the sake of any neighbors who may be watching, I'll content myself with loaning you my handkerchief."

A white square of linen was handed over her shoulder and waved like a flag. Her lips twitched. It was exactly the sort of thing Mrs. Winston would do. Grant was a good deal like his mother. It was no wonder she loved them both. "Coward." She took the handkerchief and dried her eyes, turned and handed it back. "Thank you. I'm ready to go now. Do you think the neighbors would approve if I take your arm?" She gave him a saucy grin.

"A pox on the neighbors!"

The words were a husky growl. Grant clasped both sides of her shawl, gave a quick yank that pulled her close, claimed her lips then let her go.

She stepped back, her cheeks burning, and darted a look at the nearby houses.

His chuckle made her toes tingle.

"Now who's the coward?"

He took her hand, tucked it in the crook of his arm and started down the long slope of the road.

She wanted to turn and run the other way.

"Marissa…"

She loved how he said her name. It sounded different… special. "Yes?"

"Will you be all right?" He covered her hand with his, looked down at her. "I hate the thought of you going home." His hand flexed. "If your father hits you, I'll—"

Fear twisted in her already taut stomach. She lifted her head, forced confidence into her voice. She couldn't let him know she was afraid. "I'll be all right, Grant. I'm going to talk to the board members of our church about opening a shelter. I'm sure there are members of the congregation who will sacrifice some of their time to run it."

She reached beneath the fear to find the new assurance of faith in God she was learning. "I've learned so much from your mother about faith, and the Christian way to treat others. Having the church involved will be perfect."

"Christians are only people, Marissa. They're not perfect."

She hadn't alleviated his concern for her. It was still in his voice. She tightened her grip on his arm. "I know. But God is."

"You *are* learning from Mother."

He couldn't quite carry off the attempt at humor. She rested her head against his shoulder for an all too brief moment, straightened and caught her breath as they reached the curve at the bottom of the hill and the railroad station came into view. *How long…*

The *Colonel Phillips* floated at anchor at the end of the long dock. Rowboats and canoes snubbed to the pilings along its length bobbed on the water. People strolled about on the shore area between the lake and the railroad station, clustered in small groups beneath the wide overhangs of the roof. Piles of trunks and mounds of bags sat on the ground beside the railroad tracks. Hers was among them.

"Chatauquans are going home." There was a quiver in her voice.

"Until next year."

Frustration colored his words. He turned at an angle and she walked willingly beside him to "their" spot in the dark shadow of the tree close to the station yard. "I'll say my goodbye here."

Her composure shattered. Tears slipped down her cheeks.

His arms closed around her, held her to him. He lowered his head and pressed his cheek against her hair.

"I hate to have you go home, Marissa. Two years is so long. I don't want anything to happen to you."

His husky voice added to the pain in her heart. "I'll be all right, Grant. I'll be busy working to make a place of shelter…to make sure my mother will be safe. And there will be speaking engagements to—"

A whistle blew. A beam of light split the darkness.

He lifted his hands and wiped the tears from her cheeks. "And next year at Chautauqua."

The whistle blew again. The light widened. Wheels clattered against the metal rails.

He kissed her. A fierce, desperate kiss that splintered her heart. She pressed against him, needing his strength, the sureness and security of his arms. *Next year at Chautauqua. A lifetime.* "Yes, next year at Chautauqua. If you don't forget me."

The clattering slowed, stopped. The door on the baggage car opened and crew members hopped down to the ground, lifted trunks and bags to unseen men inside who stowed them away in the dark cavernous interior. A porter shoved steps in place and helped a woman descend from the passenger car. Two men followed. The porter tugged a watch from his pocket, glanced at it and hurried into the station.

"Forget you?" Grant's voice was thick, gruff. "Never, Marissa. That's not possible." His lips brushed hers, soft, warm, tender…heartbreaking.

She slipped her hand through his offered arm and they stepped out of the tree shadow, crossed the yard and walked to the passenger car, the ache in her heart deepening with every step. His strong hand held hers, steadied her as she climbed the steps. She entered the car, turned and looked down at him. Her lips trembled when she curved them into a smile. "Next year at Chautauqua…"

Chapter Sixteen

The lamps were still lit. Grant scowled at the sight, crossed the porch and opened the door. He wasn't in the mood for conversation. But his mother cared about Marissa. She'd want to know.

He took a long breath, tried to arrange his expression so he didn't look as if he wanted to rip the world apart, and stepped to the sitting room door. His scowl returned. His mother was sitting at the end of the settee wearing a dark gray gown—no doubt "saving" the black mourning gown she'd worn to Chautauqua for when she was in public. He hated it. His mother liked red and blue and green.

What colors did Marissa like? Pain streaked through him. He'd never seen her in any but the somber black, purple and dark gray mourning gowns she wore in memory of her brother. He couldn't even imagine how beautiful she would look in a yellow gown that matched her blond hair, or a blue one the color of her eyes. His scowl deepened. Wearing mourning clothes was a bar-

baric custom! What purpose did it serve but to keep people gloomy all the time? He'd had his fill of it. He grabbed hold of the black band on his sleeve, yanked it off and strode into the room.

"Mother, I'm the head of this house now, and I don't ever want to see you in that dismal gray gown again. Father would hate it. I saw the way he looked when you walked into a room wearing your red dress. You wear *that* gown tomorrow in his memory." He walked to the fireplace and threw the armband on top of the wood waiting to be kindled on a cold evening. "You don't need to be walking around in somber colorless gowns, and I don't need a piece of black cloth wrapped around my arm to remember Father."

He sucked in a breath, turned and faced her. "She's gone."

"I'm sorry, Grant."

He nodded, looked down at his shirt she was mending—the one he'd caught the sleeve of on a nail in the barn. It seemed as if his mother always had something to do with her hands. He unclenched his and shoved them in his pockets.

"I know this isn't what you wanted…"

His snort burst out before he could stop it. "Sorry, Mother, I'm a little…angry. I'm being forced to accept a circumstance I want no part of." He yanked his hands from his pockets and strode to the window that looked out on the porch. "If her father strikes her…" His jaw muscle twitched, his hands fisted. "If he hurts her…"

There was a quick rustle, the swish of his mother's hems across the oriental rug. Her hand rested on his back. His muscles tensed at the touch. Countless times his mother had soothed his hurts with that tender touch, but not this time. Nothing would alleviate the snarl of emotions within him until Marissa was safe in his arms again.

"I understand your concern for Marissa, Grant. I was worried for her safety, too. But I've been praying as I sewed, and—I can't tell you how or when—but I know everything is going to be all right. God is going to work this out."

I can't tell you how or when...

An image of Marissa standing in the doorway of the passenger car with tear-filled eyes and trembling lips flashed against the darkness outside. "Forgive me, Mother. But I'm finding it a little hard to believe that at the moment."

"I hate to see you hurting like this." Her voice had thickened; her hand rubbed his back. "Please, Grant, trust the Lord. He'll work it out. Where's your faith, son?"

The image flashed again. But this time Marissa turned away and hurried into the passenger car. The whistle blew...

"My faith, Mother?" He turned and looked down at her. "It's on a train to Fredonia."

The passenger car rocked gently in rhythm to the sound of the wheels against the steel rails. Clackity-clack...*two years*... Clackity-clack...*two years*...

Marissa tugged the black shawl she'd draped around her head a little farther forward and kept her face turned toward the window beside her to further discourage any attempt at conversation by the woman sharing the bench seat. For once, she was thankful for the black mourning gown she wore. It explained her tears, her swollen red eyes and the sodden wad of handkerchief she clutched in her hand—or so the woman would think.

Bits and pieces of the conversations among the other passengers floated through the car identifying those speaking as having been to the Chautauqua Sunday School Assembly. The conversationalists had been comparing notes about their experiences the entire trip.

One year and she could return. They would ride the Colonel Phillips *to Fair Point together and—*

The locomotive's whistle blew. She jerked, blinked the film of tears from her eyes and searched the darkness outside the window. They were approaching the Fredonia Station. Her stomach knotted. She dabbed the wet handkerchief against her burning eyes and prepared to detrain. But she would sit on one of the benches under the wide overhanging eves of the station for a bit before she walked home. She did not want her parents to see her so…undone. And her father would send one of his employees to fetch her trunk tomorrow.

Steam hissed. The bell on the engine clanged. The car lurched then rolled to a stop. The door at the back opened. "All off for Fredonia!" The porter strode to the side of the car, opened the door at the center and lowered the steps.

She rose from her seat, avoided the glances of others getting off the train. A man stood in the narrow aisle at the end of his seat, held his hat in his hand and waited for her to pass. She approached the door and descended the steps assisted by the porter. A heaviness weighted her chest, made it hard for her to breathe. Would she find her mother well or bruised? Would her father be in his right senses or inflamed by wine? There was no way to know what awaited her at home.

Moths fluttered around the lanterns hanging from the wide eaves and threw huge swooping shadows against the brick building. The night air chilled her. She lifted the black shawl off her head, lowered it to rest around her shoulders, spurned the bench beneath the lantern and started for the one in the shadowed area by the corner away from the moths.

"Miss Bradley?"

She halted, turned.

A short, stocky man stepped away from the station door, removed his hat and gave her a brief, polite nod. "I'm Cyrus Nielsen, Miss Bradley."

"And what business have you with me, Mr. Nielsen? And how do you know my name? We have never met." She stepped to the side, glanced toward the station door.

"That's true, Miss Bradley." The man nodded, stepped back. "I'm sorry if I gave you a fright. Your father set me to watch for you. He told me to look for a young lady with golden curls wearing mourning clothes."

"My father sent you?" A cold chill ran up her spine. "Why would he do that, Mr. Nielsen? I don't understand." *Please, Lord, let my mother be all right. Please—*

"He said I was to give you this letter, Miss Bradley."

A *letter*? Why would her father send a man to her with a letter? Her stomach knotted. She stared at the sealed envelope the man removed from his pocket and held out to her. It was true. The bold *B* impressed in the sealing wax was her father's insignia. A dozen dire reasons for the letter chased through her mind. She held her breath to quell her shaking and took the envelope into her hand.

"Good evening, Miss Bradley." Mr. Nielsen dipped his head, put on his hat and walked away into the night.

She was trembling so hard she was afraid her legs would collapse if she moved. She inched her way over to the bench beneath the lantern and sat, her fingers clutching the letter, fear clutching her heart.

Men removed trunks and bags from the train, stacked them on the platform against the station wall. Hers was there, its alligator cover and domed lid plainly seen against the bricks.

Two men walked out of the station and boarded the train.

The whistle blew. The bell clanged.

"All aboard for Dunkirk and parts north!"

The porter glanced her way. She managed to shake her head, and he shoved the steps into the car, leaped up and closed the door. Steam huffed from the stack. The train rolled forward, grew smaller and smaller, then disappeared from view.

Her lungs wouldn't obey her command to breathe. The band of fear squeezing her chest drew tighter. But delay would only make it worse. She slid her fingernail beneath the wax, lifted the envelope flap and pulled out the folded paper inside.

Our Dearest Daughter,

It was her mother's handwriting. Her mother was all right! Still…why would her father send the man to meet her with a letter? She unfolded the paper, smoothed out the creases and read on.

Oh, Marissa, the most wondrous thing has happened. And, my dear daughter, it is all because of you.

It was *good* news, then. The painful constriction stopped. Air filled her lungs. She frowned, stared at those last words. Because of *her*? How could that be?

Yesterday, your father found your most recent letter about Miss Gordon choosing your lecture on the "abused victims of those who overindulge in wine or other strong drink" for her feature article in the Sunday School Journal. *I was so frightened when I saw your letter in his hand.*
And then it happened. Your father read what you wrote about the abused needing "a place where they can shelter and be safe until the imbiber sobers and the danger passes" and how "the abused require a place where they know they will receive understanding instead of judgment and not be made to feel shame" and he

cried out, "What have I done to my family! God in Heaven, help me!" and he began to weep.

I scarce knew what to think! And then he ran to his study, smashed his wine decanter and glasses upon the wood laid up on the hearth, then leaned out of the window and emptied all the rest of his wine bottles out onto the grass. He promised me he would never drink wine again.

Her father had thrown away his wine! Tears welled into her eyes. She blinked them away and devoured the remainder of her mother's letter.

Your father spent last night on his knees praying. This morning he told me to pack a trunk for each of us, that we are going to move from Fredonia, away from the many hurtful memories, and make a new life elsewhere. And that we are leaving this very day! He said he was going to give up town life and go back to farming, and that he had heard there was good land to be had to the south, near the Allegheny River. He also told me to write this letter to you explaining what has happened. His intent is to include a bank draft in your name so that you may live in the hotel until we find a place, settle and send for you. To that end, I have packed your things in a trunk to be delivered there. Your room will await you.

Your father will leave this letter with one of his trusted employees, a Mr. Nielsen, to give to you when the Chautauqua Assembly is over and you come home. There is insufficient time to reach you by post.

But to return to my story: I packed in a frenzy, uncertain of what would happen next, and then began this letter. In a short time, your father returned. He told me he had sold his business and our house, including all of the furnishings, to Mr. Ferguson, who has wanted to buy both for some time. And then he showed me the carriage and team of horses he had purchased.

Marissa, I feel I am dreaming, but it is all true. I am finishing this letter to you while your father loads our trunks and the few little things I cannot part with into the carriage.

And now it is time for us to go. But I cannot close this letter without telling you how different your father is today. He is the man I married so many years ago. He has returned to me. Please do not worry about me, Marissa, my dear. I am safe. I am well. I am happy. There may be days and nights ahead when troubles arise, but I now have hope that your father and I will face those times together.

Your father gives you his love. His provision for you is enclosed.

Be well, our dearest daughter. We will send for you when we are settled in our new home.
Your loving,
Mother and Father

It was wondrous indeed. And impossible to believe. She wanted to, but— Her father had *sold* his business and their house? That gave her pause. Perhaps it *was* all true.

She read the letter again, and then for a third time, her emotions swinging between worry and elation. In the end, it didn't matter. She did not know where her parents were, and had no way to help her mother now, should her help be needed.

The bank draft was in the envelope. She tucked it and the letter into her purse and stood. Her trunk sat alone beside the station wall. She stared at it, pulled open the station door and managed a polite smile when the stationmaster looked up from his papers with a query in his eyes. "I shall return for my trunk tomorrow."

"Very good, miss."

The hotel was not far. Flames flickered in the gas lamps atop posts that bordered the walkway, whispered their sibilant hiss as she passed. The brass knob on the ornate door was cold to her touch.

She entered the large lobby, adjusted her shawl and crossed to the long, paneled counter.

The clerk swept an assessing glance over her and lifted his lips in a polite smile. "May I help you, madam?"

"I'm Miss Bradley. I believe you have a room prepared for me."

"Oh." The polite smile warmed. "We do indeed, Miss Bradley. If you will sign here, please."

The room was spacious and well appointed. The hot bath was a glorious luxury after two weeks of washing from a bowl full of warm water in the tent. Marissa fastened the loop closures on her dressing gown—a *yellow* dressing gown. She ran her hand over the lovely bright-colored fabric. It made her feel brave to wear it. Not that she had a choice. There were no dark mourning clothes in the trunk her mother had packed for her. She yawned and cast a covetous eye toward the bed.

A blue-and-white woven coverlet was spread over the mattress. She stepped to the side of the four-poster, placed her palm on the coverlet and pushed. No crackles. She would sleep on feathers tonight. After her hair dried. She moved to the fireplace and bent forward to fluff her wet curls in front of the small fire that had been started to chase the chill from the room.

What was Grant doing? An ache spread through her at the thought of him. Was he sitting on the back porch with his mother drinking coffee and talking? Was he thinking of her? Worrying about her? What if he came to find her, to see if she was all right?

She jerked erect, horrified by the thought. Grant would go to her home and she wouldn't be there! She would miss seeing him, unless— Unless…

The notion floated at the edge of her mind, drifted closer. A perfectly lovely notion. A tempting…beguiling…absolutely wonderful idea.

She would stay at the hotel in Mayville.

A smile touched her lips. Not next year…tomorrow! *Oh, Grant…I'll be with you again tomorrow!* Energy spurted through her. She whirled around the room, then returned to her task, fluffed her damp hair in front of the fire and thought about the details. She would select the dress she would wear, then repack and have the hotel deliver this trunk to the train station the first thing in the morning. But what of her parents? The thought put a damper on her excitement. How would she get her parents' letter telling her where they had settled? She had no idea of when to expect it. She frowned, nibbled at the corner of her lip. *There has to be a way...*

She walked to the window and looked out at the street, watched a carriage pass and thought of her parents starting a new life together. *Oh, Lord, grant them happiness, I pray. Let my father's promise to my mother be true. Help him, Lord, to never indulge in strong drink again.*

A whistle blew. Light split the darkness, then swept out of sight.

The train.

Yes, that might work. Excitement bubbled up, made her stomach flutter. She would leave notice at the desk downstairs that she was expecting a letter from her parents and ask them to take it to the train station. Then she would ask the stationmaster to please give it to the porter and have him give it to the stationmaster in Mayville. The hotel there was only a few steps from the train station. She could check every day to see if the letter had arrived.

It would work. It *had* to work. Now to choose the gown she would wear tomorrow so she could hang it over a chair to let the packing wrinkles fall out of it. She hurried to the trunk and went to her knees to begin her search. She knew the very gown she wanted to wear, if her mother had packed it. The blue one, with the two-tiered, blue-and-cream-checked underskirt. The blue matched her eyes, and Grant had said he loved the color of her eyes…

Chapter Seventeen

Grant swept his gaze over the lush vines. The gray splotches of powdery mildew that dusted the leaves were scattered throughout the canopy but not yet prevalent. And it was only the vines on the lower end of the trellises in this portion of the vineyard that were infected. He needed to get those infected leaves cut off before it rained.

He cast a jaundiced look at the dark clouds gathering overhead. If they opened up and raindrops started splashing against the diseased leaves, they would scatter the spores everywhere. But at least it was something he could fight.

He slipped his hand beneath an infected leaf, folded the two sides against each other to contain the flyaway spores and severed the stem from the vine with a slash of his knife. A quick thrust of his hand deposited the leaf into the canvas bag hanging from his belt. He moved on to the next gray-splotched leaf.

Was Marissa all right? The idea that her father

might have struck her was driving him crazy! His
face went taut. He slashed the knife through the leaf
stem, jammed the leaf in the bag and moved on. The
slow, careful work was annoying. He wanted to lay
about him with the knife like some crazed pirate with
a sword!

*Women and children who are abused need a place
where they can shelter and be safe until the imbiber
sobers and the danger passes.*

What if Marissa was hurt? He cut away a cluster of
infected leaves and plunged them into the bag. If her
mother was also injured and her father was drunk, who
would help her? He crossed to the other side of the path
and started on the second trellis of vines. What if she
needed a doctor?

His stomach clenched like an unseen fist had
punched him.

*I want to continue to see you. With all my heart I
want to. But I cannot. Not as long as you have a part
in making the wine that has destroyed my family and
killed my brother. Every time I see those vines, I see
Lincoln and my mother and father.*

What if she was right? He paused his work and
stared at the trellised vines, seeing them through her
experience. Had any of the grapes he grew and sold
to the vintners made their way into the bottles of wine
Marissa's father consumed?

*Every time I think of those wagonloads of grapes
you raised I wonder how much suffering and misery
they will cause.*

He'd never thought of it that way. Never considered that the end product of the grapes he grew might be misery and suffering. A Bible verse slipped into his head. He looked at the vines and spoke the verse aloud, hearing the words not only with his ears, but with his heart. "'But judge this rather, that no man put a stumbling block or an occasion to fall in his brother's way.'"

The words were unsettling. He'd never thought about that verse in conjunction with growing grapes, but it could surely apply. He frowned and turned back to his work disturbed by his new insight. He didn't want to make another man "stumble" or cause anyone harm by contributing to the making of wine. But what was he to do? He had a debt hanging over his head and acres of grapevines. Caring for them was what he knew how to do. He had no other skill, no other way to clear off that debt and provide a living for himself and his mother. He was trapped into managing the vineyard.

He cut away more of the powdery mildew-infected leaves and put them in the burlap bag, being careful to keep the light, easily airborne spores contained when he folded the leaves. He finished the second row and crossed over to the next working steadily, methodically. The idea that he could be unintentionally bringing suffering into someone's life stayed with him. It troubled him as he worked.

He went over all the financial facts again. But it was an exercise in futility. There simply wasn't any way out of his present situation unless he could make the land more valuable so its sale would bring in money enough to pay off the mortgage and purchase another business. He gave that some thought but could come up with nothing. He was tied to the vineyard for at least two more years. But then, if he could convince his mother to move from the house she loved, he would not have to be connected to the vineyard in any way. But how could he ask that sacrifice of his mother?

"Lord, I have never intended harm to anyone by growing these grapes. And I don't want to contribute to anyone's suffering by doing so now or in the future. But I can find no way out of this situation. So unless I can convince my mother to move or You show me another way, Lord, I am bound to this vineyard."

He shook his head at the futility of the prayer and moved on to the next row. His mother kept insisting God would work this out, and he held his tongue. But there wasn't any other way. His life was shackled to the vineyard. Completely so for two more years.

Two more years.

Marissa.

That unseen fist punched him in the gut again. "Keep Marissa safe, Lord. Please keep Marissa safe."

Oh, my, flowers. Should she? Wasn't she defying convention enough by wearing the blue dress? Marissa turned the hat in her hands, tugged at the corner of her lower lip with her teeth. The blue ribbon *did* match the dress. And the cream-colored roses were—

I like it, Sissa. The flowers make me think of summer.

The memory of Lincoln, his head tipped to the side as he admired her new outfit, flashed into her head. Pain stabbed her heart. She missed her brother.

"If you were here, I'd give you a good shaking, Lincoln Bartholomew Bradley!" The empty threat she'd always made him popped out of her mouth.

Dare you to try.

His standard, laughing answer echoed in her mind. Tears smarted her eyes. "I would if I could reach you. And then I would hug you so hard…"

She firmed her trembling mouth, lifted the hat in pure defiance of the pain and settled it forward of the mass of curls that started at her crown and tumbled down the back of her head and neck. Nothing was going to make her sad today.

She pinned the hat in place, slipped the carry cords of the cream-colored reticule over her wrist and made a last survey of the hotel room. There was nothing left. Her trunk had already been carried downstairs. She ran to the window and looked out, caught a glimpse of the large trunk being loaded onto a handcart for transport to the train station. Flutters tickled her stomach.

Grant was going to be so surprised! She hurried to the pier glass, checked to be sure the cascading fabric of her bustle was in place and stepped out into the hallway. The blue-and-cream-checked pleated ruffle that formed the short train of her gown's underskirt whispered from tread to tread as she descended the stairs to the lobby.

The clerk looked up from his work at her approach. His eyes widened. He snapped his gaping mouth shut and dipped his head in a small polite bow. "Good morn-ing, Miss Bradley. We are saddened by your leaving." He glanced at his watch. "It is still early for the train."

"Yes, I know." She smiled and stepped closer to the counter. "I have a request, sir. I am expecting a letter directed to me from my parents to come to this estab-lishment, though I can't say when. And I wondered if you would be so kind as to make a note to carry the letter to the stationmaster for me? I will be happy to pay any fee for such a service."

"It will be our pleasure, Miss Bradley. There is no fee for such a small item." The clerk looked up from his note taking and smiled. "Are there any instructions for the stationmaster to accompany the letter?"

"He is to pass the letter along, by porter, to the sta-tionmaster at Mayville."

"Very good." The clerk finished writing, stepped around the counter, pulled the door open and bowed her through. "Have a lovely day, Miss Bradley."

Grant. She would soon see Grant. Be in his arms… She smiled. "And you, sir."

How different was this walk *to* the station, from the one she'd made *from* it to the hotel last night. She smiled at the people she passed, dipped her head to the gentlemen who paused to doff their hats.

Her trunks were sitting beside each other against the station building…waiting. She nodded her thanks to the gentleman who held the door for her and glided over to the desk. "If I may speak with you for a moment, sir?"

The stationmaster looked up, blinked dark eyes residing under thick, bushy, gray eyebrows, then blinked again. "How may I help you, miss?"

"I'd like to purchase a ticket for Mayville, please." She handed him the fare and received her ticket. "And I have what I believe may be a somewhat unusual request." She smiled and hurried on with her explanation before he could say no to her asking. "I will be happy to pay any fee charged for the delivery of the letter. Oh, and I have two trunks outside to be loaded on the Mayville train. Will this be enough?" She laid two coins on the counter.

One of the bushy gray eyebrows rose. "More than enough, Miss Bradley."

"I wish to include a gratuity for your kindness. And another for the porter who carries my letter to Mayville."

"That's most kind. Thank you, miss."

She nodded and turned to go, looked back over her shoulder and smiled. "You'll not forget about the letter?"

"That's not likely, Miss Bradley—" he gave her a gap-toothed grin "—not with your smile."

A whistle split the air.

She jumped, pressed her hand to the base of her throat.

"That's your train, Miss Bradley. I'll see to your trunks."

She nodded then hurried out the door as the train's bell clanged. The engine chugged by, rolled to a stop. Steam hissed. The doors on the passenger and baggage cars opened and men hopped down to the ground,

carried trunks and bags to the station, hefted hers and
stowed them aboard.

She climbed the steps the porter set into place, entered the car and took a seat next to the window, her
stomach fluttering. *Soon. She would see Grant soon.*
She smiled and looked out the window at the beautiful, wonderful, overcast day.

"Is the mildew bad?"

"No." Grant glanced at his mother, and his heart
lightened a little. She was wearing her dark red dress
his father had liked. "It's only on the vines growing
on that bit of land that flattens out at the bottom of the
slope where there's not enough airflow. With the cool
nights, the vines haven't dried out sufficiently since the
storm. I cut off all of the infected leaves I could find.
And I'll be keeping a watch."

"It looks like it might rain. Will that make the problem worse? It seems like I've heard you and your father mentioning that."

He fixed her with a look. "Mother, you used to help
Father in the vineyard. You know as much about powdery mildew as I do."

She looked right back. "Things change."

He nodded, leaned his shoulder against the porch
post and looked out over their land. "Yes. And in two
years, my situation will change. Meanwhile, she's gone.
I'm worried about her and want her back here where I
can take care of her—and pretending you don't know
about powdery mildew won't change that."

"You need some coffee."

He burst out laughing.

"Ah, proof your mother still knows what's good for you." She smiled and touched his arm. "There's some still hot from dinner. I'll get it." The hem of her red dress swished across the porch floor.

He shook his head and looked up at the darkening sky. It wouldn't be long now until the rain started. It was almost as dark as dusk. He blew out a breath and faced yet another trap. He'd have to continue managing the vineyard's business after he hired someone else to care for the vines. He couldn't ask his mother to move from her home.

The kitchen door squeaked open, banged shut. His mother had her hands full or *that* would never happen.

"Here you are."

His father's stoneware cup came into view. He slipped his two middle fingers through the handle and curled his hand around it. Hot! He grabbed it by the top with his other hand then changed his grip to the thick handle. "I was thinking about what Marissa said about women and children being abused by men overindulging in wine while I was working with the vines this morning."

"She's a convincing young woman." She blew on her coffee then looked up at him. "Marissa is the reason I started the Twin Eagle Vineyard Shelter for the Abused. Well, Marissa and God. I definitely felt Him nudging me to do that."

He'd forgotten about the shelter being formed. *Yet another tie to the vineyard.*

"But I never realized the problem existed until Marissa led Sarah and the others in that protest march against the vineyard. That march shows the strength of character and level of commitment to the values Marissa possesses." Another look was slanted up at him. "She was already falling in love with you that day, but she didn't let that stop her from keeping her promise to Sarah. I admire her for that. Oh, I guess I'll have to forget about my coffee." She put her cup on the table and smoothed her hands down over her long skirt. "Somebody's at the door. And me in my red dress."

Marissa checked the cream-colored lace that edged the high collar of her blue dress, shook out the long double-tier peplum that fell from the small waist of her bodice then touched her hat. She frowned, nibbled at her bottom lip. Perhaps she should have taken the time to change into her mourning clothes at the hotel. Her gown was too stylish, and her hat was too... frivolous. Would Mrs. Winston think her lacking in decorum, or—

The door opened.

She caught her breath, stared. A *red* dress. A smile started.

"Yes? May I—" Mrs. Winston gasped, stared. "Marissa?" She grasped her hand, pulled her inside and into a fierce hug. "Oh, my dear! Why are you here? Were you in danger? Are you all right?"

She couldn't answer. Mrs. Winston was hugging the breath from her. She hugged her back then straightened. "I'm fine, Mrs. Winston. Is—"

"Oh, yes, of course. Where's my head! He's on the

porch. Go—" Mrs. Winston stopped, shook her head. "No, let me go first."

She followed Mrs. Winston through the sitting room, her heart pounding so hard she was breathless. She paused when Mrs. Winston held up a restraining hand, stood silent and watched her pull open the door and hurry across the porch.

Grant! Her heart leaped at the sight of him.

Mrs. Winston snatched the cup from Grant's hand, stepped back and nodded at her.

She ran forward.

Grant turned, frowned. Shock spread across his face. He lunged forward and scooped her into his arms. Her silly, frivolous hat didn't matter. Nothing mattered but that she was with him again.

His lips claimed hers, translated all of his yearning, his concern, into a kiss that left her weak-kneed and clinging for support. She wanted him to hold her forever, to never let her go. The tremor in his arms crushing her against him said he felt the same.

"Your coffee is getting cold."

Mrs. Winston! How could she have forgotten about Grant's mother? Her cheeks burned. Grant lifted his head and they turned as one and looked at his mother. She grinned and lifted the cup in her hand.

"I saved the coffee this time."

Laughter burst forth. Grant's deep guffaw, Mrs. Winston's merry trill and her own bubbling ripple of happiness blended into one glorious sound. And then it stopped. Grant's hand clasped her chin, gently titled her face up. His gaze swept over her. "Did your father hurt you? Is that why you're here?"

"No. Oh, no. Father didn't strike me, Grant. I'm here because I have no home."

"He threw you out!"

It was an outraged roar. She lifted her hand and placed her fingertips over his lips. "No, Grant. Father *sold* his business and our house. Let me explain."

She turned in his arms to face his mother. "You were right, Mrs. Winston. With God, all things *are* possible." Happy tears stung her eyes. She blinked them back, wiggled her arms free of Grant's embrace, opened her purse and pulled out her mother's letter. "Please read this aloud so Grant will hear, Mrs. Winston. It will explain everything." She handed her the letter and smiled. "Father has stopped drinking wine!"

"What?"

She laughed at Grant's shocked response. "It's true, Grant. Only listen…"

The letter sounded even better this time. Or, perhaps, it was hearing it read aloud in Mrs. Winston's soft, calm voice while she was held close in Grant's arms that made it seem more believable.

"Marissa, this is *wonderful* news." Mrs. Winston folded the letter and placed it back in its envelope.

"I'm happy for you, Marissa." Grant's arms squeezed her tight then released her enough that she could breathe. "I know how worried you were about your mother's safety. But she sounds confident and happy in the letter. And your father seems truly repentant."

Grant's voice changed. She could feel the tension

come into him. She stepped out of his arms and looked up at him.

"The letter mentions a bank draft to provide for your stay at the hotel until your parents send for you." He frowned, sat on the railing and rubbed his hand over the back of his neck. "I don't mean to pry, Marissa, but is it enough? I mean, the letter doesn't say how long it will be until you hear from your parents, and I want you to know that I—that is, we—Mother and I will be happy to provide what you need, should the draft run out."

"We certainly will."

She looked from Grant to his mother and back again, her heart swelling at their love and concern for her. "Thank you, both. But you needn't worry about me. Truly. Father's provision for me is abundant."

"Still, I want you to promise that you will come to me—us—should you find you need more than has been provided."

She looked into Grant's eyes and drank in the depth of his feelings for her. "I promise."

"Well, all of this good news has whet my appetite." Mrs. Winston rose and handed her back her letter. "Have you time to share our supper before you must catch your train back to Fredonia, Marissa?"

A delicious little thrill ran up her spine. This was the moment she had been waiting for. "Fredonia?" She looked at Mrs. Winston and widened her eyes a bit as if in surprise. "Why, I'm not going back to Fredonia, Mrs. Winston." She shifted her gaze to Grant, saw the smile starting in his eyes and let her own break free. "I've made arrangements to have Mother's and Father's letter forwarded to me here, in care of the stationmaster. I'm staying at the hotel by the station here in Mayville."

Grant's grin was everything she had hoped it would be.

Chapter Eighteen

"I've always liked the rain."

Grant grinned and pushed his toes against the porch floor to set the swing in motion. "I can't think of anything you don't like, Mother—" He winked at Marissa, who was sitting beside him "—other than coffee spilled on your porch."

"Cheeky children."

He burst into laughter. "Besides that—er, me."

"Well, there's snakes and spiders and dandelion greens...too bitter." His mother gave a little shudder. "And lightning...if I'm caught outside."

He looked down at Marissa, drank in the way the lantern light played over her delicate features and made dark smudges of her long lashes. "What about you, Marissa? What don't you—"

"Someone's at the door." Mrs. Winston glanced toward the sitting room. "Who would be out in the rain?" She started to rise.

"I'll go, Mother." He squeezed Marissa's hand and rose from the swing.

The knock on the front door came again. He hurried to the entrance and opened the door. "Mrs. Swan!" He gaped at the woman's wet, bedraggled appearance.

"I-is Ruth home? Tobin has b-been at the w-wine."

"Come in…" He stepped back and pulled the door wide.

Sarah Swan stepped over the threshold and stopped. "I—I'm d-dripping. If you h-have a towel…"

He spun around and pulled his mother's cape from its hook. "This will help get you warm."

He wrapped the cape around the woman's shoulders, guided her to the kitchen and seated her in a chair. Three long strides took him to the porch door. He glanced back at Sarah Swan sitting and rocking back and forth and clutching the cape close. The coil of hair at the back of her head had slipped askew, and long wet tresses dripped water onto her shoulders. There was a lump rising at the side of her face a little below her left eye.

He yanked open the door and leaned out. "Mother… Marissa…"

They rose and hurried toward him, a question in their eyes. "It's Sarah Swan…"

He took hold of Marissa's arm as she passed by, looked down into her knowing eyes and swallowed back a surge of anger. "I'll be out here if you need me."

"Thank you." She touched his arm and went inside. The door latch clicked.

He jammed his hands into his pockets and stood

staring out into the darkness, then turned and paced the length of the porch, anger driving his steps.

Tobin has been at the wine.

Sarah Swan was so…quiet.

Rain pattered against the cedar shingles on the porch roof, spattered against the leaves of the vines. Low murmurs came from the kitchen. The ladle clanked against the hot water reservoir on the stove. He leaned a shoulder against a post at the top of the steps and waited.

A golden light leaked out into the night, glimmered on the falling rain. He glanced up and traced the spill of light to the bedroom on his left. The one across the hall from his mother's bedroom. Sarah Swan was spending the night. The first victim of abuse to come for safety to the shelter she had helped to create.

The kitchen door creaked open. He made a mental note to oil the hinges, turned and took Marissa in his arms. He held her until she stopped trembling and stepped back. The sadness had returned to her beautiful blue eyes.

"It's time for me to go. Your mother said I'm to wear her waterproof."

"I'll get it and meet you by the front door."

He stepped into the small back entry, shrugged into his mackintosh and hat, then carried his mother's waterproof to Marissa and held it while she slipped her arms into the sleeves. He settled it onto her shoulders and opened the door, wanting to drive the quietness, the sadness away from her and make her smile and laugh again.

Chilly, damp air rushed at them. He tucked her arm

in his and left the protective cover of the porch, hurried out to the street. Raindrops tapped against their
coats and splashed and danced on the walkway. "The
hem of your gown is going to be sodden."

She looked up at him and gave a little shrug.
"There's no help for it. These short trains are foolishness. The dress will probably be ruined."

The idea of it outraged him. He halted and looked
down at her. "That doesn't have to happen. I like that
gown. It matches your eyes. I'll carry you."

"All the way down the hill to the hotel!" A smile
tugged at the corners of her mouth. She broke into soft
laughter and shook her head. "I think not."

The laughter was like a healing balm. Her face lost
the sad, closed look it had worn when he first met her.
He grinned and waggled his eyebrows. "I'm willing."

This time her laughter was lighter, easier. His heart
lifted.

"So you think my gown matches my eyes?"

She was actually flirting with him! This was the
sunny, full-of-fun Marissa who had come to the house
earlier. *Thank You, Lord, she's better.* "I do. I haven't
had a chance to tell you, but you look beautiful tonight,
Marissa. But then, you always look beautiful to me."

She slanted a look up at him from under her long
lashes. "That's good to know."

He laughed and tightened his arm she held on to,
pulled her closer. "Look at me like that when we're not
under these streetlamps."

She batted her eyelashes.

He growled and led her into the wide-sweeping

turn that led to the hotel and railroad station and dock, stopped between streetlamps and pulled her into his arms and kissed her. "And one for good night." He kissed her again. "In case you can't tell, I'm very glad you're here. I didn't know how I was going to live through that separation."

"I felt the same."

Two years or *more*. The image of Sarah Swan sitting on the kitchen chair returned to him. "Thankfully— because of your father's...change of heart, we don't have to be concerned about that separation now. I can't believe you will be right here at the hotel." He started walking again, reluctant to bring up the subject of abuse again, but needing answers. He had a decision to make.

"Marissa..."

"Yes?"

"I have to ask you something about Sarah Swan."

"What is it?"

"Why was she so...quiet?"

Her hand tensed on his arm, then relaxed again. "You learn to be that way. If you yell, or beg, or cry, it sometimes makes them more angry...meaner."

His back stiffened. *What had she suffered at her father's hand?* He pulled her into the darkness at the side of the road and again took her in his arms. "You'll never have to worry about that again, Marissa. Not with me." His throat was so taut he could hardly get the words out. He held her close, listened to the rain patter against their coats and wished he could take away all of her bad memories.

* * *

Grant shook the rain off his mackintosh and hung it on a peg, removed his wet shoes and walked through the kitchen and up the stairs in his socks. His bed beckoned, but he wasn't ready to sleep yet.

He went to his dressing room and washed, put on his nightshirt and walked back into his bedroom. It was too dark to see outside, but he opened the window and stood for a minute listening to the rain falling on the grape leaves, then crossed to his bed and flopped onto his back, laced his hands behind his neck and stared into the darkness seeing Sarah Swan as she had looked when he opened the door. There were two things he knew he'd never forget: her terrible quietness and the words she spoke when she looked at him—*Tobin has been at the wine.*

He closed his eyes, tried to order his churning thoughts and pray.

"Lord, I've never seen anyone behave the way Sarah Swan did tonight. She was so *quiet*. So…defeated and hopeless. And no one should have to live that way.

"I saw the evidence of what wine can do tonight. I saw it in Sarah Swan's quietness and in the bruise forming on her cheek. I want no part of that, Lord. I won't grow grapes for making wine ever again. But I need Your help, Lord. Because I don't know what I will do, or when, or how I will do it. I need to work something out. I need to figure out a way to make a living. There *has* to be a way. Show me what to do, I pray. Because I won't have any part of making wine again."

* * *

It was still raining. Grant stood on the back porch and watched the rainwater sheeting off the roof, grateful that it gave him a reason to not be working in the vineyard. He'd not shared his decision with anyone but God, but that didn't make it any less valid.

He hunched his shoulders, shoved his hands in his pockets and scowled down at the rain-spattered floor. He was going to have to tell his mother about his decision to not manage the vineyard or business anymore. At least his mother would be all right. He'd worked that much out during his sleepless hours. He would hire a man to care for the vines and manage the vineyard and pay him with the money that was to have been his share. But how he was to make a living had escaped him. He would be free of the vineyard, but there would be no money to purchase a steamer or a business.

Footsteps and silverware striking against pans announced his mother's arrival in the kitchen. He sucked in a long breath and squared his shoulders. He wouldn't tell her now. Marissa would be coming, and he wanted something to tell her first. What a mess! Here he was, trying to do the right thing, and it could cost him the woman he loved. He had no doubt of that any longer. He wanted to be with Marissa, to have her for his wife. Two years had seemed forever to wait for her. And now… "I'm waiting for Your answer, Lord."

The squeak of the door hinges warned him his mother was coming. A handy thing. He lifted his lips in a wry smile. Maybe he wouldn't oil those hinges.

"I thought I'd find you out here, brooding over the rain and the vines."

He pulled up a grin. "Chickens brood. Men ponder."

His mother laughed and patted his arm. "Well, *ponder* this, Mr. Man. Breakfast will be ready in about ten minutes. The coffee will be ready in five minutes. I came out to tell you that should you like a cup to drink while you're *pondering*, you will have to come and get it. I am busy. We're having blueberry-sourdough pancakes and potatoes and eggs and sausage."

"That was Father's favorite breakfast."

"Yes, I know. I thought it might help." She gave him a look and went back inside.

How did she do that? He shook his head and headed for the kitchen to get a cup of coffee. She'd think it strange if he didn't. The blended smell of hot coffee, sausage and potatoes with onions frying greeted him when he stepped through the door. "Smells good."

His mother looked up from the batter she was stirring at her worktable and grinned. "I think men eat with their noses."

"Nah, too messy." He grinned at her laughter, grabbed his cup off its hook hanging from the bottom of the dish cupboard and edged between her and the stove. He put his cup down, picked up a folded towel and reached for the coffeepot.

"This milk has turned!"

He froze, then pivoted and stared at his mother, who was holding the tin of milk beneath her nose and sniffing. "What did you say, Mother?"

"This milk has turned." Disgust filled her voice.

She banged the tin down on the table. "Wait until I see Lucas Car—"

"Pasteur!" He dropped the towel, grabbed his mother beneath her arms, lifted her into the air and spun around the kitchen, laughing. "Louis Pasteur!"

"What are you talking about, Grant? You know we get our milk from Lucas Carter. Now put me down! My potatoes are burning." She pushed against his shoulders.

"Put them in the warming oven, Ma!" He lowered her to the floor, gave her a loud smacking kiss on the cheek and ran for the back entry. "I'll be back!" He snatched his mackintosh off its hook on the run, slapped his hat on his head and slammed out the door.

Marissa dried the bowl, put it in its place on the shelf over the flour bin and looked out the window for the fourth time. There was still no sign of him. But at least the sun had come out. Grant would have nice weather for whatever he was doing. She drew her thoughts back to her task and hurried to the sink cupboard. "Grant didn't say where he was going?"

"No." Mrs. Winston washed the wood spoon, slipped it in and out of the rinse water and laid it on the wood drain board next to the frying pan. "I know he's been worried about some things since his father's passing, but this morning he acted crazy. I've never seen him like this, Marissa, and I'm a little concerned."

"What do you mean by 'crazy'?" She lifted the frying pan and swiped the towel around the inside. "What did he do?"

"He picked me up and swung me around laughing and yelling, 'Louie Pastor' or some such name—"

"Was the name he yelled Louis Pasteur?"

"Yes, that's right." Mrs. Winston looked at her. "Do you know Mr. Pasteur, too? Is he a friend Grant met at Chautauqua?"

She shook her head and hung the frying pan on its hook by the stove. "No, but I'm sure he would be thrilled to make Mr. Pasteur's acquaintance. He's a French scientist of some prominence."

Mrs. Winston shook her head and slipped her hands back into the dishwater. "Well, that makes no sense to me at all." She scrubbed at a pan, then swished it through the rinse water and set it on the slatted board to drain. "Why would Grant be hollering some French scientist's name, then running out of here like his shirt-tail was afire?"

"Because *Grant* suddenly got his answer. At least he thinks he did."

Marissa spun around, met Grant's gaze and smiled. "See how we talk about you when you're not around? You're our favorite subject." She glanced down at the basket of wine bottles he was carrying and her smile died, her face drew taut. "Are those bottles part of your answer?"

"They are."

"What are you talking about, Grant?" Mrs. Winston sounded astounded. "We don't make wine."

"We haven't, Mother, but we're going to."

Grant set the basket on the floor and walked toward her with a huge smile on his face. Marissa stiffened, turned her back toward him and reached behind her for the apron strings. She would not stay—

Grant's hand, warm and hard and calloused, closed over hers, stopping her from untying Mrs. Winston's apron. "*Unfermented* wine."

"And what, pray tell, is *that*?"

She glanced at Grant's mother. Mrs. Winston looked as unsettled as her stomach felt. Grant's hand lifted from hers. She yanked the apron ties free and stepped forward, jerked to a stop when Grant's hands closed on her shoulders. "Let me go, Grant."

His grip lightened. He turned her around. She lowered her head so he wouldn't see the tears welling into her eyes.

"Marissa, you have to trust me."

His voice was tender, but firm. *Oh, how she wanted to trust him! But wine...* She lifted her head.

"To explain very simply… Wine is made by letting crushed grapes ferment. Yeast brings about the fermentation, and it is the fermentation that causes the alcohol content. That being so, if you stop the fermentation, you have *unfermented* wine. Or wine with *no* alcohol. That is what we are going to make. Or, at least, try to make."

"But I don't understand. Please, I'm trying…" She reached out and touched his arm. "Wine is wine. And wine is strong drink. I've seen—" She swallowed, blinked tears away. "How can it not be wine?"

"It is wine, Marissa. But it's *unfermented* and so it has no alcohol. It is *not* strong drink. No one can become inflamed by drinking it."

"But how do you 'unferment' it?"

"I believe I can answer that." Mrs. Winston came to stand beside them. "If yeast brings about the fermentation, then you simply kill the yeast. It's like making bread. If you make the water you add too hot, the yeast dies and the bread doesn't rise." She grinned at her son. "You're going to kill the yeast by...what... heating the wine?"

"Exactly, Mother! I'm going to heat the wine and kill the yeast, *before* it can ferment."

"Oh, Grant! Do you truly think it will work?"

He nodded. "Science says it will. Louis Pasteur did it *after* the wine had fermented to stop it from turning sour. And he applied the same principle to milk."

His mother burst into laughter. "So that's why you got so excited and acted like a crazy man when I said the milk had turned!"

"That's why." He laughed, then sobered and looked at her. "Will you help me make my unfermented wine, Marissa?"

His gaze held hers. She took a deep breath and nodded, then gasped.

"What is it?"

"I just thought..." Her lips twitched. Laughter bubbled up and burst free. "I'll be a vintner!"

Chapter Nineteen

"How are you going to make this 'unfermented' wine, Grant?" Marissa hid her wince. She didn't even like saying that name. "What do you want me to do?"

"Yes, what will we need, son?" Mrs. Winston swept an assessing eye around her kitchen. "If you tell us, we can have things clean and ready by the time you have picked the grapes. It sounds rather like my preserving and jelly-making equipment might be helpful."

"We'll need the largest pan you have, Mother. We're going to cook the grapes a little and then squeeze the juice out through some sort of cloth, put it in the bottles and cork them."

"My cheese cloth for making jelly will be useful then."

"I'll rely on your cooking ability, Mother. And you're going to need this, Marissa." Grant looked into her eyes, slipped his hands around behind her and tied the apron strings she had undone. Her heart skipped, her pulse fluttered and her cheeks warmed.

He gave her a slow, lopsided grin, leaned down and kissed the tip of her nose. The warmth in her cheeks increased to a burn.

He chuckled, turned and lifted the basket of wine bottles to the sink cupboard. "One good thing is, with all this rain we won't have to wash the grapes because there'll be no dust on them." He gave them a jaunty wave. "I won't be long."

She hoped not.

"It's good to see him happy again. He's been worried for some time." Mrs. Winston turned from the door and looked at her. "You and Grant are good for each other, Marissa. It makes my heart happy to see you together. I'm so glad God is working things out."

She smiled at Mrs. Winston's declaration of faith. It made hers more certain. "He truly is. You told me that with God all things are possible, Mrs. Winston. And I know now that you were right." She moved to the sink cupboard and began placing bottles in the hot water. "I have learned so much about having faith in God from you. I'm still working on trusting people. That's…difficult for me." She lifted a bottle from the water, placed her palm tightly over the mouth and shook it so hard the curls on her forehead bobbed.

"That's understandable, Marissa, after all you have suffered." Mrs. Winston cleared everything from the top of the long worktable and washed it off with a soapy rag. "I'm so happy for your mother and father. It's not often that we have a second chance in this life. Have you any notion of when you will hear from them?"

"No. But I don't really mind, as long as Mother is

safe now." She rinsed the bottle, set it upside down to drain and began shaking another. "I have…well… I have…"

"Grant?" Mrs. Winston laughed and rinsed off the tabletop.

"Yes, but I was going to say…you." She rinsed and set the bottle to drain, and began another. "Grant doesn't really fit too well as a—"

"A what, dear?" Mrs. Winston stepped into the pantry and came out a moment later carrying a huge deep pan filled with ladles and funnels and cloth.

"An adoptive mother."

"Marissa!" The pan clanged against the tabletop. Mrs. Winston came and gave her a fierce hug. "You have become such a large part of my life, Marissa. I couldn't love you more if you were my daughter. And if the Lord be willing— But let's leave that in His hands. He holds tomorrow."

"They won't heat any faster because we stand here and stare at them."

"You're right, Mother." Grant stole a last look at the concords in the huge granite pan on the stove. So much depended on this experiment. His stomach churned. He resisted the temptation to check the dampers once more and turned away from the stove. "I'm going out on the porch while the grapes heat. Would you ladies care to join me? There's nothing more to be done in here until it's time to strain the heated grapes." He stepped forward and held the door open for them.

"Ah, it feels good out here. The air's refreshing after

the warm kitchen." His mother started for the swing, veered off toward a chair at the table.

"Take the swing, Mother, it's more relaxing. And you and Marissa have been working hard." He plunked his right hip and thigh on the porch railing, leaned back against the post and swung his free foot back and forth.

What if it didn't work? He was so sure this morning when his mother had mentioned the turned milk and Louis Pasteur's name had popped into his head that it was God "establishing his thoughts" the way his mother talked about so often, but now...

His foot jerked. He wanted to go in and look at those grapes. Or at least pace around the porch. He'd give it another few minutes and then go in and stir them. He didn't want them sticking to the pan or burning or anything. *Lord, please let this experiment work.*

He blew out a breath, looked out over the vines. If the experiment did work, he'd have to go see Walter Taylor about increasing that mortgage or taking out a note.

"Grant..."

He shifted his gaze to Marissa, wanted to get off the railing and go over and take her in his arms. She was so sweet and beautiful...and with just enough "saucy" in her to make him ache when he looked at her.

"You've explained about the 'unfermented wine.' But I don't understand why it's so important." A frown creased Marissa's smooth forehead. "Why do you want to make it?"

So that I can marry you.

"I was wondering that myself, Grant."

His mother's gaze was fastened on him, studying him. How could he explain the dire importance of this experiment? He didn't want to tell Marissa he was without funds and had no way of making money to support her. If it didn't work… But that wasn't the only reason. Not any longer.

He started to lift his hand to rub his neck, saw his mother's gaze flicker toward it and instead waved it toward the vineyard. "There are a lot of vines out there that produce an abundance of grapes. And the sale of those grapes at harvest provides our living. It's what I've always known…what I've always done."

He locked his gaze on Marissa's and smiled. "And then I boarded a steamer for Chautauqua, saw a young lady who seemed in a bit of distress, offered my assistance and my life changed. Suddenly, all I'd known was challenged. And things I had not known of were presented in a sobering way. My eyes were opened to the abuse of women and children by men who over-indulge in strong drink, and I learned of the suffering and misery that can be the result of imbibing. I, also, learned of the possible agony of the drinker. And conviction grew in my heart until I could no longer say, 'I only grow grapes. I don't make wine.'"

He glanced at his mother and read the understanding in her eyes. She knew of the debt and that the money he should have had was gone. He took a breath and told the rest of it. "And then Sarah Swan came to the house. When I opened the door, she said 'Tobin has been at the wine.' And I saw her condition, and I knew I could never be a part of that again."

He glanced out over the railing. "But there are all those vines. And years of work to improve the vineyard. Still…there was the truth of Sarah Swan. And I couldn't reconcile the two."

He faced them again. "So last night I told the Lord I would not grow grapes to sell to vintners ever again. And I asked Him to show me what to do. This morning I believe He did. And that is why this 'unfermented wine' is so important. As Marissa said a short while ago, we will be the vintners. And our 'unfermented wine' will harm no one."

"Oh, Grant…" Marissa launched herself from the swing and threw herself into his arms. He held her close and looked at his mother over the top of her blond curls. The look in his mother's eyes was one he would hold in his heart forever.

"I've never been more proud of you, son." Her calm voice said more than her words. She smiled and rose from the swing. "And now I'm going to go check on those grapes."

"This is the last of it. When these bottles are filled and in the hot water, we're finished—except for cleaning the kitchen." Grant tilted the liquid in the large pan into the pitcher his mother held, then placed the empty pan on the sink cupboard and walked to the other end of the table. Steam from the waiting pan on the stove made a cloud behind him as he took up his position ready to seal the bottles that his mother and Marissa filled.

"Hold the bottle steady, Marissa. It wants to tip over."

"I've got it. Don't pour too fast. It's almost full."

"All right. Get ready. Here it comes."

He looked down the table and watched his mother tip the pitcher, smiled as the deep purple liquid slid off the lip into the funnel Marissa held, then streamed out the bottom into the wine bottle.

"It's almost full... Stop!"

Marissa shifted the funnel to the next bottle in line, then handed him the filled one and smiled when their fingers touched.

He stoppered the bottle, seated the cork firmly with a quick hit of his palm, then took the bottle to the stove and sealed it with hot wax. Twenty-four finished bottles sat on the eating table. This last batch would give him twelve more. *Please, Lord, let this work. And let this "unfermented wine" taste delicious.*

"Well, that was a deal of cooperation with each of us doing our specific tasks. We work well together." Mrs. Winston pushed at her hair and smiled. "We got into a rhythm that served us well."

"We did indeed." Marissa's smile made his pulse jump. "It's fortunate your mother has that long table, Grant. It would have been difficult to do the work without it."

"I'll say." Mrs. Winston shook her head and looked at him, concern and a question in her eyes. "That was only a few of the harvest leavings. Imagine bottling wagonloads of grapes. You're going to need a barn, Grant. And workers."

"If the experiment works." Grant stared at the bottles of his unfermented wine, acutely aware of his lack of experience. "So, how many days do you think it should set before we try it?"

"It's your experiment, Grant."

"True." He directed a wry smile toward his mother. "But I'm relying on your cooking skills to provide the answers to any questions that crop up."

"I see." She laughed and handed him one of the bottles. "If it's the taste you want to know about, you could open one at any time. If you want to know for certain that your experiment killed all of the yeast, well…that will take some time."

"Putting it off won't change anything, will it, Grant?"

"Only my peace of mind, Marissa." He gave her a wry smile. "And right now I don't have much of that." He sucked in a long breath and ran his thumbnail in a circle between the cork and bottle to break the wax seal. The cork came free with a loud pop. "Well…" He poured a little of the liquid in the bottle into a glass and held it out to his mother, poured more and offered it to Marissa. She shook her head.

"I—I can't, Grant. I'm sorry. I know you say it is without alcohol, but it's still wine." A shudder shook her. "Even the bottle…"

"I should have thought of that." He frowned and put down the glass. "I'm sorry, Marissa. A winery was the only place I could get the bottles and other supplies quickly. But I'll keep that in mind if—when—we begin bottling." He glanced at his mother.

"He's brought you this far, Grant. Have faith."

He nodded and picked up his glass. Marissa moved to his side, out of his way. *Please, Lord...* He took a swallow, grinned and took another. "Mother..."

She looked up from her glass and smiled. "It's delicious, Grant. It tastes like grapes right off the vine." Pride of him shone in her eyes, but that shadow of concern was still lurking in their depts. "What is your next step?"

"Well, since this has all come about this morning, I'll have to give that some thought." He emptied his glass, looked down at Marissa and smiled. "Right now I'm going to walk Marissa home." He took her hand and led her out into the hall.

"Was your...drink...really delicious, Grant?"

He closed the front door, offered Marissa his arm and nodded. "It was so good it surprised me."

"Then I think what you might do is take your 'unfermented wine' some place where there are a lot of people and give them each a taste to see if they like it. Or, perhaps, you might offer it at church for Communion. I'm certain there are a lot of people there who would give you an honest opinion as to whether they like it or not."

He stopped, stared down at her. "Those are very good ideas, Marissa."

She laughed and tugged his arm to start walking again. "You needn't look shocked. I simply took your idea of having the three of us taste it and made it larger."

"Considerably so." He squeezed her hand. "Have you any other ideas?"

"Not for the present, but for after."

His heart lurched. *Did she mean...* "After?"

"Yes, you know...for after you are making your 'unfermented wine.'" She cast a sidelong look up at him.

He swallowed his disappointment. "And what are those ideas?"

"First, I believe you should use bottles that are very different from wine bottles so that people don't get them confused. And so people like me don't connect... unpleasant...memories with them and thus refuse to buy your wine." She glanced up at him again. "And second, I believe you should have a statement on your label that states that your 'unfermented wine' may be enjoyed by children. And a second statement on your label telling everyone that there is no alcohol in your drink and therefore no danger in drinking it."

"And, again, those are very good ideas." He led her away from the hotel, guided her to the other side of the road by the railroad station and stopped at their "secret place" under the tree. He leaned against the tree trunk, took hold of her hand and pulled her around in front of him. "I never knew you had such a talent for business, Marissa. I'm impressed." He caught her hands in his and lifted them to his mouth, kissed their palms and the place where her pulse was skipping and fluttering on the inside of her wrists. "Have you any more ideas?"

"A few." She yielded when he tugged her hands and

pulled her close to him. "But it might be better to save them for another time."

"Then I'll ask you a few questions."

She stared up at him and nodded. "All right…"

"First, do you think you could live looking at the grapevines every day now that you know the grapes would not be used to make wine?"

Her hands trembled. The pulse under his fingers at her wrists raced. "I believe I could manage that."

He gave a little tug. She fell against him. His heart slammed against his chest. He slid his arms around her and kissed her temple, the warm, soft spot in front of her ear. "And do you think you would find it acceptable to live in a house with your husband's mother?" He slid his lips along her cheek, kissed the corner of her mouth.

"I think that…would be…lovely." Her words were soft, breathless. Her face turned, her lips seeking his.

His heart thudded. His pulse surged. "Then when I get this—" He couldn't resist; he captured her seeking lips, took them prisoner. "—'unfermented wine' business running—" Her lips trembled against his, parted. He whispered against their soft fullness, "—Will you marry me?"

She pulled away, leaned back and gave him a smile that took his breath. "I would not marry you while you had a part in making wine, Grant, but that's over now. Yes, with all my heart yes. I'll marry you."

He crushed her to him, pressed his cheek against her curls. The joy at the thought of having her for his own, and the need to do what was right, all but maddened him. He pulled in a long breath and prayed for strength.

"I want that more than anything, Marissa. But I can't marry you until I know I can provide for you. And that will be at least a year." He cleared the huskiness from his voice and lifted his head to look down at her. "I have to borrow the money to build a barn and buy equipment so I'll be ready to make the 'unfermented wine' next fall. But once the 'unfermented wine' is sold and I pay off the debt, I'll have enough to provide a good living. Until then, we have to wait." The words were a knife to his heart.

"Let me go, Grant." She slipped the purse cord from her wrist, pulled out a piece of paper, then looked up at him and smiled. "This is a bank draft, Grant. The one I told you my father gave me to pay for my living expenses until they settle in a new place and send for me. What I *didn't* tell you is that my father is a very wealthy man and this draft is for a very large amount. Now, since it's for my living expenses—" that saucy look he loved stole into her eyes and her smile "—and if we marry I'd be living in your home, this money would rightly belong to you. And I'm quite certain there's enough here to build a barn—"

His kiss smothered the rest of her words. She answered it with all of her love, then leaned against him weak-kneed and trembling when he lifted his head.

"It will be a loan, Marissa, to be paid back when the 'unfermented wine' is sold."

She burrowed her face into the hollow of his neck

and smiled at the husky fierceness in his voice. "If you insist."

"I do."

"Very well. And as we are making conditions—"

"Yes?"

She lifted her head and kissed his neck just below his jaw. "You must agree to change the name of your drink to 'grape juice' and never call it 'unfermented wine' again." She ended her request with a kiss to the small hollow beneath his lip.

His breath hissed from him. His arms tightened around her and his lips captured hers, sealing the bargain.

* * * * *

Dear Reader,

I love writing historical romance novels. I learn so much when I do the research needed to make the story background as accurate as possible. And sometimes during that research I find the "germ" of a wonderful story…or two.

This book began with the setting. I am familiar with the world-famous Chautauqua Institute located on beautiful Chautauqua Lake in western New York. It still holds educational classes and lectures and entertainments in the arts every summer. I've been there many times. The beautiful old buildings are still there. And you can still ride a paddle wheel steamer around the lake.

Vineyards and wineries abound in the area, all part of the Concord Grape Belt, the largest and oldest concord-grape-growing region in the world. And, a short distance away, in Fredonia, New York (Marissa's hometown in the story), stands the church where the "Woman's Crusade"—soon to become the "Women's Christian Temperance Union"—held its first meeting in the winter of 1873-1874. The next summer at the first Chautauqua Sunday School Assembly, those women met with many others from all over the country in pre-organizational meetings during which it was decided to combine forces and form a national movement.

Now, I ask you… Can you imagine a romance rife with more conflict than that of a beautiful and zealous temperance advocate in love with a rugged vineyard owner who grows grapes for wine? That story simply begged to be written.

And then there's another story "germ" that my research uncovered. Oh, Clarice, what have you become involved in?

Thank you, dear reader, for choosing to read *An Unlikely Love*. I hope you enjoyed Marissa and Grant's story. I truly enjoy hearing from my readers. If you care to share your thoughts about this story, I may be reached at *dorothyjclark@hotmail.com* or *www.dorothyjclark.com*.

Until next summer at Chautauqua,

Dorothy Clark

WAGON TRAIN SWEETHEART
Journey West
by Lacy Williams

The hazards of the wagon train frighten Emma Hewitt even *before* she's asked to nurse enigmatic Nathan Reed. Yet the loner hides a kind, protective nature she could learn to love... if not for the groom-to-be awaiting her in Oregon.

SECOND CHANCE HERO
Texas Grooms
by Winnie Griggs

When Nate Cooper saves a little girl from a runaway wagon, the child's single mother is beyond grateful. But can Nate ever let go of his troubled past to forge a future with Verity Leggett?

LOVE BY DESIGN
The Dressmaker's Daughters
by Christine Johnson

Former stunt pilot Dan Wagner has already taken Jen Fox's seat on a rare expedition, and—despite their mutual interest—she's not about to offer him a spot in her guarded heart.

A FAMILY FOUND
by Laura Abbot

As a single father, Tate Lockwood has his hands full with two inquisitive sons. But maybe their headstrong—and beautiful—tutor, Sophie Montgomery, can fill the missing piece in their motherless family...